HA!

BOOKS

SAINT WALLY
Courtney Taylor

COURTNEY TAYLOR

Chapter 1

The next thing Walter knew he was naked, and standing inside a gargantuan cathedral formed by brushed steel columns at least a kilometre in height, stained glass windows bigger than believable, and a gigantic Art Deco wall, looming directly ahead, which depicted rolling green pastures and heavenly white clouds. He couldn't remember how he'd come to be in this predicament, but dimly recalled that moments ago (or years ago it felt like) he'd been travelling down a dark tunnel, toward a growing white light.

To his left and right were thousands, no, millions of individuals, all of them naked, and lined up in queues stretching so far backward that Walter couldn't see to the ends of them. It seemed that he too was standing in one of these queues, in front of a Neanderthal-looking creature that appeared to be sleeping, even though it was standing up straight, and had its eyes open. In fact, thought Walter, as he looked around attentively, it seemed that *everybody* was standing up straight and sleeping with their eyes open. The only exceptions were the people at the very fronts of the lines...although, they couldn't all be called people. They seemed to be all manner of human, humanoid, and outrageous-looking creature, some of which were far beyond Walter's capacity to even conceptualise. As their lines each moved forward one unified stomp at a time, their millions of feet, hooves, pads, digits, suction cups, biotic shock absorbers, and who knows what else, came thundering down onto polished concrete. Walter, instinctively covering his manhood, gradually noticed that each advance of a line was preceded by a voice, never the same, calling out, 'Next!'

It was something of a surprise to learn that Saint Peter existed in the plural. There must have been thousands of them, each sitting behind a simple wooden desk and reading from a hefty book laid flat. Lined up side by side, they had long white beards, baggy grey robes, and were reaching into crystal chalices and removing something white and glowing. Walter could see that, whatever the substance was, the Saint Peters were pressing it against the foreheads of the life forms that approached them. This was obviously some kind of ceremony, and it made Walter begin to fidget.

3

For all of Walter's adult life he'd told himself there'd be nothing but darkness; nothing but nothingness. But now here was, naked, and destined for what looked to be some kind of cosmic concentration camp. The person ahead of him was an old chubby bald man who was sweating and breathing heavily. Walter couldn't blame him for being nervous. The bureaucratic yay or nay that would decree either paradise or eternal torment was only moments away. Walter sincerely hoped that the man would make it to paradise, and found that he had no such hope for himself, owing to the method by which he'd gained entry to this place.

A nearby shout of 'Next!' brought a staccato clap of thunder. Without realising it, Walter had stepped forward, and was now standing before a yellow line stencilled on the floor. The old chubby bald man had proceeded toward the desk of their Saint Peter. Walter couldn't see their Saint Peter, but he could hear him. He sounded tired–as though worn down by eons of doing the same mindless task.

The old chubby bald man leaned forward to partake in the same ceremony as all the other applicants. Suddenly, his glistening scalp exploded with a shock of thick brown hair; and his body, warped and wrinkled like wax held next to a flame, regained its elasticity and tucked up into itself. The man had been restored to his prime, and was now vigorously shaking Saint Peter's hand, thanking him with such gratitude that it seemed he'd just been informed that all of his childhood friends and long-deceased pets were waiting just around the next corner.

'It's fine, fine, fine,' was the tired reply. 'Just put this on and follow the lines. Enjoy your stay.'

The now-young man lifted a garment of clean shining linen above his own head. As it slid down over his body, it ripened into a florid outfit that perfectly represented his mood. Clasping his hands, looking about ready to lunge over the desk and hug the person behind it, he said, 'Thank you; thank you,' and then happily hurried away, revealing an elderly man whose silver placard declared him to be *Saint Peter–the actual*.

Saint Peter had a long white beard and a bald head with a snowy mullet cascading out the back of it. Pushing up his spectacles, and looking at Walter without really seeing him, he said, 'Next!'

4

SAINT WALLY

Walter stepped across the yellow line and nervously approached the famous saint. As he did so, he noticed four things upon the old man's desk. There was a large tome that was presumably the Book of life, a small crystal chalice, a healthy-looking pot plant, and a canister that looked like an obese wine bottle. Inside this last item there was a small hurricane of tiny glowing fragments. Walter was so captivated by them that he almost forgot about Saint Peter.

It seemed that Saint Peter had forgotten about Walter. The old man was staring into space as though immersed in a deep reverie. He only awoke from it thanks to strange activity on the desktop next to his own. A naked woman was jumping up and down like a lottery winner. Walter noted that only moments ago she'd been a tiny little pink person, about ten centimetres tall, who had sprinted up a staircase that had popped out of a desk leg.

Saint Peter muttered something about, 'Foetueses,' and after rubbing at his neck as if it was giving him a bit of trouble, proceeded with the task at hand. 'Lean forward and poke out your tongue, please.'

Walter awkwardly complied, and was surprised when Saint Peter leaned across the desk, tapped him on the tongue, then rubbed his fingertips together and turned a page of the Book of Life. All of Walter's personal details suddenly appeared on the new page. He angled his head to try and read them but couldn't manage it.

'Now,' said Saint Peter. 'Moorianda Bakeeleeada, currently known as Walter Alistair Matthews. Suicide. Hold on. You're not scheduled to be here till...Never mind; you're here now; might as well get it out of the way.'

As the old man continued reading from Walter's rap sheet, something quite strange occurred immediately behind him. A glowing doorway, zapping as if made of electricity, manifested in the air, and opened to reveal a youngish man with a shaved head. Walter also noticed the man's eyes. They were intensely vacant–as though he was possessed by some kind of satisfying, mind-bleaching mania.

The glowing fragments inside the canister on Saint Peter's desk began shining more brightly, and driving themselves at the glass as if to break through it. Walter was so dazzled by their resplendence that he jolted when they unexpectedly disappeared, their jar suddenly hidden beneath the folds of a dark cloak.

It wasn't until the youngish man was bowing with feigned humility and stepping back through the doorway that Walter realised he might have just appropriated something that wasn't his. By then it was too late. The doorway minimised and disappeared, and Walter recalled two feathery stumps, each the size of a toddler's forearms, protruding out of the man's back...and also an effeminate little wave that he'd given.

Apparently Saint Peter had spent a brief moment watering his pot plant. Dropping his spray bottle into a drawer and closing it, he said, 'Now. Where was I?' For several drawn-out seconds he evidently couldn't remember. Then he said, 'Ah yes, that's right, suicide.'

Walter, still feebly covering his nakedness, gradually realised that the monstrous nave was becoming quiet. The calls of 'Next!' were abating, as were the resounding stomps of the nudist queues. Glancing to his left, and then to his right, he saw that all of the other Saint Peters were looking toward the Saint Peter directly in front of him. The Saint Peter to Walter's left got up from his chair and respectfully made his way closer. Slightly bowing, he said, 'Uh, excuse me, Sheriff?'

'Yes?' said Saint Peter, snapping to attention but failing to recognise the man.

'Deputy Dooley, sir. Uh....There seems to be a...shortage of Saints.'

'A shortage?' said Saint Peter. 'What do you mean there's a shortage? This'll be something to do with the pipes. Another maintenance problem. The Saints are right...' The old man stared with bewilderment at two small vertical tubes poking an inch out of his desktop. 'I don't...I don't understand. They were here only a moment ago. I just processed someone.'

Deputy Dooley obviously didn't know what to say, so gave a jittery kind of shrug.

'This isn't some kind of a joke, is it?' said Saint Peter, looking up at his subordinate with suspicion.

'Sir,' said Dooley, straightening as if offended. 'I don't think we in the processing department take the process of processing so casually.'

Saint Peter's crooked and skeptical eyebrow gradually relaxed. Folding his arms and chattering his teeth, he looked over at Walter and said, 'Could you turn around, please. And don't cover your buttocks.'

Walter did a full rotation that revealed he wasn't concealing anything. Saint Peter said, 'I don't suppose *you* saw what happened to the canister on my desk?'

Walter nodded.

Saint Peter looked surprised, and a little bit sharply, asked, 'Well, what happened to it, then? And don't worry about your genitals. We see all manner in this place.'

Regardless, Walter kept one hand firmly in place, and used the other hand to illustrate as he said, 'A door kind of opened out of nothing, and a man with stumps coming out of his back, he took that glass jar on your desk, then went back through the door.'

'Really,' said Saint Peter, with what appeared to be both intrigue and skepticism. 'And why, might I enquire, did you not *say* anything, while you were watching this person make off with an object that was obviously somebody else's property?'

Walter's elevated heart-rate tripled, because the man who admitted people into Heaven was casting a rock of judgment in his very direction. Saint Peter looked as though he was about to wage forth invectively, but forced himself to relax, and said, 'Never mind. I'm sure this is all very new and strange for you.' Giving a laboured, perhaps apologetic smile that quickly faded, he muttered, 'There's no way there could've been a breach; this place is airtight. And it doesn't even *have* to be airtight; there isn't even any air.' (Walter stole a glimpse at the pot plant.) 'Well, if someone *is* playing a joke, then my money would be on the Vice-President. Deputy Donald?'

Deputy Dooley didn't bother correcting him, but said, 'Yes, sir?'

'Break out the *Be back in 5 minutes* signs. I'm just going to run this by the Good Lord, see what He thinks. Actually, use the One True Religioners to keep things moving. The longer we're not admitting people, the more we'll have to catch up on.'

Saint Peter turned to Walter and said, 'Would you mind coming with me, Mr.—' he checked the Book of Life '—Matthews? Just to...reinforce my side of things?'

'Um...okay,' said Walter.

'Wonderful,' said Saint Peter, clearly not really meaning that. Pushing back his chair and standing to his feet, he pointed valiantly in the direction they were headed.

Walter said, 'Um. Do you want me to go like this?'

Realising that Walter was still naked, Saint Peter said, 'Oh god no,' then opened up a drawer and pulled out a folded opaque garment. As it was handed to Walter, it flickered alive with colour, and separated into two pieces: a blue-and-white chequered shirt and a pair of black jeans.

'Non-subscriber, eh?' said Saint Peter. 'Now remember, this doesn't mean you've been sanctified. We can't do that until we've gotten back the Saints, which...Oh god I hope this doesn't get ugly.'

When Walter was fully clothed and looking like an everyday person (albeit a barefooted one) Saint Peter led him toward the Art Deco wall. Set into its base were thousands of security doors. Saint Peter was about to swipe a card and let Walter pass through one of them, when suddenly he said, 'Whoop, hang on,' and darted back to his desk. There he scooped up the Book of Life (which he'd apparently almost forgotten to bring) and severely warned the next applicant not to step past the yellow line. The groggy, apprehensive Neanderthal nodded compliantly, and relaxed noticeably when Saint Peter turned and headed back to Walter.

'Alright then,' said Saint Peter, adjusting the midsection of his robe. 'Off to meet the Maker.'

SAINT WALLY

Chapter 2

A thick white mist that tasted like some kind of ground medicine blasted Walter from all directions. This quarantining fog, as it dissipated, revealed a colossal enclosure that was like a transport terminal for the super wealthy. Golden, gleaming handrails were holding back excited crowds: Citizens of Heaven who were no doubt waiting to meet and greet their loved ones. Walter scanned the countless faces to see if he recognised anyone. The only individuals who looked even moderately familiar belonged to a group of Neanderthals. The monkey-men,-women,-and-children, were peering at him quizzically, as if wondering, *Has he changed that much?*

Saint Peter had stepped through one of the nearby staff doorways and was raking his beard to get the white dust out of it. Approaching Walter, he said, 'Now, I do ask that you stick right by my side while you're here in the Heavenly Realms. Technically you're not supposed to be up here yet.' Looking around with evident concern at the low number of Citizens exiting the Waiting Room, he held up an arm and said, 'This way, if you please. (If we can make it past those damn Mormons).' He was referring to a crowd of people who all seemed to be wearing white, antiquated swimming costumes. They were throwing high into the air one of their own—a meek-looking man who had just stepped through a doorway close to Walter's.

As they strode down a wide, ivory, mullioned corridor filled with happy groups of the recently reunited, Walter said, 'So, I take it I'm dead.'

'Not yet you're not,' replied Saint Peter, moving so fast that Walter nearly had to jog to keep up with him. 'Not till you've been processed, which is what you and I will do just as soon as we find out what's going on with the Surplus Morality. Oh my goodness, the amount of work we're going to have to catch up on.'

Making it past a chorus-line of skipping tripeds, Walter asked, 'Surplus Morality?'

'That's...Oh it's probably not worth explaining,' said Saint Peter. 'Not to be rude, but, would you mind quickening the pace just a bit?'

They entered a thoroughfare whose crystal walls overlooked a gleaming, glorious city, one that looked as if it had been dreamed up by a hyperactive ten-year-old who'd just taken a very deep sniff of the universe's finest cocaine. Thick ice-cream clouds, leaking holy shafts of sunlight, floated peacefully in the ripest blue sky that Walter had ever seen. Golden streets and highways, looking like rutilant rivers, or the routes of some giant, far-reaching circuit board, ran in myriad pathways around glittering spires and skyscrapers—buildings so broad and tall they looked physically impossible.

'Not that I want to rush you,' said Saint Peter, with obvious irritation at having to backtrack, 'but Time is somewhat of the essence.'

'Sorry,' said Walter.

At the end of the corridor, Saint Peter stopped and said, 'Just to inform you: This is the Head Office of Heaven, quite literally the centre of all Creation.' He smiled courteously, then stepped toward a pair of massive wooden doors that slid open automatically.

Revealed was an unbelievably expansive lobby, in the centre of which was an immense mezzanine structure that looked like a spiralling staircase, or, more precisely, a double-helix, one rising so high that it tapered to a needle point. The pinprick of sunshine above it was rimmed by white marble balconies stacked in the hundreds of thousands. They reached all the way down to the ground floor, and were connected by thousands of golden escalators. From where Walter was standing (because he'd had to stop to take all this in) some of the golden escalators were so far away they looked like nothing more than glinting threads of taut yellow string.

Bustling up and down the double helix of mezzanines, and across the escalators, and indeed all throughout the lobby, were millions, maybe even billions, of bizarre-looking life forms, all of them different, and deeply engaged in conversations that looked as if they were producing exciting epiphanies. The way that everybody seemed to be acknowledging everybody else prompted Walter to catch up to Saint Peter and ask, 'All of these...people...they know each other?'

'If not yet then in the future they will,' replied Saint Peter. 'That's something you probably can't comprehend at the moment. But once you've been inducted into the Spiritual, you'll understand that, despite what I said before, Time is no longer of the essence. Hence why one day, most every person you see around you right now, you'll end up being *married* to in a Physical Realm. Eternity is a very long time.'

Walter, a little bit overwhelmed by that concept, was reminded of a person from the life he'd just come from. That was why he didn't see the translucent man in the purple robe, whom he bumped into then reflexively apologised to.

'Uh, sorry about that, sir,' said Saint Peter, ducking back to get Walter. 'My friend here is a Newly Deceased. Sort of.'

'Ahhh,' said the glass man, bowing his head. 'Welcome back, my brother. I pray you once again enjoy your time in the Heavenly Realms. And do not trouble yourself, my brethren, for we all make mistakes.'

A few paces later, Saint Peter said, 'That man is what we in Heaven call an Apotheothorist. Such Souls have lived so many lives and donated so much Surplus Morality that they've become purified. Thus the transparency. But like I said, stay close by. Wouldn't look good for the department if I lost you, would it.'

On the other side of a group of purple pygmies who were dressed as if they'd just stepped off a bamboo space ship, Walter saw regalia he recognised, and again catching up to Saint Peter, asked, 'Is there, uh, religion, up here?'

Saint Peter gave a slightly humoured laugh and said, 'Always one of the biggest surprises for people. And the answer is yes—but only at first.

'You see, if a person was to pass through the Gates of Heaven and become a *completely* new creation, then that would negate the very purpose of their having gone down to a Physical Realm in the first place. Because what's the point of becoming a Physical if you're just going to forget the entire experience? You might as well stay up in Heaven, skip the whole ordeal and get the same result—minus all the pain.'

'So the people who stick to their beliefs...' asked Walter.

'Simply do so,' said Saint Peter, 'because the memories and beliefs they've acquired in their Physical lifetimes have been encoded into their sub-DNA—also known as a Spirit, or a Soul, or a Morphogenetic field. It's their true and eternal identity, which always looks different, depending on the Dimension it's just come from. The purpose of Heaven—or one of its purposes, anyway—is to serve as a kind of rehabilitation place, where Souls come and get refreshed, then venture back into the Physical, usually opting for lifestyles drastically foreign to them. This is because during their time in Heaven, Citizens learn about the interconnectedness of everything in

Creation. You see,' added Saint Peter, to point out the principle, 'the Spiritual life is not a stagnant one.'

A plume of flame shot out the back of a chariot when Saint Peter said, 'God's office, please.' The vehicle rocketed away from its bay and launched into the air, its wheels spinning so fast they became invisible. Golden escalators whooshed overhead and underneath as the chariot ascended in wide circles, so quickly that sound warped and crumbled away. In its absence was some kind of broadcast that was humming beneath the visible world. A gruff but kind voice was saying, *'What do you call a circumcised Bible? The Old Testament!* Heh heh heh. An old one but a good one. But here We go; in the news: It seems the people of Dimension 2127435—that's the one where cutting your nose hair is a crime—have gotten together and decided to make it a law that if a person denounces Me, then he or she therefore denounces reality (which is also a crime). Now I have a few contentions with this new ruling, and let Me explain why.'

As the disembodied voice continued, the chariot rose above the mezzanine structure, and Walter saw that a tremendous bronze water feature stood magnificently upon the top of it. The gleaming statue depicted a scraggly homeless man who was holding up a cardboard sign reading *Repent!* Walter chuckled when noticing that a sparkling waterfall was coursing down the front of the man's rumpled metal pants.

Saint Peter, seeing what Walter had laughed at, said, 'Oh you'll simply love the Man Who designed that tasteful, urinating honorific.'

COURTNEY TAYLOR

Chapter 3

'Pietro!' exclaimed three Angel secretaries, sitting behind ornate golden desks and painting their fluffy white wing-tips.

'Hello, ladies,' said Saint Peter, as a pair of frosted glass doors closed behind him and Walter.

'You haven't graced us with your presence for a very long time now,' said Brittany.

'A *very* long time,' said Chelsea.

'Alas, ladies, I have to work. Tell me, Amy, is the Good Lord in?'

'He's been expecting you, Saint Peter.'

'Thank you very much,' said the old man, giving a flirty little bow. 'You girls rest easy for the moment. We'll be back out here to say hello again in no time.'

The Angels giggled and swatted in his direction, then went back to painting their wing tips.

'*All things bright and beeeeeautiful,*' sung Saint Peter, quietly and conspiratorially, as he and Walter traipsed toward a magnificent doorway framed by frills and friezes and genuine lightning bolts. 'Well, maybe not *bright.*'

The huge doors, made of a single diamond cut down its middle, were stenciled with golden letters reading, *God, Designer and CEO of All Creation.* Saint Peter stopped in front of them, took a deep breath, smoothed down his robe, and combed his fingers through his beard. Looking at Walter, he said, 'I think you'd better tuck in your shirt.'

The old man was about to knock, but a familiar voice called out, 'Come in! Unless you're a Jehovah's Witness!'

The diamond doors rolled away from each other and revealed a colonnaded room with a dark marble floor. The first feature that Walter noticed was a bejewelled elephant head, mounted on the pillar directly opposite the entrance. The second feature he noticed was a large glass desk whose surface was rippling. Behind this watery tabletop was an extravagant throne, turned away from them and rocking on a swivel base.

'Uh,' whispered Saint Peter. 'Don't say anything unless God says something to *you*, all right?'

Walter, his hands suddenly shaking, nodded nervously, and followed Saint Peter into a spacious, modishly-furnished chamber whose floor-to-ceiling windows provided a view that momentarily stunned him. Apparently God's office was so high up that the curvature of the planet was visible. Only, there wasn't just one visible planet, but countless numbers of them. They stretched away to infinity, and were lined up so closely they appeared to be touching. Some in fact were merging, while others possessed contours that Walter's eyes couldn't grapple with. The precisely-organised planets appeared to form neural-like pathways that led toward Heaven. It seemed that God's office, or the paradise it looked out across, was some kind of multidimensional centre of gravity.

The clearing of Saint Peter's throat was enough to prise Walter from the overwhelming view. He hurried in pursuit of the old man, feeling frail, ridiculous, reverential, and terrified.

Stopping before the watery desk, as prompted to by Saint Peter's example, Walter questioned what he should do with his hands, and decided to place them behind his back, until questioning if that might appear too arrogant. He put them in his pockets but then changed his mind. He clasped them, then let them dangle, then clenched them, then went back to clasping them. He couldn't wait for the rocking throne to turn around. But at the same time he was incredibly afraid of whatever might be sitting within it.

Finally, the plush golden throne swung around smoothly...and revealed a heavyset Man with a thick white beard and a hoary mane of hair. Walter thought he looked like Zeus–only pudgier.

'*What?*' shouted God, jumping up from His throne as if outrageously offended. His beard was aflame with holy energy. His eyes crackled with anger. The literally fulminating Deity stalked around His desk and made His way closer. He was large, looming, and furious; but His rage abruptly vanished, and He said, 'Petey! It's good to see ya. I'd ask how you are but I already know.'

'Greetings, my Lord,' said Saint Peter, carefully stepping around the lion and lamb-skin rugs spread out on the floor. 'I'd like to introduce you to—'

16

'Walter Matthews, eh?' said God, levelling His thick white eyebrows in Walter's direction. 'Suicide. Tsk tsk tsk. I hate it when a member of such a fearfully and wonderfully made species tries to terminate itself. But I gotta admit—ya hafta have balls to do it, especially...'

He looked to Saint Peter, who said, 'Off a balcony. Twenty-seven stories.'

God whistled as though impressed, then said, 'Just checkin' to see if y've been payin' attention, Sheriff.'

'Of course, my Lord,' said Saint Peter, holding the Book of Life close to his chest and rocking on his heels.

'So,' said God, as He cracked His back. 'What's on your mind, holy man? Oh that's right, the Saints have gone missing. That is correct Walter, I'm all-knowing. Of course I know where the Saints are. And yes, I know who took them. Well, it's probably quickest for Me to get 'em back Myself. I know that deep down you wanna come along, but, you haven't really had legitimate clearance to be up here, so...' God looked at Saint Peter—seemingly humoured but at the same time reproachful.

'Sorry about that,' said Saint Peter. 'Mr. Matthews saw who took the Saints, so...'

'It's all right, Sheriff,' said God. 'I'm flattered to think y'thought y'could get away with it. But anyway, it was Lucifer.'

'Oh,' said Saint Peter.

'Well, it wasn't Lucifer *specifically*,' said God, stirring the air as if He resented technicalities, and then jouncing toward the door with His hands in His pockets. 'It was that young convert o' his—the one who cut off his own wings—acting on Lucy's behalf.'

'But I thought Lucifer was busy in the Reincarnation department,' said Saint Peter.

'Re-*education*,' said God, correctively. 'But you know the way that Angel is. He's a Contrarian. And nothing's ever good enough unless the limelight is on you-know-who.'

'So, uh, what do *I* do in the meantime?' asked Saint Peter. 'Until You come back with the Saints, I mean.'

'Nothin' ya *can* do,' said God. 'Just sit here and relax. Wait for Me to get back. And don't worry about your family, Walter—they're gonna be Honkus Doriticus.'

God waved His hand at the diamond doors and they rolled open. A doorstop materialised at the base of each. Grinning in a charmingly wolfish way, He said, 'Just leave this thing open, all right? I've been doin' a bit of experimenting, and all o' those subatomic particles—not good for the sinuses.'

He winked and saluted, then turned and made for His personal elevator, which made a *ding* as it opened. Stepping inside and folding His hands, God cleared His throat and called out, 'Amy, cancel My one o'clock with Chuck Darwin. I'm not in the mood.'

SAINT WALLY

Chapter 4

In the muddy streets of a thatched village immersed in darkness and light raindrops, an Angel who prided himself upon his taste in all things *thingsical* was debuting his newest song. Obviously *Tender Fragile Soul* was destined to become a classic: The Angel's three cronies were so taken by it that they'd stopped what they were doing in order to listen with their full attention. Even the red-headed villager they were brutalising was gazing up at Lucifer with admiration. Although, maybe the simple man simply admired Lucifer's black, futuristic-looking, self-made kimono cloak; or his white-blonde hair and delicate features. Or maybe he admired the graceful flapping of the Angel's white fluffy wings as they moved about like the arms of a conductor, in time with a tune that was *not* similar to that of Achy Breaky Heart. Those who said otherwise would suffer the same fate as the villager: Lucifer would pull back his designer boot and kick them right in the pollinator, without even pausing his song.

'Don't inform my Soul, my tender fragile Soul, I simply don't believe it'd comprehend.

'Prepare yourselves, boys,' shouted Lucifer, 'here comes the final line, the climax, the thematic culmination!

''Cause if you inform my Soul, my tender fragile Soul, it might explode and bring my end.'

The end of the song was punctuated by a scream from the red-headed villager. Lucifer drew in his wings and dropped lightly onto the mud. Pausing ceremoniously, he looked around at his three cronies and said, 'Gentlemen. Those last words are *new* last words. Notice the way I incorporated what's *actually* going to happen into the song?'

'Brilliant,' said one of his followers, a dowdy man wearing a cream-coloured suit and matching fedora. 'Absolutely brilliant.'

'Thank you, L. Ron,' said Lucifer, graciously dipping his head toward his longtime henchman, L. Ron Hubbard. 'I trust your opinion because you've placed your faith in *me*.' To another follower, he said, 'And what did *you* think, Oosama? Could you make an award-winning video out of *that* little number?'

Osama bin Laden, who still had hold of the nearly-unconscious villager, replied, 'Was good. Was very— inventive. Is that right word?'

'That is *indeed* the right word, Oosama,' said Lucifer, rolling his hand thankfully (and thinking to himself that Osama had a voice like a faraway fog-horn—and it wouldn't take long for *that* to become annoying). 'Very perspicacious of you.'

Lucifer turned to an Angel who had a shaved head and mutilated wings. The Angel closed his eyes and trembled almost perversely as Lucifer repeatedly said his name.

'And how 'bout you, Clip Clip Clip Clippety Clip Clip Clip? I can't leave *you* out of this discussion, now, can I? What did *you* think of my little foray into "musical prophecy?"'

Clip opened his intensely vacant eyes and said, '*My* opinion, is that the subtextual wit inherent in that manipulated verse was— *sublime.* The fact that it referenced the Book of Beelzebub—also known as, *It's only the Second Act: The autobiography of a Questioning Angel*—was, *daring,* needless to say. But I think the *true* profoundness lies even deeper, because when you compare the two texts—*Tender Fragile Soul* and *The Book of Beelzebub*—you'll find that one says, "Rise up and take a stand," while the other says, "He might explode and bring my end."' Turning to Osama and L. Ron, Clip said, 'Stand back and answer me this one, gentlemen: Which Being is considered the "Soul" of All Creation?'

Osama, who had spent a few weeks in Hell before Lucifer had "rescued" him, tentatively said, 'Allah?'

'That's *right,*' said Clip. '*God* is the "Soul" of All Creation. And if the "Soul" doesn't *understand,* then that means...'

'That means *God* doesn't understand,' said L. Ron, obviously proud of himself for catching on so quickly.

'Exactly,' said Clip. 'And what does the song tell us the "Soul" is going to do if it *doesn't* understand?'

'It might..."explode and bring my end," yes?' said Osama, brightening at the thought of pyrotechnics, a subject he was passionate about.

'And what do you think the word "my" represents?' asked Clip.

L. Ron and Osama looked at each other, both without a clue and trying to hide it.

'*I'll* tell you what it represents,' said Clip, beginning to pace around in the mud. 'It represents everything. *Everything*. And that is why we need to *remove* the "Soul." Because if we don't, then it's going to explode, and when it *does*, it's going to take *everything* with it. The Book of Beelzebub predicts this. It says, and I quote, "a state of dissension should inevitably come about because Heaven isn't satisfied—if it was then I wouldn't be having these thoughts.""

'Chapter 14, verse 32,' said L. Ron, confidently.

Clip nodded, impressed, then said, 'The fact that we four are standing here—'

'Five,' said Osama, waving the floppy arm of the villager.

'The fact that we five are standing here,' said Clip, 'in a state of rebellion, plotting against the society that has caused us to feel like outcasts...doesn't that say the Book of Beelzebub was right; that we are, in fact, rising up and taking a stand?'

Osama and L. Ron, not sure if they should nod, both nodded.

'And if the Book is right about *that*,' said Clip, 'then isn't it safe to think that the Holy Prophet who wrote it might also be right about *other* things? Namely that all of Creation will explode if we don't take God out of it?'

'Uh...yes?' said L. Ron and Osama, both in complete bewilderment.

'Then let me just say one last thing,' said Clip, speaking mostly to his beloved leader. 'I don't think Lucifer's statement, which instructs us we need to act boldly in order to save Creation, was just— prophetic. I think it was...*genius*.'

Lucifer stroked his totally smooth chin and said, 'You know, that's pretty much exactly what I was trying to get across when I sang it. *Now*. Let's get back to brutalising!' He pulled back his foot, intending to unleash another round of booted fury; but before he got the chance, a blinding flood of white light, accompanied by a *ding!* noise, caused everyone present to turn around and gape.

Osama dropped the villager (who went plüp into the mud). Clip and L. Ron hugged each other for safety (though they would have called it solidarity). Lucifer only smiled.

Treading closer toward them, backlit by holy light, was a tall, dusky, thickset figure Whose beard and eyebrows began crackling like electrical stormclouds. The shadows upon God's face receded until His visage was brighter than the blinding elevator standing open behind Him. The red-headed villager sat up in the mud, beheld this frightening apparition, and screamed. That scream followed him as he launched to his feet and sprinted away into darkness, the mud flicking up behind him like small subterranean mortar bursts.

Lucifer, miffed by such undignified noise pollution, cleaned out an eardrum before saying, 'Well well well. Didn't expect to see *You* down here. Did we, boys.' He and his cronies tried to chuckle as they backed away from the Almighty. 'And why *are* You down here? *We* haven't done anything.'

'You know I know everything, Lucy,' said God.

'Or so You say,' said Lucifer.

'And you know I can't lie,' said God. 'So now the question is: Why do you think I would?'

'To make Yourself feel better?'

God laughed merrily, then went deadpan and said, 'I do miss your wit. But I came for the Saints.'

'The what?' said Lucifer.

God glowered and the Angel quickly wilted.

Opening up his trench coat with a flourish, and then reaching between his legs, Lucifer unclipped an object that was dangling from his belt. This object, the canister of Saints, he threw upward and trapped against his chest. His grinning face was now speckled by white light, cast by luminous particles that were swimming around inside the jar in a dense constellation. These particles, the Saints, began driving at the glass as though to break through it to get to Lucifer.

'Is this what you want?' asked the Angel, with a dull smirk. His face crumpled resentfully when no answer was returned. Nodding prissily, he said, 'You know it's rude to not answer a question when someone asks it.'

God raised an arm and beckoned for Lucifer to hurry up and bring forth the goods. The Angel, obviously delaying his delivery, stepped forward and said, 'You've met my friends, haven't You?'

'Clarence, Osama and L. Ron,' said God, without even glancing at the cronies. 'Three paragons of wasted potential. Now hurry up and get snappy, Byelzy. I'm workin' on a new Dimension.'

Lucifer stepped sideways, his feet squelching in the mud, and said, 'You know, when I was working down in the Re-education department—you remember how I was down there doing the whole tour-guide thing? Well, yeah, that's what I was doing, and anyway, one day I was showing around a bunch of Atheists—who of course were all trying to convince themselves that everything around them was just a death-bed hallucination or something—when all of a sudden, completely out of nowhere, this question just *came* to me. At first I was a little bit scared by it. I thought, I shouldn't be thinking that! But then I began to think, *Why* shouldn't I be thinking that? And the only answer I could really come up with was: I shouldn't be thinking that because God doesn't *want* me to be thinking that. Because maybe if I ask Him for an *answer*, He won't be able to *give* it.'

'You know somewhere in that Book of Mine,' said God, 'it recommends people *don't* try to test Me.'

Speaking hesitantly—as if to make his words seem less bold—Lucifer said, 'That could be construed as a— a kind of smokescreen, yes?'

'Even if it is,' said God. 'What's it to you?'

'Well, nothing really,' said Lucifer. 'Because I'm just a humble choir director, who happened to be demoted for having "tampered with the song choices."'

'Just like I told M'boy when I gave his chemical set to the Israelites,' said God. 'Sometimes you need to get yourself some more understanding. Because Yahweh doesn't do things arbitrarily.'

'See that's what I mean,' said Lucifer. 'In *my* opinion that just demonstrates You're a *kill*joy. A dictatorial control freak. A kid who doesn't want other kids to use his toys.'

'You're entitled to your opinions, Lucifer,' said God. 'But this is a three-year-long conversation We're getting into right now. And all I have to say is: give Me the Saints.'

'A *please* would be magical,' said Lucifer.

God's expression said there was no chance of it.

Lucifer asked, 'Aren't you just a *little* bit curious, about what the question is?'

Wearily, God replied, 'Lucy, if it will shut you up, you can ask Me *two* questions.'

Lucifer happily drummed his digits on the canister, then put a finger to his lip and said, 'All right. How to word this? Okay. Here it is, exactly as it came to me: If you're God, and You can do *anything*, can You make a rock so big even *You* can't lift it?'

God pondered that for a moment, then said, 'Of course I can. I can do anything.'

'Prove it,' said Lucifer.

'I don't have to prove *Shiite* to anybody,' said God.

'Then isn't this just the whole *smokescreen* thing again?' asked Lucifer.

'What if it is?' asked God, chuckling heartily.

'Well,' said Lucifer, 'I know You like keeping secrets, but, testing this out practically—it could be a very positive thing. Maybe it could put an end to all the *bickering*, because, well, why would the Physical Citizens rebel if their faith has been...reaffirmed?'

'You haven't read the Book of Exodus recently,' said God. 'Have you.'

'I *skimmed* through it,' said Lucifer. 'You know me. I'm more of a *visual* learner. Which is why, I think I need a demonstration.'

God considered Lucifer's proposal, then said, 'If I do it, will you and your friends promise to go straight back to the Re-education Department, without My having to command you to?'

'Of course,' said Lucifer, as if it was simply the natural thing to do. 'I mean, I can't speak *for* my friends, but, whatta ya say, fellas? Do we promise to go back to Hell if God shows us His little party trick?'

The cronies nodded. L. Ron was bold enough to say, 'Of course.'

'Well, there's *their* answer,' said Lucifer, stepping backward and waving for his followers to do the same. 'Might I suggest...maybe...reinforcing the ground, so You don't fall through it?'

God did exactly that by pointing at the ground beneath His feet. It solidified into a perfectly smooth disc, the size of a table-top, and the same colour as the soil.

The Almighty snapped His fingers, and there appeared before Him a small floating pebble, which he plucked out of the air and held up as though inspecting a jewel.

Glancing away from it, casting a tired, deprecating gaze upon Lucifer and his cronies, He said, 'You asked for it, fellas: a rock so big even I can't lift it.'

The pebble pinched between God's thumbtip and fingertip expanded and dropped down onto His palm. Growing even more, it went from cannon-ball-sized to house-sized in only moments, and soon became so big that when God lifted it above His own head it blocked out the night sky completely. The shadow it cast became so profound that, were it not for God's natural radiance, and the glow of the Saints, the entire surrounding region would have been consumed by total darkness.

'You should get a load o' the planets this thing is knockin' outta the way,' said God, as a bead of sweat emerged from His brow.

'Impressive,' said Lucifer, reaching up and flicking the still-growing boulder. 'But need I state the obvious that: You're still lifting it.'

God hunched His shoulders and sent a rush of energy into the rock. The groaning, cracking and bulging it had so far demonstrated intensified remarkably.

Lucifer turned to his cronies, gave them a wink, a thumbs-up, and mouthed the words, 'It's gonna come down any second now.' Turning back to God, he focused with relish upon the strain being exhibited, and noted that a bead of sweat, clinging to the Almighty's brow, was ripe enough that it was about to drop.

'Oohp,' said the Angel, when the droplet slipped off God's face. Suddenly remembering his priorities, he spun around and shouted, 'Hit the proverbial deck!'

The bead of sweat plummeted toward the ground; and when striking the reinforced soil, rebounded off it, ricocheted of the underside of the boulder, and then slammed into nearby mud, blasting open a crater so big that a house fell into it. Lucifer and his cronies dropped to the mud, all of them save for L.Ron, who, thanks to his relatively privileged upringing, didn't have quite the same amount of street smarts as the others. When God's arms buckled and the boulder crashed down onto His shoulders, L.Ron was struck in the upturned face by the heaviest object in all of Creation. He crumpled into the mud, right next to Osama, who said, 'Elly. Are you okay?'

The weight of the rock pushed God to his knees, and tipped Him forward as if forcing Him to bow. His anguished, straining face was glowing like a scorching ember. His knees had made indentations in the reinforced soil. Jagged cracks were radiating outward from them.

26

'Hold tight, fellas!' shouted a supine Lucifer, his eyes going googly as the rock descended toward him. 'It's gonna happen! It's gonna happen! Please God let it happen!'

Clip looked up at the boulder above him, awed by the size of it. Osama, terrified of being crushed, said, 'Ohhhhhhh Allah.' Naturally, an explosion followed.

The rock on God's shoulders detonated into a greyish, plasma-like substance that deluged onto the ground; and from there, seemed to activate, in such a way that it clawed at the air, swirled the mud into mousse, and caused bipolar wind currents that tore the shoes off L.Ron's feet. Those deluxe black-and-tans flitted backward and forward, slapping Lucifer and his followers as they were dragged downward into a horrid eddying bog. Lucifer was screaming; Clip was sobbing; Osama was confused; and L. Ron was unconscious. The maelstrom in which they found themselves was centred around God, Who was battling against a howling convergence of ash-coloured surges: colliding blasts of power that were crystallising. In not long, God appeared to be trapped inside an enormous frosty object that looked like a poorly cut diamond. It was groaning as though under extraordinary pressure, and flashing magnificently whenever God launched a lightning bolt that failed to penetrate its interior.

With no greater warning than a slight decrease in atmospheric pressure, the object collapsed inward, and sent out a shockwave, so strong that the mud burying Lucifer and his cohorts evaporated. They floated momentarily amid suddenly-clean air, and then splatted onto fresh mud. Each was traumatised in his own distinct way. For instance, Clip began laughing like a lunatic when he saw that, by some kind of miracle, the nearby thatched houses were still standing.

The rumbling caused by the implosion eventually faded. The world became silent: So silent, in fact, that Clip had stopped laughing in order to hear it.

Lucifer staggered to his feet, coughing and waving at the air as if annoyed by nearby smokers. Through slowly dispelling haze he saw an object glinting in the moonlight. It was a shiny glass cube, two metres high, long, and wide. Inside it was a tall, thickset, out-of-focus figure.

The Angel began laughing, and shouted, 'That's what *happens* when you try to defy Reality, boys! Ya get caught out!' Snapping his fingers he said, 'There's going to be a monument—right here—where future generations will come to see the very place where God himself was— Yaaaahhhhrrr,' cried out Lucifer, falling to the ground like a swooning maid, reacting because God had lunged like an angry tiger and slammed His shoulder against the glass.

Clip snapped out of his trauma, then flapped his useless wingstubs and ran over to his leader, shouting, 'Are you alright?!'

'Of course I'm alright,' hissed Lucifer, being helped to his feet, but pushing at his follower with weak little slaps. His aura of command no doubt established by this protest, he overcame a shiver and made his way to the glass box. There he smiled at God and tapped his fingertip on the glass, saying, 'Did you notice something, Lordy? Despite your best efforts, this thing didn't even *crack*. It appears to me that you're *contained*—like— like an animal: caged and...and *neutered*.'

The Almighty became a picture of composure, and folded His hands nonchalantly.

Lucifer wasn't impressed, and said, 'I don't think You're gonna be so casual about this whole situation when You're—how should I say it?—pondering Your past mistakes as You slide deeply into exile.'

With a voice that the glass couldn't muffle, God asked, 'You really think you can contain Me, Lucy?'

The two conscious cronies were unnerved by the resonating sound of God's voice, which seemed to come not from within the box but from everywhere. Lucifer, appearing not to notice that, only snorted and said, 'Well, on the grounds that right now You're...as You *are*, I think it's safe to say I'm doing a pretty good job *so far*. Don't you agree? And allow me to inform you, before you start monologuing about how You're the Alpha and Omega and the Centre of the Universes and all of that done-to-death *ordure*: Even if this brilliant little plan of mine doesn't work out the way I specifically *want* it to, it is still going to be infinitely worth it. Because from here on in—no matter *what* happens—when all of the Redeemed Universes see this face, every single being is going to know that *there* is the Angel who once sang in the very face of God Himself.'

'And look what became of him,' said God.

28

Lucifer overcame a bout of faux dejection, then said, 'Well, I may not have *your* sympathies. But I do at least have *these*.' Ripping the canister of Saints from out of his cloak, he held it up to the cube and said, 'Whatta you think? Have they got enough Goodness to atone for the sin of kidnapping God? I seriously hope so. And yes, I know all about the repercussions: the Karmic balance being unbalanced, et cetera, et cetera.'

'We're talkin' bad things, Lucy,' said God. 'Monsoons and tidal waves, perverts and politicians.'

'And *I*,' said Lucifer, 'am gonna have a front row seat. I'll be watching the entire thing from one of those Private Box thingies that privileged people have at sporting events. Or actually, now I'm thinking about it, I'm going to be more of a *participant* in this whole little spectacle, because I have been getting a *lot* of ideas that're all to do with wreaking havoc and making a mess and just generally desecrating everything You've created. And then, even though I've done the most heinous—don't you just love that word?—and extravagantly God-defying misdeeds that've ever been perpetrated, You're still gonna have to let me back into Heaven. Because as You said: You don't lie. And what *that* essentially means is: if Your system works a certain way, then that's the way Your system works, and You can't change it. And guess what. Soon everybody's gonna know that.

'Anyway. Enough of this discussion about having found an insanely beautiful little loophole for anarchy. I need to get going, because I am just itching to get out there and really *earn* my atonement.'

Lucifer pulled out a silver cigarette lighter and said, 'Fellas. Let's get to work. This Old Man needs to be mobile.'

COURTNEY TAYLOR

Chapter 5

'It's a shame the Good Lord hasn't got the time to chat,' said Saint Peter, heading toward a lounge chair made of white cloud. 'He's really quite a character. Makes *me* laugh, anyway.' Sitting down and taking off his sandals, he pulled a footstool closer and put his feet up on it. 'Aw, there we go. I really need to get one of these. Hydrates your feet, apparently. Now, don't worry, the Good Lord won't be gone for long. He'll get the Saints and then He'll...' Saint Peter yawned and closed his eyes. Several seconds later he was asleep.

The levitating orb holding up Saint Peter's feet was made of liquid and soil, and was one of many artefacts that Walter could see from where he was standing. He didn't want to move from his position, in case he might be smote, but soon couldn't resist the temptation, and gingerly took a step. He quickly noticed that the floor beneath his bare feet contained millions of stars and galaxies, embedded in the dark marble like incandescent seeds in black ice. He felt dizzy, and had to look elsewhere as he made his way toward the colonnades.

Photographs and memorabilia from different Dimensions were neatly organised on the shelves of the pillars. Looking closely, Walter saw a blueprint of the first ever snowflake, and a terrarium containing some kind of tiny nascent life form. A rock with the word *Ebenezer* carved into it was paper-weighting some hand-written psalms. A bottled sacrifice (of which there were many) had within it a strange creature that looked like a leopard crossed with a dugong. It was laid out on a miniature stone altar, above a plaque that read, *For God, in anticipation of His unfailing commitment to the advancement of our Tribe.*

There were several photographs mounted on the colonnades, one of which seemed to take pride of place over all the others. It showed God and a young boy aged about twelve. They were grinning happily, floating in darkness, and holding onto a flag that read, *I AM was here, so was JC, 0∞.1 seconds ABB.*

Walter looked closely at the boy, noted his ethnic features, and gave a small, half-surprised laugh.

That was when the room began to shake.

The surface of God's desk rippled like a pond in an earthquake. The objects on His shelves clattered around and threatened to fall. Saint Peter's feet rolled off the footstool, struck the floor and jolted him awake. 'Oh, goodness,' he said. 'What's going on?'

Walter was standing in the middle of the room for fear of being accused of breaking something. The rumbling eventually faded away. He looked at Saint Peter and asked, 'Was that normal?'

'Define normal,' replied Saint Peter, sitting up and yawning. 'My money would be on the Vice President. He's probably got his hands on something he shouldn't have.' He yawned again and said, 'I should probably make it look like I'm doing something.'

The question that unexpectedly rose to the surface of Walter's mind was: 'Those things that Lucifer took.'

'The Saints,' replied Saint Peter.

'The Saints,' said Walter. 'They're...people? In that canister?'

'No, no, no,' said Saint Peter, waving away that idea. 'The only reason certain people have the title of Saint—myself for instance—is that it's, well, a bit of an in-joke, really. Allow me to quote the Zohar when I say, "Were it not for the pure souls above, the world could not endure for even a moment." What exists inside the canister is Surplus Morality: quite literally the Spiritual embodiment of Good, which is generated in a Physical Realm, then handed over when a righteous person moves from the Physical and into the Spiritual. The reason you thought the Saints are *people* is probably because many Spirituals, during the time in which they don the Carnal Capacitor uniform, often get the deed and the doer confused. They think that because such-and-such does good things, such-and-such is therefore Good, and by extension, a Saint. When in fact, it isn't the person per *se* that is Good, it's the charge generated by the things they're *doing* that is Good. Because that's why Good things are ultimately done—not to make *people* Good, but to have Good existing. Does that make sense?'

Walter, quite confused, half nodded.

Saint Peter got to his feet and wandered around the room, saying, 'I suppose I should explain. Being a Physical, you probably know that every action has an equal and opposite reaction. What you more than likely don't know, is that every Physical action also produces a Spiritual vibration, which can be either Positive or Negative, depending on what was done. Spiritual beings—in whichever Physical uniform you find them—are like self-charging batteries. They store up the Positive vibrations they generate during their Physical lifetimes, and then, if they're benevolent, they hand over their Goodness so that others who didn't quite make the balance can use it to fill the void in their affected sub-DNA. This process of reckoning and renewal is known as "undergoing atonement."'

'You said *if* they're benevolent,' said Walter.

'Yes. Well. These days, what with free will, it's becoming something of a popular trend for people to retain their excess Morality. They store it up for future Physical lifetimes—under the notion that if they dig themselves a Karmic hole, they can use the Saints to stimulate the Laws of Attraction so as to get themselves out of it. Personally, I think it's a matter of people indulging themselves. Which is frightening if you think about it. But all that aside, the Saints are the leftover essence of Good, and they're used to keep the flow of Souls circulating. Without them, nothing would exist.'

'And what would be so bad about that?' asked Walter.

'What do you mean?' asked Saint Peter.

'Why does Good have to exist?' He shook his head, correcting himself, and asked, 'Why does anything have to exist?'

'Aha,' said Saint Peter, becoming almost enthusiastic. 'That's actually not such a silly question. First of all, let me just say that everything exists because the Divine Maker wants it to. If you have any problems with that, He is very open to discussion. And secondly, the reason Good has to exist is the very same reason Evil has to exist—because they're both part of a system that creates the charge that powers everything you see around you now.'

Walter's confusion must have been evident. Saint Peter took off his spectacles, cleaned them on his robe and said, 'Here comes a quick lesson that's all to do with the way things work. Or as God likes to call it, the Turds and the Trees. In the Physical Realms, the Positive and Negative Spiritual vibrations are at war with one another. Good chases Evil, which in turn tries to dodge and attack Good. That's all movement, so what's created is kinetic energy, which, when fed into a transducer, is converted into the power that keeps everything up here running. Every Citizen of Creation makes a contribution, and the worlds keep turning because of their efforts—Good or Bad.'

Walter was quiet. Then he asked, 'So...Good and Evil fighting each other; that's pretty much what keeps the lights of Heaven running.'

'Exactly,' said Saint Peter.

'That's a bit— exploitative— don't you think?'

Saint Peter cleared his throat, put his spectacles back on and said, 'Well. I don't know if that's the word *I'd* use, but...' *Ding!* 'Ah. That'll be the Good Lord now.'

Saint Peter treaded over to the entrance and peered across the expansive foyer beyond it. 'That's strange,' he said. 'God's elevator is empty. However. The Good Lord *is* known for His humour. Better brace yourself for something unexpected.'

Walter followed Saint Peter across the anteroom, toward God's luxurious elevator. It was set into a wall that was decorated with a gigantic gilded mural of Atlas, who, instead of being weighed down by one big planet, was easily juggling thousands of them. Saint Peter leaned inside the elevator, looked around within it, and glanced upon an envelope. It was stuck to the ceiling, held in place by stickers with tongue-in-cheek smiley faces on them. The old man reached for the envelope but found he wasn't tall enough. 'Would you mind?' he asked. 'I'm holding the Book of Life.'

Walter stepped inside the elevator, peeled the envelope off the ceiling and passed it to Saint Peter. Out of it came a Polaroid photograph. There were words on the back of it. Saint Peter read them, then looked closely at the image on the other side, and gasped.

'What's the matter?' asked Walter.

The old man was looking for words but couldn't seem to find any. Thrusting the photo into Walter's hands, he slapped himself on the forehead and muttered about retirement.

The photo showed three individuals who were obviously going for the old-time law-enforcer look. They were brandishing machine guns, and proudly standing in front of a large glass box. Inside that box was God, Who was grinning and giving two thumbs up. This made Walter think that maybe Saint Peter was right: maybe God was playing a joke. The thought that followed was: Nothing new about that.

Two of God's captors were familiar to Walter. One was the angelic thief from the Waiting Room. The other was Osama bin Laden. Figuring that the latter must have escaped from Hell, Walter turned his eyes to the photograph's most salient member: an Angel with white extended wings, and a haughty, puffed-up posture. Presumably it was *his* flamboyant cursive on the blank side of the photo, which read:

As you can see, we've kidnapped God. And guess what! You're not ever going to get him back. But if you'd like to try, then one of the offerings you can make is this: Every time the Angel Lucifer is spoken to/about, *or written* to/about, *there should be a capital H prefixed to* Him, Himself, His, *and all other variations—including a capital Y for* You, Your, Yourself, *and all of the et cetera. Thank you very much for taking the time to read this note. We pray it finds you* panicked. *Which is exactly how you* should *be feeling.*

Yours sincerely (notice the capital Y*), Lucifer.*

'It *has* to be a joke,' said Saint Peter, pacing around with his arms folded. 'Although Lucifer and the Good Lord haven't been on the best of terms recently. It's not very likely they'd be in cahoots on a prank like this. Although perhaps the Almighty's set it up to look that way. He's pretty mysterious, after all.'

'What should we do?' asked Walter.

'Well, I'm not sure what the protocol is. But I'm thinking perhaps we should consult...' Saint Peter gulped. 'The second-in-command.'

Chapter 6

The door read *Jesus H. Christ, Vice President of All Creation,* and slumped over the desk that guarded it was an Angel bodyguard/secretary, either asleep or deeply drunk.

'Probably a bit of both,' whispered Saint Peter, as he reached for a large golden doorknocker. It was a life-sized lion's face, standing out in relief. Saint Peter knocked lightly by waggling its jaw.

There was no answer from the other side of the door. The old man muttered something about times for special liberties, and turned one of its handles. He and Walter slipped inside the VP's office.

Walter heard Saint Peter fumble around with some switches on a wall. One of them activated the blinds of several tall, vast windows. Sunlight flooded the room, doing so in mangled patches because some of the blinds were damaged. Those patches of light fell upon eclectic and sometimes upended pieces of furniture, and illuminated a multileveled working space that was more like a penthouse. It would have been swank if it wasn't covered with strewn rubbish. It had balconies, a brass fireman's pole leading to the levels above and beneath, and, outside, visible through one of its windows, a lengthy glass lap pool that extended out from the building like a transparent bridge reaching to nowhere. The pool was filled with floaty toys, as well as a sun-baking creature that looked like a polar bear.

Saint Peter looked around and apparently spotted the person he was searching for. The man was on the other side of the room, stretched out on a lounge chair. Even from a distance Walter was surprised. The man was long, lean, scraggly, and appeared to be wearing a wife-beater singlet. As they made their way closer, past video game cords, junk food wrappers, and harnesses whose bungee cords hung from the ceiling, he saw that the man was littered with homemade tattoos. The most prominent one, on his forearm, read, WTH<u>W</u>JD? As well as all that, he was missing two of his top front teeth. This was made known by the fact that his mouth was hanging open as he snored wheezily.

Saint Peter said, 'Heht-hem,' and received no response.

He gently kicked the man's boots and again received no response.

He opened the Book of Life at its halfway point and slammed it closed.

'*Aaah!*' shouted Jesus H. Christ, awakening and gasping for breath. He looked around like a drugged and frightened animal reacting to sunlight, and shielded his eyes with a canopy of fingers. The viciousness of daylight evidently waned a fraction: enough for Jesus to rasp, 'Petey. How are ya?'

'I'm well thank you, sir. Yourself?'

'I got nothin' to complain about,' said Jesus, heaving himself to a lazy sitting position. He took a deep, fumigating sniff of the air, and swallowed as though he had a sore throat. 'What's goin' on? I didn't think we had a meeting or anything today. I was just...relaxing. After a big, uh, business thing.'

'Which was followed by a rather big night, I take it,' said Saint Peter.

Jesus stretched his facial muscles, then yawned, nodded, and turned his attention to Walter.

'Uh, yes,' said Saint Peter. 'Walter, this is Jesus Christ. Jesus Christ, this is Walter. Walter is Newly Deceased and yet to be processed. He's up here because, well, he's involved in a— a course of affairs that has proven to be quite strange. To say the least.'

'Fertilise my curiosité,' said Jesus, searching his pockets, amused by his own quote.

'Well, it seems,' said Saint Peter, all but cringing, 'or it doesn't seem...It's happened that, well, the, uh, Saints have...gone missing. Or to a finer point...they've been stolen.'

'That's a pretty abnormal thing to hear,' said Jesus.

'I was watering my pot plant,' said Saint Peter. 'It's a Bonjevavarian evergreen, and, I was only looking away for a moment, but when I looked back up they were—'

'Petey,' said Jesus, holding up a calming hand. 'Shiite crappens. Y'just gotta deal with it. Have y'told Dad about it? I'm guessing y'haven't.'

'We *have* told Jehovah,' said Saint Peter, as Jesus began searching the cushions of his couch. 'He told us not to worry about it; that He'd go and get them back. He went down to— I don't know, wherever He went to— and when His elevator came back, He wasn't with it. We found this.'

Jesus received the Polaroid and gave it a cursory glance. He was more interested in the cigarette he'd just found beneath his couch cushions. Once that latter item was lit, and he was drawing deeply from it, he had a more thorough look at the photograph. Consequently, the cigarette almost fell out of his mouth, and he didn't quite know what questions to ask. 'When did...How did...?'

'Not even five minutes ago,' said Saint Peter. 'And I'm quite certain it's not a joke.

'As your father isn't here, I believe the recommended procedure is for me to inform *you* of what's happened, and you're the one who takes it onward.'

There was a loaded crackling pause—like a wick burning toward a bomb—and then Jesus said, 'Is that a good idea?'

'Whether or not it's a good *idea*...' said Saint Peter, obviously unable to think of a way to finish that sentence.

Jesus scratched at his dark facial fuzz and hauled himself to his feet. Walter noticed that as he spoke, his eyes repeatedly glanced at a specific corner of his office, where a knocked-over bird cage was pinned to the ground by a toppled plinth.

'Uhhhh,' said Jesus, seemingly for a distraction, 'd'you think, maybe, we should run all this past the board?'

'That is completely your decision, sir.'

'Petey, don't call me that. How would y'like it if I called you clerk? Or...Peter?'

'What would you have us doing?' asked Saint Peter, widening the placement of his feet.

'Um...' said Jesus, his mind evidently a total blank. 'Uh...You're in the Waiting Room, aren't you.'

Saint Peter nodded.

'And the people in the Limbo Lines, they're still Physical, aren't they.'

'Well, they haven't yet signed away control of their Carnal Capacitors,' said Saint Peter. 'So you're right. Technically.'

'I'm just thinkin',' said Jesus. 'If things go from bad to badder, y'might wanna get in early and start pickin' out the One True Religioners. Store up their Morality 'cause, you know, if somethin' *really* bad happens we might hafta use it.'

'That's a good idea,' said Saint Peter. 'But we'd be storing it up at the expense of admitting people into the Echelons. Is that something we're prepared to do?'

'Uh,' said Jesus, rubbing his chin. 'Did Dad tell you where He was going?'

'He just got in His holy elevator and went,' said Saint Peter.

'That's a bit o' good news,' said Jesus. 'I can just hit the refresh button. And tell me, how is—' He snapped his fingers and Saint Peter reminded him. 'How is Wally involved in all o' this?'

'He was waiting to be processed and saw who took the Saints.'

'Aw yeah?' said Jesus. 'Who was it?'

The question was levelled at Walter, who didn't provide a speedy enough answer on account of being a little bit star-struck.

'It was that young Angel who clipped his own wings,' said Saint Peter. 'The one who's always following Lucifer around.'

'Clarence,' said Jesus. 'Hell. Not a good thing if *that* idiot's flappin' around. Last time I saw him was after his "baptism," when Lucifer had given him his new name. Now he wants to be called "Clip," 'cause of how he circumcised his feathers.'

'Oh how inventive,' said Saint Peter.

'Tell me about it,' said Jesus. 'Okay. Gotta figure out how to do this. I reckon I'm gonna go to wherever Dad went, 'cause there might just be a few— residues lyin' around. Information n' that sort o' thing. Petey, you go back to the Waiting Room n' pick out the One True Religioners. For the time being store up their Morality and only let *them* through. We might get a backlog o' Limbo Lines, but I reckon that's something we can catch up on just as soon as everything's Honkus. Uh...' He snapped his fingers and then it came to him. 'Walter. What're you doin'?'

Walter shrugged.

'All right then. D'you wanna come with me? 'Cause I'm gonna need someone to make me feel like I'm not totally on my own.'

Saint Peter bit his teeth and said, 'Technically he's not supposed to be up here.'

'Technically,' said Jesus, as if he didn't have a lot of respect for that word. 'Petey, y'got my word that if the powers-that-be come crashin' down, it's not your apexial they'll be landing on. I'll sign off on it. Is that okay with you, Mr. Wally?'

Walter looked at Saint Peter, who reluctantly said, 'I suppose you'd just be biding your time in the Waiting Room.'

'All right then,' said Jesus. 'Let's go.'

As Walter shadowed Jesus into God's holy elevator, Saint Peter, seemingly doing his best to sound confident, said, 'Uh, good luck, and everything.'

'Why thank you Petey,' said Jesus, reaching for the refresh button. 'Behave yourself while we're gone.'

COURTNEY TAYLOR

Chapter 7

Through the parts of the elevator windows that weren't frosted decoratively, Walter saw hundreds of worlds sweep into view for barely a moment. There were smoggy conurbations, jungles that were orange like fire, a place where all of the trees appeared to be made out of water, and then, *Ding!*, the doors opened upon a world whose grey sky pressed heavily onto a hamlet of charred houses. The two men stepped out of the elevator, their feet sinking into mud, the Son of God muttering resentfully because these shoes were his favourites.

'Typical,' said Jesus, as they squelched down the main road of the recently razed village. 'Lucifer no doubt. Really is a son of a pervert. Well, obviously there's no sign of anything. Looks like he did all this for fun, or to cover his—' *Ding!*

Jesus spun around as the doors of the holy elevator began closing. He took off running but didn't get to them fast enough. They closed, leaving nothing but vacant space, space that Jesus tried to kick before howling, '*Craaaaaaaaap!*'

Walter didn't know what to say, but finally decided upon, 'I take it we're stuck here.'

Jesus was bent over as though he'd just run a marathon. Looking up at Walter with a stink-face expression, he said, 'My HP card. I left it back in the Spiritual Realms.'

'What's an HP card?'

'Heavenly Privileges. It's what you use to...' He waved away the explanation as though it wasn't worth the effort, but then stood up straighter and said, 'It's pretty much what y'get if you're involved in the running of Creation. Makes things a hell of a lot easier, 'specially in the Physical Realms. It's how back in the day I did the whole walkin' on water thing, which— Well, I'm sure you've heard all about *that*. Anyway, I'll see if I can circumvent this ugliality.'

Jesus began to whistle the tune *Swing Low Sweet Chariot*. The way he was looking around made Walter think he was trying to call an animal to him.

After a solid minute of whistling the same tune, Jesus looked confused. He also looked as if he wasn't in the mood for answering questions, so Walter asked only one: 'What should we do now?'

Red-headed villagers in old-fashioned clothing were venturing out from charred hiding places, seemingly having recognised Jesus' tune. The VP looked at them and said, 'Well, I reckon we might do a bit o' recon action, see if these people can point us in the direction o' some kind o' civilisation. Hopefully that'll help us get a ride back to Heaven.' Waving a lazy cross at the approaching villagers, he yelled, 'My sympathies!'

An hour or so later, Jesus and Walter were trudging along a dirt road that seemed to be running through the legitimate middle of nowhere. Jesus, grumbling about how you should never take directions from in-breds, glanced over at Walter, recognised Walter's expression (obviously a familiar one) and said, 'Don't expect too much, Chief. But it seems we *have* got plenty o' time for questions, so, do your worst. I've heard 'em all before.'

Slightly embarrassed by his own transparency, Walter thought about what he wanted to ask, then said, 'If we don't get the Saints back, what's gonna happen?'

'I'm surprised ya didn't ask about something to do with the New Testament,' said Jesus, smiling dryly. 'And I like the way ya said "We," Wally. Ha ha. *Wee Wally.* That's your name from now on.' His smile fell away and he said, 'If we don't get the Saints back, what's gonna happen, worst-case scenario, is, all o' the Physical Universes are gonna be destroyed.'

'What?' said Walter. 'How?'

'Aw, it's been a while since I've been at school,' said Jesus, 'but let's see how we go.

'You've got a thing called the Ality fabric, which is a Spiritual material that binds but also separates all o' the Physical Universes. This...kinda *skin*...is held together by the connectedness of all the Souls that live inside Creation. Creation being pretty much everything. Does that make sense?'

Walter nodded.

'Okay then,' said Jesus. 'Now. The way it goes is, every single Spirit—from a Universe Soul to the Soul of a cockroach—has a proportion o' Good and a proportion o' Bad. It's the whole Ying-and-Yang whatever. Anyway, if the Good and the Bad inside o' the Spirits get chucked outta balance, then the Spirits'll produce some pretty weird reactions, depending on which way their levels swing. Too much Good and it's all about Peace and Love; there's absolutely *no* self-interest so no one's strivin' to achieve anything. (Needless to say that's pretty unproductive, for them and for Heaven). Too much Bad and the Spirits become *totally* Selfish, which means all they do is concentrate on 'emselves. That's when the Ality fabric starts dissolving, 'cause if the Souls holding it together aren't doing their jobs by holding hands, then the mechanism breaks down. That's just a simplification, but...Am I makin' sense?

Walter, poised to say *No*, nodded.

Jesus evidently noticed Walter's confusion, and said, 'All right, here's the process: When the Spirits become Selfish, they get inverted, 'cause they're only looking inward and concentrating on 'emselves. If they do that for too long, they start acting strangely. That's when we start calling 'em Angry Loners. As y'probably know from the world you've just come from, Angry Loners are usually the type o' people who, I dunno, do things like— urinate on kindergarteners and set 'em on fire.'

'So you mean,' said Walter, 'these Angry Loners begin to attack one another. And that's why the fabric dissolves?'

'Exactly,' said Jesus. 'They're not keepin' their Universe together. And on top o' that, when Bad chases Bad, what y'get is a kind of vibrational echo, which feeds on itself, and produces a sort of concentrated Evil—a chemical called Bad Karma. I'm sure you've heard of *that* phrase, yeah?'

Walter nodded.

'And I'm also sure,' said Jesus, 'that you woulda seen this Spiritual substance in action in the Physical Realms. Y'ever seen a person who looks so worn down by life that y' can actually see the disappointment and the bitterness wearing away at their faces? Well, that's 'cause their bodies are bein' eaten alive by a manifestation o' Bad Karma. And if humans—'cause you're a human, right?—could live to the age of a-hundred-and-fifty, then these people with the BK inside of 'em wouldn't be able to do it. 'Cause it's been gauged that afflicted Physicals, when they make it to the year-1-21-mark, become so consumed by the Bad Karma inside 'em that their entire Physicality gets claimed by Spiritual bitterness. You'd literally see their Physical bodies crumpling up into sick and bitter, twisted little wads, which'd then keep getting smaller and smaller till there was nothin' left but tiny little balls o' shriveled-up hatred. And yeah. That's what's gonna happen to the Universes if we don't get the Saints back into 'em. Bad Karma'll manifest, then generate, then drag everything Physical into it. It'll be the Big Crunch, or whatever they call it. Did that make sense?'

Walter nodded, soberly.

'But that's just the worst-case scenario,' said Jesus. 'And we should probably set our sights on a topic o' conversation that isn't so morbid. I don't wanna be gettin' bummed out by all this— Ohw! Check it out! Can you see that?'

Walter looked in the direction Jesus was pointing, where ahead of them, on a distant road meeting theirs at an angle, a horse-drawn cart was about to cross paths with their own.

'What'd I tell ya, Wally?' said Jesus, clenching a victorious fist and smiling toothlessly. 'Everything happens for a reason. Or at least I like to say it does.' He took off in the direction of the faraway cart, yelling at its driver. Thirty or so seconds later he was rasping as if having a panic attack, referencing his own name, and saying, 'I gotta cut back on all the communions I' been showin' up to.' He laughed like a mewling goat and began to cough.

Walter, jogging alongside him quite comfortably, asked, 'Did you just use your own name to...blaspheme?'

'Ha ha,' said Jesus, wheezily. 'Come on man, it's predictable. And I hate that word. It sounds like a perfume. *Blaspheme*— the new fragrance by *Jesus Christ*. Heh heh heh. All right. This guy'll probably think we're lunatics if he hears us talkin' about different Dimensions. Might get us kicked off our ride, so don't say anything. Okay?'

When they made it to the cart, they said *hello and thanks for stopping and jeez it's a miracle we ran into you*, then climbed onto its empty tray and plonked themselves next to a blue, majorly-permed sheepdog. Their driver, a thickset man in his late fifties, looked like a country farmer trying to push the barriers of fashion. He was wearing a large pink beefeater's hat, a bright red cravat, and an orange cape. Embroidered on the back of his cape were two faces: a smiling Asian man and a smiling chimpanzee. Words stitched beneath them read, *Surely one must bear the Mark of Cain.* Jesus snorted dryly and shook his head.

Half an hour later, as their driver rambled on about land councils and the merits of garlic capsules, Walter gazed out at scenery that hadn't changed even slightly, his thoughts again taking him to the world he'd left behind. Hopefully the news of his death was finding its rightful avenues. He was worried that people he hadn't been close to were finding out about his passing before those he had been close to. That occurrence had always annoyed him. It didn't seem to pay credit where it was due.

A noise distinctly flatulent distracted Walter from his thoughts. Looking over at Jesus, the blue dog, then at Jesus again, he asked, 'Did you hear that?'

'Hear what?' asked Jesus, who was answered by a drawn-out repeat of the same flatulent sound.

Beyond the peak of a nearby ridge there appeared a shiny moving object that looked like a periscope. The top of it opened like a blooming flower, and out of it came a brown vapour, along with the vulgar noise that had piqued their interest.

Jesus leapt to his feet and shouted, 'HA HAAR! I thought we were stuck in some Dad-forsaken Dimension where technology doesn't exist! Thanks a billion ya cult-lovin' maniac!' He ruffled the driver's furry pink hat till it toppled off his head, then leapt out of the cart, landed heavily on the dirt, hitched up his jeans and ran up the hill.

'Sorry about that,' said Walter, dropping onto the road, picking up the driver's hat and giving it back to him.

''S all right,' said the driver. 'I've got a cousin with a mental illness. Likes to do funny things in public places. You fellas take care o' yourselves. And make sure you keep to the paths of righteousness. Otherwise you'll end up with somethin' incurable.'

'Thanks very much,' said Walter, smiling and waving as the man drove away. Turning and jogging up the hill in pursuit of Jesus, he made it to where the Son of God was looking out across a long straight river of bitumen.

'What'd I tell ya, wee Wally?' said Jesus, giving another toothless grin. 'Providence.'

COURTNEY TAYLOR

Chapter 8

Cars and trucks with glass-encased organic engines were going past at a healthy rate, but none of them were stopping. In fact most were speeding up when they saw the two hitchhikers, probably because Jesus, with his thumb out, was self-consciously covering his scars, so looked as if he was trying to hide a pair of handcuffs.

'I know you're not wearin' any shoes, Wally,' said the Son of God, as he moved to a less conspicuous position, 'but it might be more productive if people see *you* first.'

Walter stepped closer to the highway, held out his thumb and said, 'Please don't be offended by this, but, you're not really what I expected you to be.'

Jesus smirked and replied, 'Y'wouldn't believe how often I get that, m'man. All I can say is, y'got the Bible to thank for all o' the misconceptions. And before you ask what I mean, here's the answer I usually give the masses. Let's just say that that little interDimensional pamphlet, in whichever format it comes, is a Spiritual Stimulus Package (which is what the ladies consider me to be, heh heh heh); a guidebook that'll help keep your Physical Universe on the straight and narrow. To explain myself, before you ask me to explain myself. Religion—being something that it isn't Good or Bad, but which'll swing in either of those directions—is chucked into the Realms that need a bit of a kick-start, in the hope that its influence'll move things in a more "active" direction. It doesn't always, but, most of the time it somehow manages to.'

'So...none of it's true?' asked Walter. 'The Bible, I mean.'

'Aw, it's all true,' said Jesus. 'But which Dimension that truth was extracted from is where things get debatable. 'Cause the Book's a shlocking together of happenings-filled-with-principles that've cropped up in Dad-knows-how-many Dimensions, some of which haven't even been created yet. And all o' these principles overlap each other with their meanings and reflected realities. So, well, what *that* means is, even up in Heaven we don't fully understand what refers to what. Which is why a lot o' people, when they make it back up to the Echelons and witness Physical History, get a little bit confused. 'Cause a lot o' the Bible's written in code, so...but anyway,' said Jesus, annoyed by the amount of brain work he'd just had to do. 'The nutshell of what I'm saying is: The reason people have a somewhat...*unrealistic*... perception o' me, is 'cause the version o' me that cropped up in the Bible is, well, censored, or sanitised, so the proper flow of how things *should* be, still manages to— I dunno— be the dominant thing happening. If that makes sense.

'And before you ask the question, "Is this a case of what the people don't know won't hurt 'em?" let me say that I don't know. It *could* be that, or it could be like my Old Man always says: Just because it hasn't happened *yet*, doesn't mean it's not *gonna* happen.'

'I was gonna ask what *did* happen,' said Walter. 'Why did your adventures get— sanitised?'

'Adventures,' said Jesus, smiling. 'That's exactly right.' He seemed on the verge of giving an answer, but in the end drew air between his teeth and replied, 'Look, it's a long and detailed history, which I've had to recount about five-hundred-thousand-million times. If I can get outta repeating it now, then, that's what I'm gonna do. But yeah. Y'wouldn't believe some o' the things that get cross-referenced and, uh, obfuscated. I'll use myself as an example. In the Physical they see me as the Only Begotten kinda son. But in Heaven I think I'm viewed more as the Prodigal. A lot o' people think that whole Wayward Kid parable actually refers to the Sodom and Gomorrah incident, which, to enlighten you:

'When I was a kid, me and my Dad used to go around settin' up Universes. We'd get a whole bunch of ingredients like antimatter, different gases and elements, then we'd light up these big zero-gravity bonfires and throw things into 'em, just to see what'd happen. It was heaps o' fun. And anyway, I musta been about nine or ten, and I wanted to find out what'd happen if I mixed, I can't even remember what the substances were, but I made a bonfire in a Realm that relied on oxygen. I didn't *mean* to kill anyone. And to my ten-year-old brain that didn't even matter 'cause beings get reincarnated. But yeah I was out in the desert, away from any towns or anything, and I threw in a can o' somethin' really flammable, and there was a big reaction. The whole surrounding area had to go into quarantine for "scientific" reasons. A certain radius had to be "sterilised" and that's the Rain of Fire episode. It's also the reason I ran off and tried to hide from Dad, which some people think is one o' the inspirations for the whole Adam and Eve bein' naked thing. Anyway it all worked out in the end. I came back to Heaven and said sorry; Dad told me not to play around with dangerous substances on my own, especially in the Physical Realms; and after that...Yeah. It was all smooth.' Jesus sniffed as if clearing his throat and said, 'We should probably keep a better pace. That'll tell these drivers we're not a pair of unmotivated vagrants.'

A short time later, a white sedan with spherical wheels pulled over to the side of the highway. 'Ha ha,' said Jesus, doing a loping dance that made his greasy hair lash around. 'I told ya we'd get a ride.'

They jogged over to the idling car, whose heartbeat they could hear as they approached. Jesus crouched down to speak with its driver, but suddenly backed away and said, 'Oh. You, um, look pretty jam-packed.'

Walter didn't know what Jesus was talking about, because except for the driver—a man in his thirties who had a shaved head—the car was empty.

Jesus shook his head and said, 'I, um, don't wanna be eaten by orange dinosaurs. Wally, those dinosaurs in the backseat, they're gonna eat me 'cause they think I'm tryin' to join their band.'

The driver said, 'Is he all right?'

'He's got...mental problems,' said Walter, because Jesus was winking at him erratically.

The man had a good look at Jesus and obviously felt sorry for him. He said, 'You know there's a hospital pretty close to here. If you need me to take you there...'

'*Hospital*?' said Jesus, brightening but still feigning craziness. 'Don't take me to a hospital—that's where they experiment on your brothers of Hercules, your Testiclees. And I wanna keep mine. They're my friends.' He stepped away from the car and walked around with his arms out wide.

'Thanks,' said Walter, as Jesus began doing slack pirouettes. 'But when he gets like this he's pretty unreasonable. We might just keep walking till he gets tired.'

'Well, good luck then,' said the driver, with noticeable concern. 'And watch out for trucks. Lots o' mavericks on this highway.'

'Thanks,' said Walter. 'And thanks for the offer. We appreciate it.'

51

The man nodded firmly and politely, then flicked his indicator and pulled back onto the highway.

'What was wrong with that fella?' asked Walter, when the car was a small white dot in the distance.

'He had a shaved head,' said Jesus. 'I don't like that about people.'

'What, is Jesus Christ prejudiced?'

'No,' said Jesus, defensively. 'It's just, I don't like bald people. They remind me o' Buddha. The fat bald degenerate. But don't worry, Wally. There'll be another ride. 'Cause like I always say: Fortune favours the beautiful.'

What eventually came cruising down the highway was a horse-drawn carriage, only, the galloping horse was suspended in the air by a harness, its hooves connected to rods that turned an octuplet of rubber-rimmed wheels. Sitting in the vehicle's cab, behind a rectangular glass windshield, was a couple in their late thirties. The man had dark hair and a tiredly satisfied expression. The blonde, pink-skinned woman looked as if she was analysing a bundle of receipts.

'Ha ha!' said Jesus, when the vehicle pulled over to the side of the highway. 'What'd I tell ya?' He ran in its direction, slowed when he was close, then sped up again when he saw that the driver wasn't follicularly challenged. Clambering into the back of a wood-paneled cabin, he came face to face with a three-year-old girl who was rigged up in a car seat. She looked at him as if he was an oddity. Regardless, Jesus tapped his forehead as if taking off a hat, and said, 'Good day, madam.'

'Where are you gentlemen off to today?' asked the lady in the front, after introducing herself as Mary and her husband as Andrew.

'Uh,' said Jesus, fumbling with his seat belt as Walter climbed inside. 'You know that, uh, hospital, down that way?'

'St. Christopher's?' asked Andrew.

'Yeah, I think that's the one,' said Jesus. 'Unless there's a closer one. We're, uh, visiting a friend of mine.'

Andrew guided the vehicle back onto the highway, then slightly raised the volume on a wireless radio that looked as if it had been cobbled together with components foreign to each other. A newscaster was saying that yet another disagreement had claimed yet another group of civilians in yet another faraway conflict. Jesus said, 'End Times, m'man. Just like always. Heh heh heh.'

'Yeah they keep pushing back the date on that one,' said Andrew. 'Bet they're all wishing they'd invested in real estate. Either of you gentlemen religious?'

Jesus shook his head and said, 'Can't take yourself too seriously. That's what *I* think.'

'Amen to that,' said Andrew.

'And what about you, Walter?' asked Mary.

Walter shook his head and said, 'Same boat.'

Mary wiggled her fingers at her daughter, who smiled and kicked her legs like she was trying to get a go-kart moving.

'Hey, there's *your* mother,' said Jesus. 'Y'wanna see *my* mother? They've got the same name—I just realised that.' He pulled down his grubby singlet and unveiled a tattoo on his chest. It depicted a serene Mother Mary who was brandishing a cigarette and a handgun.

'That's very...elegant,' said Mary.

'Thanks,' said Jesus. 'She wanted me to get it.'

'How about kids?' asked Mary. 'Either of you guys got any?'

Walter shook his head. Jesus gave a bouncy noncommittal shrug.

'Married?' asked Mary, looking at both of them.

This time Walter gave the noncommittal shrug.

'Aw, it's hard to find a girl, ya know,' said Jesus. 'Y'never know if they like ya for who you are or who your Dad is.'

'I take it he's rich?' asked Andrew, looking at Jesus in the rearview mirror.

'And famous,' said Jesus.

'Aw yeah? Would we know him?'

'Andrew,' said Mary. 'He probably doesn't wanna say.'

'Nah, it's all right,' said Jesus. 'He's Humphrey Bogart.'

A short time later, as they passed a billboard that read,

Jesus

coming soon

Andrew was defending himself from his wife, who was telling him not to be so rude.

'I'm just *saying*,' said Andrew. 'Even if he *is* illegitimate—the mathematics doesn't sound right.'

SAINT WALLY

Chapter 9

'Good luck, Walter, Mr. Bogart,' said Andrew. 'Hope your friend gets better.'

'Thanks,' said Jesus. 'And thanks for the ride. And good luck with the child-raising. She's a cutie.'

After waving at the toddler, who blushed and hid her face, Jesus closed the carriage door then tapped his fingers on its window. The horse-propelled locomotive-looking carriage pulled away from the pavement, revealing a bumper sticker that read, *Honk if you're Holy.*

'So why have we come here?' asked Walter, as they walked up a hill toward a hospital.

'Like I told *them*,' said Jesus. 'We're visiting a friend o' mine. And if anybody asks what we're doin', just say we're lookin' for the prophylactic dispenser. Heh heh heh.'

It took a bit of sign-reading, but eventually they found the Intensive-Care Unit, which for some reason was imbued with weak darkness—as if it was twilight in this place only. Jesus, cringing on account of his squeaking shoes, was about to explain the gloom, but grabbed hold of Walter's arm and pulled him into an adjacent corridor. A nurse in a white uniform hurried past them. Jesus whistled with relief and said, 'Anyway. Physical beings can't see Spiritual beings, but 'cause me and you are still a little bit physical, they can see us a little bit.'

'You mean, we're all blurry?' asked Walter.

'Nah,' said Jesus, as they stepped back into the main corridor. 'We just haven't got the same essence as them, so we're not really very...memorable. We can talk to 'em and interact like normal people, but when we walk away they usually can't remember us.'

'So the people who gave us a ride,' asked Walter. 'They won't be able to remember us?'

'The little girl probably will,' said Jesus, leaning into one of the rooms and looking around. 'She's closer to her re-entrance date, so hasn't forgotten about the Spiritual Realm. But to her parents we're just gonna be like a gap in their memory. It's like when I came back to earth to visit all my friends and they didn't recognise me. Y'remember that story?'

Walter nodded.

'Well, that's pretty much what happened. I was half Spiritual, so wasn't really "All There."'

Jesus looked into another room filled with an occupied bed but obviously not what he was looking for.

'Anyway. Sorry. The reason this place is dark. Two reasons, really. One is 'cause lots o' sad things've happened here. All o' that pain and grief comes pulsin' outta the Carnal Capacitors, sorta saturates the Spiritual atmosphere. It's the same thing with haunted houses n' happy homes; different emotions, though. The other reason—lots o' people've died here, which means there'a been lots o' cuts in the Ality fabric. That's how people make it back to the Spiritual Realm: they travel through a rift that connects 'em with the Death Duct, which takes 'em straight to the Outer Darkness, where they travel around Creation and come back into it and...Well, I might have to draw it for you. When we get back to Heaven remind me to do that. But the darkness we're seein' now—it's only 'cause the Ality fabric's a bit weak around here. Nothin' to worry about, though; unless you're a sensitive, overly-excitable type, like a psychic or a schizo; or a tribal person.' Peeking into another room, vaguely irritated, he said, 'Looks like nobody's dyin'.'

'If this friend of yours isn't here,' said Walter. 'What would be our next move?'

Jesus went to answer, but then halted, his eyes going wide. He grabbed Walter by the sleeve and pulled him down the corridor. Opening a door and entering the room beyond it, they came upon a dark hooded figure with white fluffy wings. The figure was standing in front of an intubated patient, holding up a golden sickle-sword that Walter knew was called a khopesh. He correctly surmised that the person wielding it was the Angel of Death.

Jesus stepped deeper into the room, and with mock snobbery, said, 'Hello, darling.'

The cloaked figure turned around...and Walter was very surprised to learn that the Angel of Death was in fact a young and very attractive dark-haired woman.

'Well, if it isn't the Son of God,' said Death, removing her hood, and looking at Jesus as though he was a very salty surprise.

'How are ya, Grimmie?' said Jesus, grinning. 'Made anybody blow snot out their noses today?'

'Not yet,' said Death. 'But now that I'm looking at you I think I might've just found a candidate.'

'Walter,' said Jesus, 'this is Death. She and I met while I was hangin' out on the cross. Bad memories. Except for meeting Grimness, of course.'

'We actually met before that,' said Death. 'It's just he can't remember it.'

'The Gomorrah incident,' said Jesus. 'Apparently.'

'Exactly,' said Death. 'And hello, Walter. I think I might've met you before, actually.' In Jesus' direction she said, 'Although we might not've been introduced back then, because introductions take time, which I, apparently, don't have a lot of, because some people say I'm a workaholic.'

'Aw I wouldn't be *that* drastic,' said Jesus. 'Go-getter is a much less abrasive term.'

'Because the effects of diseases and obesity and things like earthquakes,' said Death, 'and not to mention all of those religious lunatics who so enjoy killing each other—they're very non-abrasive, non-time-consuming things to deal with, aren't they.' Pleased with her own riposte, Death twirled her khopesh and said, 'So what're you gentlemen doing down here in the Present, anyway?'

'Well,' said Jesus, scratching at the back of his head. 'It's kind of an annoying story, but the sum of it is: we're on a top-secret mission kinda thing, and I've been locked outta Heaven again. But I just remembered: Before we go back, we gotta go see Mohandas. Would you mind helpin' us out with that?'

Death, acting as though she hadn't quite heard that properly, said, 'You want *me*, to take *you*, to see *Mohandas*.'

Jesus nodded, almost guiltily.

'Are we talking about the same Mohandas,' said Death, 'who is constantly practicing auto-asphyxiation erotica and "accidentally" almost killing himself, which means that *I*—'

'That *you* have to go out of your way to— yes,' said Jesus.

'The same Mohandas,' said Death, 'who has sold bogus OTR "secrets" to how many cult leaders, who have all influenced thousands of people to commit suicide, which is a mess that–'

'That *you* have to deal with,' said Jesus.

'That's right,' said Death. 'That *I* have to deal with. The same Mohandas—'

'I'm pretty sure it's the same person we're talkin' about, Grimmie,' said Jesus. 'So please don't give me any more examples. Otherwise we'll be here till— till *I* come back.'

'Hmph,' said Death. 'At least he admits it.'

'Yes,' said Jesus. 'I do. Because Mo has...he's got his problems. But right now me and Wally really need to get to him.'

'Why?' said Death, who then said, 'Look I don't *care* why. It's not my problem. And the fact that you asked *me* to take you to see him.'

'It's not *that* big a deal, is it? Look, Grimmy, if it's about how busy I've been.'

'I really don't wanna hear this,' said Death, turning toward the patient in the bed. 'It's not my problem anymore.'

'Well, what we're dealin' with right now is gonna be *everyone's* problem if me and Wally don't get things into action. And I woulda called y'sooner than now, but, I've got responsibilities, too. Ya know?'

'You've been busy,' said Death, as if it was understandable. 'For almost a millennium.'

'Don't use that on me again,' said Jesus. 'Time's different everywhere. *You* know that.'

Walter saw that Jesus was floundering, so built up some nerve, and attempted to capitalise on the Time's Different Everywhere factor by saying, 'He *has* been with me for quite a while.'

Death looked at Walter, then at Jesus, and then said, 'Are you serious? With *your* Dad's beliefs?'

'*No,*' said Jesus, cringing. 'No-no-no. Walter, that's not— He means we're very busy, 'cause...'

'Because why?'

'I don't want tell you.'

'Oh my. I knew it.'

'No you *didn't* know it, Death. I am not a sodomite. Walter and I were...We were...Well, we're...we're down here for a reason.'

'You've said that,' said Death. 'But what you *haven't* said is what that reason is. And that leads *me* to think that the generosity of the good ol' Grim Reaper is being exploited once again.'

'We're on a— I dunno— a quest,' said Jesus.

'A quest,' said Death. 'What is this? Some kind of double-adapting role-playing *board* game?'

'Death, you *know* me. I am not a double-adaptor.'

'I've got'oo admit,' said Death. 'I have sometimes wondered.'

'You have *not*,' said Jesus. 'See now you're just makin' stuff up to suit your own purposes, which—' He closed his eyes as if praying for patience. 'I am not gonna get dragged back into this sort o' thing.'

'Then why don't you just avoid it,' said Death, 'by telling me why you're down here and why you need my help, because I do *not* want to be an enabler for some kind of misadventure that you're only...*worsening*.'

'Grimness,' said Jesus, remonstratively. 'Be realistic. Look. Right now you are the only one in this room who can pervade every single area of every single Dimension. You are part o' the system; and as the Vice President *of* that system, I am telling you you have *got* to take us to Mohandas.'

'And now we're back to Mohandas,' said Death. 'And what we're *not* back to is the reason why you want me to take you to Mohandas.'

'Fine,' said Jesus. 'If this is how you're gonna be, then how 'bout you just take us back to Heaven so we can get *ourselves* to Mohandas. It'll chop up valuable time because I'll have to sign for another Privileges card, but if that's what we have to do to save Creation, then that's what we have to do to save Creation.'

A voice coming from the doorway said, 'Excuse me. I don't think you're supposed to be in here.'

The trio turned to see a young female nurse, who was looking back and forth from Jesus to Walter and not seeing Death.

'And *now* look!' said Jesus, swiping at the air. 'This woman's gonna be callin' security 'cause she thinks I'm insane! D'you seriously want the fate of the Physical Dimensions going completely to hell just because you can't forgive and forget?'

'Forgiveness,' said Death, derisively. 'Also known as *Good ol' JC's get outta gaol free card*. That's the only reason you started spreading that message.'

The nurse, who was hearing only one side of the argument, stepped out of the room in what appeared to be a huff. Walter closed the door behind her and leaned against it.

'Death,' said Jesus, speaking slowly and calmly. 'That woman just went to call security, which means that Walter and I, who are both partially Physical, and thus able to *interact* with the Physical, are going to be arrested. If we are killing time in some pathetic little gaol cell, do you know what *else* we'll be killing? *Everything.*'

'All I'm hearing is vagueness,' said Death.

'Well how's this for vagueness?' said Jesus, with ultra seriousness. 'We're down here on Earth because the Saints have been stolen, Dad's been kidnapped, and Wally and me are tryin' to figure out how to get everything back to normal.'

Death's face went completely sour, as though she was thinking that surely this son of a God was lying through his missing front teeth. But then she glanced at Walter, who was leaning against the door with his eyes cast downward, and chose to withhold her diatribe. Cautiously, she said, 'Your dad's been...kidnapped? Are you serious?'

'More serious than I have been for a very long time,' said Jesus. 'We don't know how it happened, but it happened.'

Death scowled and said, 'You're not making this up, are you? This isn't some kind of prank?'

Jesus scoffed and rubbed at his brow.

Walter said, 'He's not lying, and he's not a sodomite. He's just busy.'

After a long pause, Death mumbled, 'Now *that'd* look good on a T-shirt.'

Jesus clasped his hands, buckled at the knees and said, 'Thank you, Grimness.'

'But I am not going near Mohandas, all right?' said Death, holding up a declamatory finger. 'I do not wanna have to speak to that misogynistic philanderer.'

'That's fine,' said Jesus. 'You can just drop us off near him.'

Deciding that that was appropriate, Death lifted her golden blade and cut a vertical gash into the air. It was tall enough for an adult to step through, and looked like a sky blue eucalyptus leaf rimmed by golden light.

Cheekily, Jesus said, 'How 'bout when all this is over, me 'n you take a bit o'—'

Interrupting him, Death smiled politely and said, 'I don't wanna be hearing any of your "how 'bouts." Okay?'

The VP seemed miffed and confused—doubly so when Death looked over at Walter and said, 'Be safe.'

'We will be,' said Jesus. 'Guaranteed. 'Cause you know what I always say.'

'Good,' said Death, smiling with civility, obviously not wanting to hear what Jesus always said.

Jesus, seemingly hoping for at least a small grin, gave a lazy salute and stepped through the rip. *'Whooaaa!'* he cried out, when his foot unexpectedly met nothing but air. He dropped about five metres and splash-landed in a crystal blue ocean.

'That's for Lazarus,' said Death, leaning out of the rift, grinning smugly at Jesus as he coughed, spluttered, and feebly treaded water. 'Don't worry, Walter. His friend'll be by pretty soon.'

'Thanks very much,' said Walter, approaching the rip and stopping at its edge.

'Manners,' said Death. 'How refreshing. You're welcome.'

Walter jumped through the gash and splashed into the other Dimension, where Jesus was floating on his back and spitting up a fountain of water.

'Bye now,' said Death. 'And good luck with everything. And remember to call someone else if you get in trouble.' Touching the blade of her khopesh to the bottom of the rip, she lifted it and zipped up the tear in the Dimensional fabric.

SAINT WALLY

Chapter 10

'She's somethin' special, isn't she?' said Jesus, as he and Walter swam in what seemed to be a completely arbitrary direction. 'See, Wally, that's another example of misconception right there. People think I conquered Death, but, let me tell you, it was *she* who sallied forth toward *moi*.' He cackled and nearly went under the water, then reclaimed his technique and said, 'Oh god, what I'd give for an HP card right now. Y'know how she got that thing? The blade, I mean. My Dad gave it to her. "In recognition of professional excellence, for the slaying of an untold number of first-born Egyptians, man and beast." Yeah we had some good times.'

Walter blinked and winced because someone else's thrashing around had splashed salt water in his eyes. Jesus appeared to notice, and said, 'Maybe I'm only sayin' this 'cause y'don't seem to have the nay-sayin' gene, Wally, but...I didn't leave my Heavenly Privileges card back in Heaven. I lost it in a card game a couple o' nights ago. Y'know the one where if y'get four o' the same then y'have to grab a spoon, and the one who misses out has to have a drink? Yeah. Well, Lucifer came along and sat down, said things'd be more fun if there was more at stake. I of course agreed. Typically.'

'So I'm guessing that's how he broke into Heaven,' said Walter.

'It's what I'm guessin' as well,' said Jesus. 'The restricted access parts, anyway.'

'Do you think your Old Man knows about all this?'

'Well,' said Jesus, 'He is omniscient, so...I dunno. But anyway. What's done is done is dead. Me and you'a gotta focus on the future.'

'Which has something to do with Mohandas?'

'I'm hoping so,' said Jesus. 'A couple o' months ago, Dad made MK the executor of, I dunno, "some crappy thing," and He told me, if there was ever like a "communication breakdown," then Mohandas was the man to see. At the time I thought Dad was just settin' up a middle-man, so He didn't have to deal with me. Now I'm thinkin that's a pretty...idiosyncratic kind of reaction.'

Five hundred metres south of the water-treading duo, a luxurious power yacht was charging through the ocean. Its captain was a tall, dark and handsome Sheikh, whose attention was more on the large-breasted women he was entertaining than on the direction he was steering. Deciding out loud that he'd greatly like to see some female wrestling, he yanked the boat's steering wheel hard to port, causing the dozen or so women in bikinis to tumble across the deck. The Sheikh laughed out loud, and had no idea that he was now heading directly toward Jesus and Walter.

'What'd I tell you, Wally?' said Jesus, upon seeing the boat now approaching them. 'Fortune favours the beautiful. The Rolls Royce o' rescue vehicles...of *course*.'

'It's coming at us pretty fast,' said Walter. 'Do you think they have seen us?'

''Course they have,' said Jesus. 'What're the chances o' bein' clobbered by the one boat in the whole damn...' He abandoned his sentence, because the yacht wasn't slowing down.

'Uh, maybe we should swim downward,' said Walter. 'Just in case.'

'Probably get hit by the propellers if we do that,' said Jesus.

'As opposed to the boat itself?' asked Walter.

The yacht looked like a sleek ivory arrowhead, and sounded as if it was powered by a jet engine. It was almost on top of them; but still, Jesus said, 'We're not movin' anywhere, Wally. I'm the one who gives the go-ahead about the laws in these sorts o' Dimensions. We're stayin' right here.'

The Sheikh pursed his lips at a young brunette, then swaggeringly faced forward. '*HOLY MOTHER OF CHODHU!*' he screamed, when he saw that two human heads, one of them quite scruffy, were bobbing in the water directly in front of his speeding boat. He spun the steering wheel in a panic, and again a pile of women rolled across the deck, this time so vigorously that some of them lost hold of their champagne glasses. The boat nearly capsized, but it *just* missed the two men in the water. What didn't miss them was the vessel's wake, which surged forward and slapped them in their faces.

'Whoo!' shouted Jesus, invigorated, and rising and falling with the swell. 'That was close, ay, Wally? Closer than was comfortable.'

The captain of the yacht was furious. Putting his vessel into a lower gear, he circled around, killed the engine, stormed downstairs and shouted, 'What the bloody hell do you think you're bloody doing, floating around in the middle of my private bloody ocean?' He did an abrupt double-take, then said, 'Jesus Christ. Tiffany, get the rope ladder!'

———

Women in bikinis helped Jesus and Walter clamber up onto the deck. Jesus, emanating torrents of salt water, grinned at the Sheikh, held out his arms and said, 'MK.'

'JC,' said the Sheikh, smiling widely. He was about to hug Jesus, but then pulled back because, 'Oh hang on, you're all salty. This robe is silk, man.'

After they'd settled for high fives, the Sheikh said, 'You know Mr. Vice President, my less-charitable urges were telling me to leave you in the water. What the bloody hell are you *doing* down here?'

'G.,' said Jesus, 'I shall elaborate. But first. Walter, I'd like you to meet the Reincarnation of Mahatma Gandhi.'

The aquiline Arabian, about six foot five and very well groomed, gave a lazy-eyed upward nod and said, 'Mahatma means Great Soul. You can call me Mahatma.'

They adjourned to one of the yacht's drawing rooms, where large windows showcased a row of finely-sculpted women sunbaking on the deck. Gandhi didn't want his white couches getting wet, so Jesus and Walter were seated on plastic covers.

'*Chodhu*,' said Gandhi, when Jesus finished telling him about everything that had happened. 'This is bad news. Who's in charge of things right now?'

Jesus raised a hand, and a woman in a sarong slipped a cocktail into it.

'Oh,' said Gandhi. He indelicately changed the subject by saying, 'Bianca, next time serve the guests first! Walter, are you comfortable?'

Walter received a cocktail he hadn't asked for, and nodded.

Jesus sniffed his drink, and evidently not pleased with it, leaned forward, put it on a glass coffee table, and said, 'Dad once said to me, if I was ever in the doo, I should come to you and you'd "enlighten" me.'

'Hmm,' said Gandhi, stroking his beard as if thinking deeply. 'The ways of your Father are indeed mysterious. But I feel He was referring to something He once gave me. It was a Christmas, birthday, whatever present, for you. He said He didn't want me seeing what it was because I'd ruin the surprise. Of course I *did* look, and, well, it was such a lame gift that I simply didn't feel the urge to *ruin* the surprise. I actually forgot about it, and that's why I never gave it to you.'

'What was it?' asked Jesus.

'Not much more than a piece of paper,' said Gandhi. 'A document about...I can't even remember, that's how unexciting it was. But your Father told me to guard it with my life, for one day it would prove very beneficial.'

'A piece of paper,' said Jesus, looking thoughtfully at Walter, who had no intention of drinking the cocktail he was holding. 'Dad mighta left us some kind o' heads-up as to what's happening. G., we need to get our hands on that thing. Would you mind takin' us to it?'

'Sure,' said Gandhi. 'I can take you right now if you like. I'm not doing anything.'

Neither Walter nor Jesus was sure if he was being sarcastic or accommodating.

As Gandhi steered his yacht past palatial homes set upon stretches of man-made beach, he pushed up his sunglasses and asked, 'Have you spoken to Mother Teresa recently?'

'She's back in the field,' said Jesus. 'Takin' care of a bunch of Albino orphans. Some Dad-forsaken village in who knows where.'

'She's a very driven woman, that one,' said Gandhi. 'I often tell her she needs to slow down and do a bit of relaxing. Otherwise she'll end up all bitter and twisted, resenting every life she lives. Just like the Apostle Paul. That snake-biting...' He trailed away into expletives. Jesus smiled as if he could empathise.

Gandhi soon added, 'You know *I've* thought about going back once or twice. But I don't know. I'm having too much fun where I am.'

'You should,' said Jesus. 'Especially now. With the Saints missing and everything.'

Gandhi smiled, lowered his sunglasses and said, 'Something I learned the first time I found myself in Heaven: There's no point worrying about anything, because ol' Yahweh's got it all covered.'

'Of course, back then, nobody had ever *kidnapped* Yahweh before.'

The yacht gurgled toward a small island blooming with tennis courts, palm trees and swimming pools—a tacky but extravagant holiday hideaway rimmed by all manner of expensive water vehicles.

'Money doesn't get you invited to a place like this,' said Gandhi, as he and his harem led Jesus and Walter across a network of piers. 'You have to be either very famous or very attractive. *You* might not be either of those things, Walter, but that's okay; you're a friend of JC's. I'm sure we can make an exception. No I'm actually just kidding—you're not *that* bad looking.'

Inside a gaudy boathouse was a glass elevator, the steel track of which headed up the incline of a man-made mountain. Gandhi snapped his fingers and the women disbanded.

As the elevator tracked toward a stone mansion that looked like a monastery, Gandhi said, 'I had it imported from Portugal, brick by brick. You're going to absolutely love it. The whole thing's been redecorated. Sort of my own individual style. Lots of different influences.'

Exiting the elevator and leading the way over to two enormous pine doors, Gandhi kicked one open like he was an action hero, and revealed a cavernous room that was part hunting lodge, part modern museum, all castle, and no taste.

He led them along a balcony that looked down upon a wooden labyrinth of tall bookshelves. Of the ancient tomes stacked upon them, Gandhi said, 'I haven't actually read any of these. I just bought them because I find women are impressed by them.

'All right. You guys wait here. I put the paper in one of my vaults, which for privacy reasons only *I'm* allowed into. And before you ask, no, it is not a dungeon containing child pornography. But if that's your thing, I don't judge. Amuse yourselves; but don't touch anything.'

Jesus and Walter looked at each other as if moderately impressed, then headed off individually to have a look around.

Walter found a spiralling staircase that took him down to the lower level. Making his way past garish suits of armour and wonky fluorescent sculptures, he arrived at a collection of knotted-rope underwear, which, according to a small plaque, had been worn by sixteenth-century monks for no other reason than to arouse their own discomfort. He shook his head at the craziness of some people, quietly entered the maze of bookshelves, and soon discovered a small reading cove.

On the farthest side of it there was a stone chimney rising to nowhere. Hanging upon it, in a pool of sunlight, was a painting of Jesus Christ, sitting on a rock and cradling a lamb. Walter had to smile, as the holy and innocent-looking character in the frame was nothing like the one he was travelling with.

A gravelly voice coming from behind him said, 'Did you know that that man is actually the forefather of several current Middle Eastern dictators?'

Walter turned and saw a stout man with a tired demeanour, sitting at a heavy wooden table and clutching a gossip magazine. Getting up from his chair and ambling closer, the man said, 'I used to be a follower. Devoted to his life and teachings. But then I found out that he did not actually come to Earth to save it, but for a holiday. Every person who ever brought this depiction of him into the world should be angry with themselves. And you yourself would be wise not to place stock in such...illusions.'

The man gave a pained and knowing smile, retrieved his gossip magazine, and left. Walter noticed something on his person that glinted in the sunlight. It was a small golden planet, grape-sized, and attached to a leather necklace. He also noticed that Jesus, standing behind a bookshelf, had overheard the man.

'I've got it!' yelled Gandhi, his voice echoing. 'Where *are* you guys?'

The three of them met in the reading cove, where Gandhi said, 'All right, here it is. Can you believe I forgot which drawer I was keeping it in?' He slapped a piece of paper onto the table. It was a document titled, *The Nine Down Three Across Anyooal Perort on Upper Eshelon Counteractivity*. They each read about three paragraphs and came to the same conclusion, which Gandhi summarised perfectly when he said, 'I told you it was a lame gift. It's gobbledygook. And can you believe that's actually a real word?'

'It's gotta make sense,' said Jesus. 'It came from Dad, and He never does anything without a reason. But what the hell does that mean? *Loors that dead to loors that dead to windows?*'

Walter put his finger at the top of the page, counted nine lines down and three words across. Reading out loud, he said, '*And then it shall come to pass that Lucifer will be called to account at the Pates of...* How do you say that word? G.E.A.R.L. *Gee-earl?*'

'Jirl?' said Jesus.

'Girl!' said Gandhi, brightening. 'The Pates of Girl.'

Jesus snapped his fingers and said, 'The Gates of Pearl. The Pearly Gates. *Lucifer will be called to account at the Gates of Pearl.* This thing's a prophecy, for sure.'

Gandhi scoffed and said, 'What, you think Lucifer will be rounding up a few last-minute converts from the back of the Limbo Lines? Why would he be at the Pearly Gates? He's Spiritual; can't die.'

Jesus picked up the letter and looked at it closely, as if trying to see words beneath the words. 'I dunno,' he replied. 'And I don't know why this memo's all mixed up, but...one o' Dad's secretaries, Chelsea, she's dyslexic, a bit sensitive about it, too. I'm bettin' *she* was the one He was dictating to.'

'That still doesn't clear away the obvious insanity,' said Gandhi. 'Like I said, why would Lucifer be at the Pearly Gates? He's Spiritual.'

Jesus scratched his head and said, 'We're gonna have to think about that.'

SAINT WALLY

Chapter 11

In a city called Metropopopolis, Lucifer led his three cronies through a showroom filled with shiny luxurious cars. They were accompanied by six young female groupies, each wearing red plastic devil horns. Lucifer had his arms around two of the sashaying women, and was quoting a poem he'd written just recently.

'And there I'll be, little ol' me, up in Heaven, just wait and see. Sanctified and Glorified, thanks completely to the Religified. But that'll be when the deeds are done, when the fun's been had by everyone.'

The rebellious Angel smiled maniacally when setting his eyes upon a gleaming red vehicle that looked like a sports car crossed with a fighter jet. Pinching at the air, he said, 'I like that one.'

Twenty-four seconds later he was in the driver's seat and spinning around the showroom, leaving tyre-marks and black smoke. The two groupies seated next to him applauded when he shouted, 'To the orphanage!'

The crimson mechanical beast exploded through the showroom's display window amid an eruption of broken glass. It slammed onto the pavement outside, skidded, and then roared down a darkened city street. Close behind it were expensive vehicles driven by Clip, Osama, and L. Ron. L.Ron didn't have any groupies, and the schizophrenic motorcade he belonged to didn't have the slightest concern about slow-moving cars, on-coming traffic, pedestrian crossings...or nuns. In fact, Lucifer screamed with joy when he saw a group of them chattering on a footpath, and swerved outrageously to meet them. Portly women in black and white fabric cartwheeled up onto the vehicle's bonnet, flipped off its roof, flew off its sides, and fell beneath its tyres. A straggler squealed as Lucifer swerved repeatedly. He finally got rid of her by using the car's windshield wipers.

After congratulating himself for his resourcefulness, Lucifer turned to his two groupies and asked, 'What coloured child would *you* ladies like to pick?'

Chapter 12

Jesus and Walter were sitting at a bar—one of several in the top floor of Gandhi's renovated, relocated monastery. A flat-screen television, mounted above a wall of delicate-looking bottles, was showing amateur footage of a recent earthquake in some undeveloped nation. Jesus was rotating a carton of cigarettes he'd just put on his tab, murmuring, 'The Gates of Pearl. The Gates of...' He trailed off and didn't finish what he was saying.

Walter noticed a vague despondency settling onto Creation's VP, and asked, 'You heard what that fella said. Yeah?'

'What?' said Jesus, crudely feigning ignorance.

Walter said, 'Remember that famous saying by—I can't even remember who—*Nobody can make you feel inferior...*'

'*Without your consent,*' said Jesus. 'I know. Eleanor Roosevelt. Or one of 'em. She says it to me every time I run into her. That woman seriously needs to hurry up and get herself reincarnated.'

Gandhi, who had been organising a pool party, sat down on a stool and said, 'Or like *I* once said: *They cannot take away our self respect if we do not give it to them.* I like my way of saying it better. Ball-breaking Eleanor Roosevelt.' To the bartender he said, 'Do you know how to make a hand grenade? Well, prove it, my man. What are you guys talking about, anyway?'

'Just tryin' to come up with some ideas about what to do next,' said Jesus, slipping the cigarette carton into his jeans pocket before grabbing a packet of matches from a bowl on the counter. 'Walter thinks we should go back to Heaven, see if anyone's heard anything.'

Gandhi spun on his seat and asked, 'You're thinking maybe someone has seen Lucifer?'

Walter nodded.

'Well, he does like being seen,' said Gandhi.

'*Called to account,*' said Jesus. '*Called to...*' Snapping his fingers as though an idea had suddenly hit him, and pointing at the bartender as he tallied numbers on a cash register, Jesus said, 'Of course. "Called to account." Dad wasn't telling us Lucifer'd be at the Pearly Gates. He was telling us we'd find him by checking my account details. All we gotta do to find Lucifer is view the transactions on my Heavenly Privileges card. Why didn't I think o' that?'

'It sounds pretty obvious now you've said it,' said Gandhi. 'But what— are you saying he's got your HP card?'

'Long and boring story, G.,' said Jesus. 'I'll tell you 'bout it later. Right now we' gotta get back into Heaven. Would y'mind swipin' us in?'

'Ooh,' said Gandhi, cringing as though he didn't want to admit this. 'See I was thinking about that, and, I've only got a *Carnal* account, which means only one Spiritual transaction. I was going to use it in case I got like AIDS or something.'

Jesus looked unimpressed; and to cement that notion, said, 'Mohandas. My Father is God, the Being Who created all of the Universes. I'm quite positive that when He *gets* back, He'll be more than glad to *pay* you back.'

'In the meantime, though, I won't have my Spiritual transaction,' said Gandhi. 'What if I end up in some hospital bed, having to endure pain? I've been sick before, man. Let me inform you, it's not fun. Look, I'm not saying you *won't* get Him back. I'm just saying I have to consider all of the possibilities. That's the *wise* thing to do.'

Jesus held out a hand and said, 'Mo. Give me that card before me and Wally beat the testosterone outta you. I am not joking.'

Shaking his head reproachfully and muttering about the abuse of power, Gandhi reached beneath his silk robe and came out with his wallet, which he opened so slowly that Jesus snatched it away from him.

When Jesus had found the right card, he threw the wallet back to Gandhi and said, 'Thank you, Mohandas.'

'Just make sure your Dad does pay me back, okay?' said Gandhi, as Jesus swiped the card at thin air, thereby producing a glowing doorway. 'Took me how many lifetimes of good deeds to *get* to that balance. And, uh, if you're expecting me to go with you...My girlfriend— well, she's not really my girlfriend— she's got a fashion shoot tomorrow. If I hadn't said yes I'd be with you for sure, but...one must always honour one's prior commitments. Sorry. And JC? I'll need my card back, man. What's the point of philandering if I'm not clocking up any points?'

It was a joke that went unappreciated. Gandhi received his card and slipped it back into his wallet. Trying to smile, he said, 'Good luck with everything, yes? And say hello to Mother Teresa for me. If you see her.'

Jesus gave a salute that didn't come with eye contact, then stepped through the glowing doorway, with Walter right behind him.

COURTNEY TAYLOR

Chapter 13

'Oh thank Jehovah,' said Saint Peter, breaking away from two of his Deputies.

'Petey,' said Jesus. 'What's been happening?'

'Well, we've been doing what you told us to,' said Saint Peter, as he led Walter and Jesus toward the Waiting Room. 'We've been collecting the Surplus Morality from all of the OTR certifieds—and also the Aborted Children.'

'Good,' said Jesus. 'And good work on the foetuses. I wouldn't have even thought o' that.'

'Sorry,' said Walter, as he hurried to keep up with them. 'OTR means One True Religion, yeah? What does that mean, effectively?'

'If you're OTR certified,' said Jesus, 'y'can pretty much check *yourself* into Heaven. They used to have their own special line, but...I'm not too sure why Dad changed the rules on that one.'

'Because following the New Testament overhaul,' said Saint Peter, 'God decided to no longer discriminate. Though as always, things would be a lot easier if we did. Right now we're having to go through each and every Limbo Line to try and weed out the favoured ones. Extremely tedious process.'

'The reason the OTRs are special,' said Jesus, 'is 'cause their Morality doesn't need to be treated. It's been contained in such a "wholesome receptacle" that the Saints are practically super-charged.'

'So, which religion is it?' asked Walter, as they came to a security door.

'You're a Physical,' said Jesus. 'We're not allowed to tell you *that*. But anyway it's in the Bible. Have a read of it.'

Saint Peter swiped his card through a scanner. A security door slid upward. The trio stepped onto a gridded balcony overlooking the billions of naked Citizens in the thousands of unmoving Limbo Lines.

'So the ones at the very front,' asked Jesus, 'they're awake, aren't they.'

'Correct,' said Saint Peter. 'And they're also subject to normal bodily functions and cravings, which is why we've been handing out sandwiches and bottled water. Also, we've set up some portable toilets.'

A pair of Deputies was trolleying one of those portable toilets toward a bouncing life-form that had a head like a Chihuahua. The poor creature badly needed to relieve itself, but couldn't step beyond the yellow line, for fear that the Citizen behind it would step forward and awaken, thereby advancing the queue.

Jesus laughed dryly, and said, 'And just in case everything hits the fan and people are still comin' into a blocked Waiting Room, are we gonna have enough space to fit 'em all?'

'Well, one of my Deputies had an idea about that,' said Saint Peter. 'On the floor we've got limited space, but up in the air—' he gestured toward the high ceiling '—we've got quite a *bit* of room. We were thinking of perhaps commissioning some scaffolding. Then we could have Limbo Lines upon Limbo Lines. If you get my meaning.'

Jesus clapped Saint Peter on the shoulder and said, 'That's not a bad idea, Sheriff. Although hopefully it won't come to that. Dad left us a message.'

———

In a stupendously airy spire (one of many rising from Heaven's Main Office) there was a mammoth, stone, flat-topped pyramid. Hovering above it, like a calm UFO, was a gigantic glass brain with a white fluorescent halo.

'Dad got tired of answering inane questions,' said Jesus, to Walter, as they and Saint Peter ascended the crowded steps of the ziggurat. 'So to avoid em, He replicated His brain and made it public access.'

They were cutting the queues by hurrying past people, and for this Jesus felt badly. He could see that many Citizens were recognising him, and found himself recalling a T-shirt he'd once had printed. It read, *Crowds. One day they'll lay out the green carpet, three later they'll swap you for a reprobate.*

The final steps led to a sweeping, mist-covered plateau. About to step onto it were two Rabbis. The skinnier one was saying, 'But if I have fourteen apples, and *you* have fourteen apples, then would not the logical conclusion be -'

'Sorry to interrupt, gentlemen,' said Jesus, 'but I'm gonna have to be quite rude and commandeer your place in the line. Important official business, I'm afraid.'

The two Rabbis turned around and looked at Jesus skeptically. The skinnier one said, 'Do you know how long we have been walking up this thing? Apologies, but, our belief permits us not to respect your authority. So if you don't mind...'

The pair turned away and was about to proceed; but Jesus, with noticeable steel in his voice, said, 'Gentlemen. If you would like to make a complaint about my appropriation of your place this queue, let me tell you where y'can lodge it. It begins with *your* and ends with *sphincter*. *Comprehendé*?

This time when the two Rabbis turned around, they evidently saw that the VP's dark eyes were blazing. The chubbier one went to say something but thought the better of it. The skinnier one stepped aside, held out an arm, and sarcastically said, 'Harmony, respect, welcome to Heaven.'

'Thank you,' said Jesus, stepping forward.

The moment they entered the mist, a dazzling beam of golden light shone down and engulfed them. There were many other people engaging with the Info Brain, but they seemed far away, and unimportant - even though they were involuntarily breezing past on all sides, like the pieces of some fast-moving, highly-complex, mandala-themed strategy game.

'Uh, Dad,' said Jesus, looking upward, 'we're gonna have to access my Heavenly Privileges page.'

God's booming voice replied, 'I hope you' got your password, sonny boy.'

Some of the mist configured into a keyboard made of cloud. Jesus approached it, cracking his knuckles, but then reconsidered and said, 'These things stress me out. Somebody else wanna type?'

Walter stepped forward to potentially help. However he was removed of the duty by a barging Saint Peter, who said, 'Aw, look, it's in Tongues; an Unprocessed person won't be able to read it.

'All right, Mr. Vice President. What's your middle name?'

'Hosanna,' said Jesus. 'And no, it's not a girl's name.'

'And the account number?' asked Saint Peter, typing adroitly.

'Account number is: 777 777 7...1. And the password is...aw, hang on. I can never remember it. No, it's a number. Try my birthday—010101.'

God's voice intoned, 'The password you have entered is incorrect. Perhaps make sure your caps lock is off.'

'That's annoying,' said Saint Peter. 'Maybe you got your password wrong.'

'I'm pretty sure that's what it is,' said Jesus. '010101.'

Saint Peter tried again—more carefully—and was quickly given the same result: *The password you have entered is incorrect.*

'Maybe it *is* the caps-lock thing,' said Jesus.

The old man tested that option, then calmly said, 'So, obviously you don't have your card with you.'

'Lucifer has it,' said Jesus. 'And it's a long and boring story...that began not so long ago. The last couple o' days are a bit...blurry. I mean, the only thing I can remember about last night is, at one point, me n' Joe Smith Jr. thought it'd be funny to swap underwear, so—' he sighed disappointedly '—Maybe I did tell someone my password, and they went and changed it on me.'

'Or maybe they simply guessed it,' said Saint Peter. 'It wasn't exactly complicated.'

There was a plaintive pause; and then Walter asked, 'So whatta we do now?'

'I'm not sure,' said Jesus.

'Finding God is the important thing, isn't it?' said Saint Peter.

'Well, right now in that department,' said Jesus, 'we're so far up Shiite Creek we could get out and walk. Maybe we should focus on finding Lucifer. Realistically, the only thing I can think of that'll give us a heads-up as to where *he* is, is this.' He held up the Polaroid.

'Should we have it analysed, do you think?' asked Saint Peter.

'Might be a good idea,' said Jesus. 'But...'

'But you're thinking the board will catch wind of what's happened,' said Saint Peter.

Jesus nodded, and said, 'I should probably be the one to break that wind to 'em. Probably shoulda been the first thing I did, now I'm thinkin' about it. But...Well, that's the next thing we're gonna do. Right after this.'

Jesus overcame his obvious disdain for typing. Stepping up to the keyboard again, he jabbed at it, and brought up a page called, *The Pilgrims' Passage Information Index.*

'What are you looking for?' asked Walter.

'Contact details for my bro,' said Jesus. 'Geoff son of Joseph.'

'You think he might be able to...help pull our canoe?' asked Walter.

'Hopefully,' said Jesus. 'And hopefully we don't have to start carrying it. Anyone got a pen?'

Chapter 14

Walter was peering through a glass wall that crowds of people—including Jesus—were interacting with. Beyond it was a gigantic crystalline room, in the centre of which was a kilometres-high diaphanous ball that was pulsating, owing, Jesus had said, to the new information about Time and Space that it was absorbing.

Encircling the huge ghostly sphere were thousands of doorways, each resembling the three-piece aggregates of Stonehenge. The millions of Citizens filing into and out of them, all to witness selected moments of recorded Physical history, were called Pilgrims. One of those Pilgrims was named Geoffrey Son of Joseph.

'Hey what's that number you've got?' asked Jesus, referring to the digits scrawled on Walter's forearm. Walter read them out and Jesus pressed them into a grid diagram on the glass. 'All right. Let's hope he picks up. Sometimes it takes him months to get back to you.'

There was a dial tone; then the smiling face of a thickset bearded man appeared in the glass and said, 'Hi, you've reached Geoff son of Joseph. Leave your name and number after the f— *beep*.'

'Geoff. It's Jesus. I'm outside the Pilgrims' Passage. When y'get this message call me back on this number. Quickly. It's important.'

'Ah. There you all are,' said Saint Peter, lifting up his baggy grey robe as he hurried toward them. 'Here we go. God's elevator's last known coordinates.'

'Thanks,' said Jesus, taking the slip of paper, and bouncing impatiently on his feet. 'And sorry y'had to go all the way back to Dad's office to get it. Wasn't thinkin'.'

Suddenly the glass read, *Pilgrim calling.*

'It's a miracle,' said Jesus, tapping the *Accept Call* icon. 'Geoff! Y'there?'

Geoffrey son of Joseph belonged to a throng of Pilgrims that was gathered so populously inside a darkened cave that their bodies merged to form a veritable cloud of witnesses. The heavyset bearded man, like every other spectator, was grouped around a supine convulsing man who looked like a goat-herder, and had, floating in front of him, a holographic tab filled with historical trivia.

'Bro,' said Geoff, speaking into a golden planet trinket that was laced around his neck. 'Guess where I am now. Visiting the 37th reincarnation of Judas. And guess who it is.'

'That's all fascinating Geoff, but listen, I need you to go to these coordinates at this time. I'd go myself, but, 'member how I got banned? For tryin' to superimpose myself into all o' those political assassinations?'

'Yeah, that was hilarious,' said Geoff. 'Woulda been classic if y'pulled it off. Messiah with a machete, haha. Where do you want me to go?'

'Okay,' said Jesus, who then read out, 'Dimension 114792364. Planet 1458934. 31/47N, by, 35/13E. 4 hours, 23 minutes HST from the Present.'

Geoff set the coordinates on his little globe: doing so by twisting the knob on its top and adjusting the glowing numbers on its latitude and longitude beams. 'That's pretty recent,' he said. 'So what's goin' on?'

'You'll find out soon,' said Jesus.

Geoff pressed a button on the globe. The cave and the people within it swept through him as if they were ghosts. In their place appeared thatched houses and drizzle-filled darkness. Geoff was standing in the middle of a muddy street, not far from Lucifer and his henchmen, who were cowering against each other—trying but failing to look bold and defiant.

Jesus, Saint Peter and Walter, watching via the glass screen, didn't have a clear view of what was happening, thanks to the nighttime darkness, as well as Geoff's inability to keep his globe steady.

'Hey, your Dad's down here,' said Geoff. 'I thought He was taking a break from makin' appearances. What's goin' on? He doesn't look very impressed. And He's talkin' to Lucifer, who as always looks like a transvestite. Kinda like you, J., ha ha.'

'Geoff,' said Jesus, ignoring the good-natured jibe. 'I'm gonna need you to describe what's happening. Tell me everything you see, everything you hear. And yes, I know Lucifer's got the Saints. Try not to be too melodramatic, all right?'

'Lucifer's got the...Okay,' said Geoff, recovering from that information. 'Lucifer just asked your Dad a question. It's the old one about, *If God can do anything, can He make a rock so big even He can't lift it?*'

'What'd Dad say in reply?'

'He said He can. And it looks like now He's gonna do it. Okay. Your Dad is...He's making a rock. Wow. It *is* big. And He *is* struggling.'

'What's Lucifer doing?'

'He's just watching. The other guys with him, they look worried.

'Okay, your Dad, He's still struggling, and—*whoa!*—*haha!*—one of Lucifer's friends just got hit in the head with the rock.'

'Dad dropped it?'

'Well...'

'Geoff just say it.'

'That rock is...It's pushing Him down. I don't think He's gonna be able to hold it.'

A plangent vibration suddenly shook the glass wall, and was followed by a noise that was like a thousand raging rivers colliding.

'Yikes,' said Jesus, running his finger across the suddenly-hazy screen so as to turn down its volume. 'Geoff? Can you hear me? What's happening? We can't really see anything.'

The roaring noise lulled for a moment, and then roared even louder before ending abruptly. Geoff gasped.

'What is it?' asked Jesus.

'Your Dad. He's...in a box. Like a glass box. How did this happen?'

'I have absolutely no idea,' said Jesus.

'This is crazy,' said Geoff. 'And Lucifer's goin' up to the glass...he's taunting Him.'

'Probably not too smart,' said Jesus.

'Ha,' said Geoff. 'That's what he just learned. But your Dad's still in that thing.'

'Just keep watching. See what happens.'

'Okay,' said Geoff. 'Okay. Uh. Lucifer's setting fire to some of the nearby buildings. And two of his people—'

'I know who they are,' said Jesus. 'You don't have to tell me.'

'They're trying to get God and His box onto a cart. They're struggling. He must be pretty heavy, your Old Man.'

'Don't tell *Him* that,' said Jesus.

'All right this is a bit weird. One of the guys is walkin' behind the horse, stepping on its—whatta y'call em?—hoofprints, so you can't see 'em.'

'Why would he do that?' asked Jesus. 'No point hiding the evidence. We're watching it right now.'

'I dunno, bro,' said Geoff. 'But they've just opened up a doorway. Lucifer must have an HP card or something. I thought you told me he was on probation. Okay, but anyway, they're goin' through the doorway—God and the horse and everything. The fella at the back is still stamping out the hoofprints.'

'Can you follow them?'

'Nah, man. Can't do it. They've gone somewhere Spiritual. The Database doesn't record up in the Echelons.'

'Because we only record the fleeting moments that can't be replaced,' said Jesus, like an unimpressed, unswayable bureaucrat.

'So what happens now?' asked Geoff.

'I'll have to think about that,' said Jesus. 'D'you wanna come back to the Passage? That's where we are.'

They met Geoff beneath a giant billboard of God, Who was posing as though advertising an expensive watch, above words reading, *Who Luvs ya, kiddies?* The two half-brothers ran up and back-slappingly hugged each other. Jesus became serious and said, 'Anyway. This insane predicament I'm havin' to deal with. Let me introduce you to the fellas helpin' me. Walter, this is Geoff, the oldest of my Physical half-brothers and sisters. He's younger than me but he looks older.'

'Same mother, different fathers,' said Geoff, as he and Walter shook hands and said hello. 'And I only look older 'cause my beard is more robust; J can only grow a *wuss*tache.'

'And Geoff,' said Jesus, 'I think you know Saint Peter.'

'Of course,' said Geoff, holding up his hand for a high five. 'How could I forget the guy who pulls a gun on me every time I make it back to Heaven?'

'Some people continually struggle to accept their mortality,' said Saint Peter, smiling politely, and reluctantly submitting to the hand slap.

Geoff rubbed his palms together and said, 'But before we rescue your Dad can we get some food? I feel like I haven't eaten since diarrhoea killed the dinosaurs.'

SAINT WALLY

Chapter 15

In a Biblically-themed restaurant that Jesus said he often visited because here people thought he was just an actor, the Vice President and his guests were seated in a somewhat private booth lined with framed-and-autographed photos of scriptural dignitaries. Walter looked closely at a photograph showing a young man sitting in front of a huge birthday cake. He was surrounded by a crowd that included God, Jesus, shirtless Angels wearing sunglasses, a giant, and several cheeky-looking donkeys. There was one candle upon the cake, and white icing calligraphy that read, *Happy New Birthday Methuselah!!!*

'And what might be your commandments?' asked their barefooted waiter, who was attired in wild animal skins and a bandoleer of dead grasshoppers.

'I'll have the 5,000 feeder,' said Jesus, not even glancing at the menu, 'and a large Holy Water with no ice. Actually, I'll have *two* large Holy Waters with no ice; you guys look pretty busy. Thanks.'

'No ice,' said the waiter, who, when turning to Walter, received an order for, 'The sweet and sour scrolls, please.'

'Those things are pretty small,' said Jesus. 'I reckon get about five of 'em.'

'Thy wills be done,' said the waiter, when he'd taken the rest of the orders.

As they ate their meals with an unholy amount of gusto, Jesus told Geoff about everything that had happened. Geoff, between mouthfuls, said, 'Well, this explains some of the crazy things I've been seeing in recent memory files. You wouldn't believe the amount o' Dimensions that are trying to legalise bestiality. It's insane.'

Saint Peter, having just finished a large plate of Golden Calf fillet, wiped his mouth with a napkin and said, 'Anyone for dessert? I am not waiting around for that waiter.'

'Oh, man,' said Geoff, speaking through a mouthful of manna. 'How do you eat so fast but stay so skinny?'

'I'll ponder that question while I'm standing in line,' said Saint Peter, rising to his feet. 'Anybody want anything?'

'Could you maybe get some Red Sea Salt?' asked Jesus. 'We've run out. Thanks.'

Geoff wiped his fingers on the Great Sheet beneath his meat platter and said, 'But this is bad. Not just for the Physical Realms.'

'For everybody,' said Jesus. 'I know.'

"Cause the whole Bad Karma-chemical thing,' said Geoff. 'Remember the time your Dad put that Dimension into lockdown?'

Jesus' blank expression forced Geoff to say, 'You don't remember that? It's the whole reason He made the Spiritual incomprehensible to the Physical.'

'What happened?' asked Walter.

Geoff took a sip of non-alcoholic wine, then said, 'Okay. J.'s told you about the Ality fabric, yeah?'

Walter nodded as Geoff rotely said, '*Physicality and Spirituality are bound by the word Ality and therein lies the re*ality. Yeah. Well, back in the Day, the people of some Dimension—I can't remember which one—managed to build a technology that allowed 'em to perceive the Spiritual.'

'You mean,' said Walter, 'they could see...ghosts?'

Geoff replied, 'They could see ghosts, which are Present Pilgrims, and the Souls of the Universes; they could see everything. And typical Physicals, what was the first thing they decided to do?'

'They experimented,' said Walter.

'Exactly,' said Geoff. 'They learned a little bit about how the Realm worked and why it worked, and then they got the idea to use the whole Good and Evil charge-dynamic as a means of generating power for them*selves*. This kinda sounds a bit like the whole Forbidden Fruit, Knowledge of Good and Evil, and also the Tower of Babel thing, yeah? I mean, the Physicals built a machine that got 'em to the top of the tree; they picked the fruit and even though they didn't understand what it was, took a bite out of it.'

Jesus snapped his fingers, saying, 'Now I remember what you're talking about. It's the whole lobotomy so they don't hurt 'emselves thing.'

'A shallower state of awareness is how your Dad termed it,' said Geoff. To Walter he said, 'It's the reason why Physicals these days usually can't see miracles when they happen. Their brains are in a sort of low-energy mode.

Anyway, about this technology. When the Physicals broke through the Ality fabric and learned they could interact with the Spiritual Realm, what they decided to do was stimulate the Evil, so that Good would generate more of itself in order to keep the balance. The theory was that if you had more Good and Evil fighting each other, then you'd generate more Moral energy. And since Moral energy's cheaper than any other kind—why not?'

'But something went wrong,' said Walter.

Geoff nodded and said, 'When they stimulated the Evil inside the Soul of their Universe, they thought Good was gonna rise to the challenge and fight it. But it didn't, because Good doesn't just *happen;* people need to *make* it happen. Evil was thriving and everyone was just standing back, waiting for the problem to solve itself. They didn't realise *they* were the ones responsible for the balance.'

'And when they did,' said Walter, 'it was too late?'

'That whole Physical Universe went into lockdown,' said Geoff. 'There was so much Evil it completely smothered the Good. And since every Dimension is interdependent upon every *other* Dimension, and they all exist in the same space—that is, inside of each other—God had to isolate the poisoned one. Otherwise...'

'What would've happened?' asked Walter.

'Pretty much exactly what *started* to happen,' said Geoff. 'Bad Karma saturated all the Physical Dimensions, then leaked into the Heavenly Realm. Spiritual beings began to have, how should I say it? Carnal urges.'

'You mean,' said Walter, 'they started having...intercourse?'

Geoff and Jesus shook their heads like worldly older brothers. Geoff said, 'What I mean is: when the Bad Karma started coming through the Heavenly vents, the Citizens began thinking more primitively, more tribally. They busted up into selfish little groups, and if God hadn't done anything—'

'Then they would have beaten the hell out of each other,' said Walter.

'Exactly,' said Geoff. 'And eventually, their loss of perspective would have slowed down the whole Soul Cycle. 'Cause after all, if everyone in Heaven is busy fighting, and no one's choosing to be reborn into a Physical Realm, then there are fewer people out there battling Evil. So...'

'So nobody'd be making any power for Heaven,' said Walter.

Geoff nodded and said, 'The lights'd go down; all of Heaven'd be stuck in darkness.'

'And you can't have that,' said Walter. 'Even if it means millions of Dimensions—'

'Billions,' interjected Jesus.

'Billions of Dimensions,' continued Walter, 'are plunged into pain and anguish—you can't have the lights of Heaven going out.'

Holding up his hands in mock self-defence, Geoff said, 'Just wait till you've been processed, Wally. That's when you'll see the light. When it gets tipped onto the whole situation, makes even the ugliness look all right. But in the meantime, just remember: Bad vibrations originate from the mind, so maybe be a bit conscious about the depth of your thinking, because if you haven't been atoned yet, you'll only go crazy trying to work things out.'

'And also remember,' said Jesus, 'that Geoffrey I wish you'd'a kept your mouth shut about all o' these problems we're gonna have to deal with. I'm startin' to get paranoid, thinkin' we might start seein' behaviourisms up here in the Echelons.'

On the other side of the restaurant, a group of chattering beings, each from a different Dimension, and some with robes wrapped around their heads, began pointing at a solitary man in the adjacent booth. It wasn't long before these Sikhs and Hindus were picking at their meals and throwing morsels at him. Jesus happened to see this, and said, 'Speak o' the damn occurrence. Not really keepin' to the rules, are they.'

He stood to his feet, but Geoff grabbed him by the forearm and said, 'Bro, things are a bit unpredictable at the moment.'

'When I'm in town,' said Jesus, 'when aren't they? Heh heh heh.' He turned and made for the other side for the restaurant.

'If this doesn't go down very well,' said Geoff, 'we're both gonna have to go over there and start swinging. Okay?'

'Whatever happened to turning the other cheek?' asked Walter, bemusedly.

'The original quote,' replied Geoff, 'was: Turn the other cheek so I can hit that one too—ya son of a spastic.'

'Excuse me, gentlemen,' said Jesus, when he made it to the table of Hindus and Sikhs. 'Would you all please be so kind as to stop doing what you're doing? Management is receiving complaints.'

'What are we doing?' asked one of the smaller Hindus as he threw a French fry. 'We are not doing anything. Except for minding our own business. And we do not appreciate being interrupted whilst we are doing so.'

Jesus looked at each of them; and still smiling politely, said, 'Gentlemen, if you don't stop victimising one of the customers of this fine establishment, then I'm afraid I'm going to have to have you all rein*car*nated...as women.'

The entire party stopped smiling, and looked at Jesus as if he was an abomination. The biggest member said, 'Don't be letting that costume get to your head, my man. You're nothing but a gimmick, and not a very good one. Now go back to serving patrons and leave us be.'

The group cackled and waved Jesus away. One of its smaller members picked up a broken-bread bread roll and threw it at the man in the nearby booth. That man, who was wearing a Hawaiian-style shirt, and had a quite familiar moustache, made no protest when the bread roll bounced off his chest. Adolf Hitler only picked up a napkin, wiped a splotch of mustard off his collar, and continued eating his lonely meal.

Jesus scuffed his foot on the floor and said, 'Leave you be, eh? Leave you be. Well, as a Citizen of the Heavenly Realms, I don't think I can do that. Because the man at that table is *also* a Citizen, which means that *he*, like *you*, has been brought to balance. And I should know; I was the one who signed off on the whole deal.'

A Hindu with a mauve complexion wobbled his head and said, 'I am thinking you might have been in the job for too long, *waiter*. This is a very clear case of identity crisis.' He and his peers burst out laughing and gave each other high fives. Jesus only said, 'What makes you think I'm *not* the Vice President?'

One of the smaller Hindus got to his feet and stepped up close to Jesus. The Son of God was a full foot taller than him, but even still, the Hindu was brave enough to point an untrimmed fingernail in the VP's face. 'Do you even know what that man has done?' asked the Hindu. 'He re-appropriated our symbol for sunrise. And that is not something we are *down* with.'

The only reply Jesus gave was a smile: A smile that revealed a blank gummy gap where his two front teeth should have been. The Hindu lost his expression of belligerent indignation and stepped backward. As he sat back down next to his fellows, their smug expressions slid off their faces, for they too had noticed that a scar on Jesus' wrist refused to peel or flake as he rubbed at it with his middle finger.

Jesus rose on his toes and said, 'Excellent. And please allow me to say, on behalf of everyone else in the Heavenly Realms: I hope you all enjoy the rest of your meal. For dessert, might I recommend anything with...beef in it?' Addressing Hitler, he said, 'And sir, I trust your meal is adequate?'

Hitler bobbed timidly in his seat, then nodded and replied, 'Sacrificial lamb-burger. Is güht.'

'Marvellous,' said Jesus, before turning and heading back to his own table.

'Prime example of leaving the flock to get the one,' said Geoff, as Jesus approached. 'And of not givin' a Shiite about the status quo, which is how JC's Dad likes to operate.'

Jesus slipped back into his seat, took a sip of Holy Water, and said, 'Should really get rid o' the 'stache. Attract a lot less attention that way.' Looking back at the Hindus, he shook his head and muttered, 'Daddamn trouble-makers.'

A few moments later, the voice of someone trying to be polite said, 'E-excuse me. Are you...Jesus Christ?'

Jesus groaned quietly and muttered, '*Wanted* to keep a low profile,' then turned around in his chair and came face to face with his own face. It was framed within a golden ID card, a card held up by none other than Lucifer himself. The Angel qualified his original query by adding, 'Because this photo just *really* doesn't look like you.'

The courteous smile on the Son of God's face immediately came unstuck. Jesus tensed as though about to leap forward and snatch hold of his HP card. Lucifer sensed this and backed away, accidentally bumping into his three cronies, who wobbled as a result, but continued their best efforts to look like unimpressed lawbreakers.

Jesus got to his feet and said, 'Well well well, if it isn't the prissy son of a pervert who wouldn't stop moaning about the fact that he only got one debatable mention in the Good Book.'

'That's riiiight,' said Lucifer, watching Geoff and Walter rise from their seats. 'Because the only thing worse than being talked about, is *not* being talked about.'

'What the Hell are you doing up here?' said Jesus.

'Oh, I just thought I'd drop by,' said Lucifer, 'and tell you to come with me. Or else.'

'Or else what?' said Jesus, sneering at Lucifer's three cronies. 'Look around yourself, Lucy. You're on Spiritual ground. My turf, sissy man.'

'Tsk tsk tsk,' said Lucifer, shaking his head dolefully. 'That really is your problem, Mr. Vice President. You pull back the slingshot and let go of the rock before you even think about where it's heading. That's why *I* should have been the one to get the executive job. Because *I* have vision. But anyway, we don't want to be rolling around in the muck of the past, now, do we? Because as I was about to say—or else you won't get to hear my proposition: The one that perhaps entails my throwing you a life-line.'

When Saint Peter finally received his Milk-and-Honey shake and Mount Sinai sundae, he carried his tray back toward a now-empty table, and wondered out loud, 'Where in the name of My Own Dear Chastity have they gone?'

SAINT WALLY

Chapter 16

Lucifer led the way to a nearby corridor, where, away from the irritating eyes of the inquisitive public, he brought out Jesus' HP card and produced a glowing doorway. It opened to reveal a coarse, far-reaching desert drenched in twilight. The Angel rolled his hand as if to humbly allow everyone else to step through the doorway first. Nobody trusted him, so he said, 'Fine. *I'll* go first.'

Lucifer stepped onto the dirt. It crunched beneath his feet. He spun around like a ballerina, and when everyone had joined him in this new Dimension, he clasped his hands and cheerily said, 'I'm happy we could all make it here. I'll close the door because leaving it open would arouse suspicions, yes?' He swiped the card and the doorway disappeared.

'You said we could have the Saints,' said Jesus. 'Where are they?'

Lucifer laughed merrily, as did his cronies, and replied, 'Well, my very generous contribution to the *Let's help Jesus Christ in his Quest to get back his Dad and not look like a complete* Fool *foundation*, is just on the other side of that hill. I also left a little surprise for you. Kind of an *évocateur* of memories.' With theatrical discretion, he added, 'Potentially it's quite embarrassing for you, so, you might not want your two *protégés* to be there when you see what it is.'

Jesus scoffed at the Angel, then became pensive as he looked toward the hilltop that blocked the rocky horizon.

Lucifer, disenchanted by the VP's slowness in complying, said, 'Allow me to rephrase my demands: Go over that hill. Alone. And find what I've left for you. Otherwise you won't be getting your over-privileged little digits on the Morality I'm currently in possession of.'

Jesus turned to Walter and Geoff and said, 'If these morons try something stupid, don't be delicate about restraining 'em.'

'We won't be,' said L. Ron, causing Clip and Osama, and even Lucifer, to giggle.

Jesus said 'Pff,' and proceeded up the rise.

Lucifer watched Jesus disappear over the hilltop, then perked up noticeably and said, 'Tell me something, boys. What with the fact that I've kidnapped God...Does this mean that by extension now *I'm* the King of Creation?'

'That's how *I've* always thought of you,' said Clip, trembling perversely.

Jesus hopped down several rocky ledges that took him into a desiccated valley filled with thorny bushes. After looking around for about four seconds, he threw up his hands and said, 'There's nothing here!'

'There is!' Lucifer called out. 'You just haven't looked hard enough! Come *on;* I didn't even try to hide it!' Confidentially to everyone present, he said, 'I'm afraid he's always been impatient. That's why he had to have Angelic supervisors when he was a kid—so he didn't throw a tantrum and get himself lost. Which he did, you know, on more than one occasion.'

'Like you'd know,' said Geoff. 'You were too busy doing your nails, and trying to take credit for mental illnesses.'

Jesus stumbled into a thorny cul de sac – 'A zareba,' he muttered, momentarily impressed by his own knowledge. Ahead of him, sitting on the ground in this small clearing, there was a person. No, it was an object, one that looked like a person. It was a plastic inflatable woman, of the kind used for strange and lascivious purposes. Jesus realised Lucifer's purpose for the doll upon getting close to it. Taped to its face there was a piece of paper, which he managed to read in the diminishing light. It read, *Call me Sweetie and serve me Cold, I'm a Dish best delivered by the Cunning and the Bold.*

'That weasely son of a –' Jesus spun around and sprinted in the direction he'd come from. Making it to the top of the hill, he yelled, 'Get Lucifer! He's planning something!'

But it was obviously too late. Lucifer, smiling evilly, was pointing a silver handgun at Jesus. His cronies were training machine-guns upon Geoff and Walter.

Clip, Osama and L.Ron unleashed a barrage of bullets that shredded the air, spat up plumes of dust, and sent Walter to the ground. Jesus ran toward them, but was stopped when a bullet sliced through the air and collided with his shoulder. He fell to the dirt, feeling as if molten worms had dug a nest inside him. Staggering to his feet, he was shot once again by Lucifer, who was proclaiming his own confidence by holding his gun in a saggy-wristed fashion.

Lucifer twirled his pistol like a lazy gunslinger and brought out the HP card. Opening another doorway, he said, 'Boys! Hurry *up*! We have *got* to keep to the schedule!'

Clip trained his ear toward his leader's voice, and while doing so, was kicked in the jaw by Geoff. Clip had been practicing his káráté moves on Geoff's stomach while Osama and L. Ron restrained him. But now Clip was falling like a drunken pine tree, and hitting the ground so heavily that he sent up a cloud of dust.

In a move so fluid it appeared to have been choreographed, Osama and L. Ron dropped Geoff, picked up Clip, and bustled him through the Spiritual doorway. Lucifer, who of course had already stepped through it, gave Jesus a twiddly-fingered wave and said, 'Bon voyage, el weenie Vice Presidenté.'

Acid-bellied rage surged through every single atom of Jesus Christ's being. He launched to his feet and stagger-sprinted toward the doorway. It had begun closing: its borders minimising to meet at a central point. Jesus focused on that central point, gritted a roar between his teeth, lunged forward, and punched with all his might.

The Son of God's fist collided with Lucifer's groin. There was a terrified squeal and a blinding flash of white light. Then the doorway disappeared...and so did Jesus' forearm.

The distal portion of the VP's arm was blue and opaque—as if it belonged to a ghost.

'Are you...alright?' asked Walter, who was clutching at his own chest, and breathing as though coping with substantial pain.

Jesus didn't reply. He was so enraged that he had no words.

Geoff said, 'Yeah he's alright, Wally. He's a Hybrid, same as you; hence the adverse reaction to the bullets. But don't worry: the Spiritual's gonna regenerate the Physical. You're unkillable, the pair of you.'

'Second time today we've been stuck in a Physical Realm,' said Jesus, shaking his head and standing to his feet. 'I am telling you that has got to be a record.

'Y'know what I shoulda done? I shoulda gone over that hill and just waited. Just waited to hear what that weiner was gonna try. And then I shoulda run back over here when he didn't expect it, and colossa-smacked him right in the face.'

'Maybe someone shoulda just colossa-*kicked* him,' said Geoff, 'right between the knees, 'cause that's obviously where he's hiding the Saints.'

'I *thought* he was walking strangely,' said Jesus. 'I really did. He was...*waddling*. He had the Saints *on* him–the whole time.'

'Look at what happens when you don't listen to your own instincts: when you try to be..."wise."'

'Ahr well, bro,' said Geoff. 'To quote a certain someone: *What's done is done is dead.*' He paused a moment, then asked, 'So whatta *we* do now, do you think?'

Jesus smiled thinly in Walter's direction, and said, 'Usually that's Wally's question.'

A crimson smear portending the nearness of night had appeared on the horizon. Jesus cast his eyes on it and said, 'I s'pose we'd better make a fire. Otherwise us two Hybrids are gonna freeze our prostates off.'

Chapter 17

The doorway closed and Lucifer stumbled backward, away from Jesus' forearm, which was lying on the floor like a forgotten piece of armour. The Angel gushed, controlled the urge to start weeping, and fanned himself with his feathers.

Standing taller as though to pronounce his own dignity, Lucifer composed himself, then turned to his two conscious cronies—Osama and L.Ron—and said, 'Gentlemen, congratulations. We have just laid the *second* foundation of my visionary scheme. The Vice President is out of the equation, and you, and me, and we, are soon going to be the most infamous Citizens in all of Creation. *Now*. Do you, my beloveds, remember an experience we had just recently, when we and— several young ladies who didn't have a lot of respect for themselves— took a trip to a place of inner-city under-privilege?'

'You mean when we and those...*loose women*,' said L. Ron, disapprovingly, 'adopted those orphans?'

'The orphans,' said Osama, 'with father issues?'

'*Specifically* with father issues,' said Lucifer. 'That's right, Oosama. Well done. What, may I ask, did we *do* with those orphans?'

Osama, who thought the question was so simple that it had to be a trick question, cautiously said, 'We fed them— laxatives, and— de-robed them. Then we told them to run naked through that hospital, and poo in as many places as possible!' He smiled hugely, saying, 'And we said we would give them all the ice cream they could eat if they did that. But...oh. We forgot to give them the ice cream.'

'And after we "forgot" to do that,' said Lucifer, 'what did we do with those orphans?'

'We put them on a bus,' said L. Ron, 'and then parked it on top of a mountain and left them all there.'

'*Precisely*,' said Lucifer. 'Because *I*, dear subjects, was looking nine steps ahead—at the *third* foundation we four are going to lay.'

He kicked out his leg like a drill-sergeant doing a 180, stepped over Clip and said, 'Contrary to popular opinion, gentleman, an orphan is quite a valuable thing. Because in many a world there is many a person who will happily lend you their services in exchange for a fresh young mind to inculcate and a fresh young bride to inseminate. Oosama. You're taking a trip back into a Physical Realm, to visit some of your old friends and do a bit of recruiting. We're going to need people to document our historical achievement. Otherwise, posterity is going to suffer *enormously*.'

COURTNEY TAYLOR

Chapter 18

Geoff and Walter were collecting firewood, while Jesus, down in the valley that Lucifer had sent him into, was again whistling *Swing Low Sweet Chariot*.

'He must have that song stuck in his head,' said Walter, snapping a dead branch over his knee.

'JC didn't tell you about the Holy Spirit?'

Walter shook his head.

'D'you know much about the Bible and that sort of thing?'

'I'm not a theologian or anything, but I think the puppets at Sunday school did a pretty good job.'

Geoff laughed as if he thought this was gonna be great, then said, 'You remember how in the Good Book, JC was down at the river of whatever, getting baptised, and then the Holy Spirit came down from above?'

'Like a dove,' said Walter.

'Exactly,' said Geoff. 'Only that's where they obscured it for some reason. The Holy Spirit's actually a parrot. An albino parrot.'

Walter was genuinely surprised, and said, 'The Holy Spirit's a literal bird. Literally?'

Geoff confirmed it with a cluck of the tongue, then said, 'Sent to keep JC outta trouble. A gift from his Dad as a celebration of sobriety. Which didn't last too long. Well, the celebration did. But yeah, that's how come J. was sort of on the straight and narrow from that point on.'

'You mean with his ministry?'

'That's right,' said Geoff. 'He had that bird on his shoulder right up until the day he ascended into Heaven. It told him what to say, how to say it, how not to get in trouble. Whenever he *did* get in trouble, it was only 'cause he ignored the damn thing.' Geoff laughed. 'That's why he got crucified—but don't ask him about that. It's still a sensitive issue.

'But the baptism. I was there that day. It was one of those intervention things. JC was drunk as all anything, so we threw him into the water to wake him up. Then he surfaces, lookin' like a drowned Arab, and we all tell him he has to quit drinking 'cause he came down to Earth for a purpose.'

'You mean he was in the water,' said Walter, 'because he was...sobering up.'

'He'd had a big night the night before,' said Geoff. 'And J-the-B—that's what we call John the Baptist—was telling us that J-the-C needed to get himself together, otherwise he'd miss his window of opportunity. I can't actually remember the specifics, but J-the-B was ranting on about Universes aligning and the perfect time for the perfect will of God—complicated stuff; still goes over my head. So anyway, something had to be done about J.'s imbibing, so we all got together down at the river and said what we needed to say. Then J. said, *Okay, I'll try to be a better person,* and that was when the Holy Spirit came down from the sky and landed on his shoulder. God said you've made the right choice; this here is to celebrate that. All you have to do is whistle this tune, and if y'ever need help making the right decision, the bird'll be there to give you advice.'

'So, technically,' asked Walter, 'it's...'

'A pan-Dimensional being,' said Geoff. 'Which means wherever it is in all of Creation, it hears J. whistling and comes swooping down to offer its services.'

'How come it isn't swooping down now?'

'That is a very good question,' said Geoff, pausing to think about that.

'You guys wanna see what Lucifer left us?' called out Jesus. He was ambling over the hill, clutching a bottle of bourbon and the plastic inflatable woman. In reference to those two objects, Walter said, 'Least we're gonna have a good time, eh?'

'Walter,' said Jesus, as he laid the doll on the ground and sat down on top of it. 'I'm shocked. You've been hanging around Geoffrey too much. And I heard all the whispering. What's he been telling you?'

'I was just informing Wally about our friend the Holy Spirit,' said Geoff. 'We were wondering why it's not making an appearance.'

Jesus got to work on the bottle's lid, and replied, 'I don't know. But...I'm thinking I might've offended it. Last night, I can't remember much. And when I woke up this morning the HS' cage was knocked over. It was empty, so, I'm thinkin' that right now my nanny might be irritated with me.'

Seeing that Geoff needed some matches, Jesus reached into his pocket, retrieved the packet he'd nabbed from Gandhi's bar, and threw them over. Geoff got to work at lighting the tinder.

The lid came off the bottle; Jesus took a swig. 'Ahh,' he said, when he'd finished. 'I'd offer you some Geoff, but, Spirits can't imbibe in the Physical, can they.'

'That's just mean,' said Geoff, as he blew on the tinder and a fire bloomed into life. 'And are you sure you wanna be drinking that?'

'It'll be all right,' said Jesus. 'Help me relax. And it's not like I can get my hands on any more of it.' He passed the bottle to Walter, who received it but then thought twice and passed it back. Jesus looked surprised, and said, 'You sure? It's the one good thing about bein' a Hybrid: You're ambidextrous when it comes to partaking of the two Realms.' Settling back against the inflatable woman, he asked, 'You're not a *closet* religious nut, are you? Unlikely, given your uniform.'

Walter shook his head and said, 'Just not a fan.'

Jesus nodded, then said, 'I think that's good. Self restraint n' all that sort o' thing. *I'd* be more like that, if I was more, I dunno— *disciplined*. I'd use my time for important things. Things like...'

'Lighting fires,' said Geoff, as he threw the packet of matches back to Jesus, and then began feeding larger sticks to the flame.

'Exactly,' said Jesus. 'Nothin' like a good fire. Jeez, I reckon the last time I lit one woulda been over two-thousand years ago.' He grinned and said, 'Hey, Geoff. Did you ever visit the time when Dad made Elijah burn his own crap?'

Walter said, 'I think that was actually Ezekiel.'

'Really?' said Jesus. 'Yeah y'could be right. Anyway. Man that was funny. He took us all down there to watch—the whole Creative Department—we were laughin' like nothin' else.'

'I did go back to see that,' said Geoff, crawling away from the campfire, which had begun popping and grabbing hold of the logs on top. 'That Ezekiel is one seriously frazzled man.'

'He's a lunatic,' said Jesus, snickering. 'That's why Dad's always playin' jokes on him.'

Walter, who knew he probably shouldn't say this, said, 'From what I've seen so far, it seems like God's playing jokes on more people than just Ezekiel.'

Geoff and Jesus looked across the fire. Jesus said, 'Somehow, I don't think that was an unconscious slip. I think that was a cool and calculated ditch at a representative o' the Hierarchy. But that's fine by me, Wally. Say what you want, 'cause we have definitely got the time to listen.'

Eventually Walter said, 'What more do I have to say? I mean, I think it's pretty obvious that your Old Man, for His own, edification, or whatever, has forced billions of, not just humans but, animals, into a realm of pain and suffering and...loss. I mean, what would the Human Nations council, or whatever it's called, say if they could have a sit-down meeting with the Man in Charge? How He can rationalise something like Creation...' Walter shook his head as if he thought it was shameful, then said, 'And the answer supposedly only comes when it's all over—when you die and get processed into Heaven, where, I dunno, life makes so much sense that you choose to go back into the Physical Realms and "generate more power," thereby justifying your having been there in the first place because you've *chosen* to be there. I don't think I need to say anything more. It's making me irritated. And I *do* feel pretty outta my league in saying all o' this, but...There it is.'

Jesus looked deeply into the fire, his dark eyes reflecting its orange form. Presently, he said, 'I know how y'feel, Wally. It is all pretty unfathomable. Which is how Dad made it, 'cause that's how He is. But...just remember what those Daddamn Televangelists are always saying: "Physical life's just the tip o' the iceberg." And the fact that you're here now, on the other side—'

Walter interrupted him, saying, 'Doesn't excuse the fact that I've had to say goodbye to every single person I loved in the previous life.'

Jesus quietly assented, then said, 'But to be defined by such a limited...*glimmer*. That's pretty insane, don't you think?'

'Something even more insane,' said Walter, 'is the thought of an eternity of connecting with people I'm destined to be ripped away from. And to then say that it's all okay because you'll just go into another life and make more friends, different friends...I'd rather have nothing. To just be nothing. Than have to go through that.'

Geoff broke the silence when he said, 'Remember, though, Wally, detrimental vibrations come from the brain, so just go easy on all that deep-thinking till you've been processed. Yeah?'

Jesus waved at Geoff as if he was a nuisance, and said, 'We haven't got any answers for you, Wally. Yes I'm the Son of God, but even *I'm* sometimes lost in the mystery. People come up to me at parties and say, *What does this mean? Is it literal or metaphorical?* and I'm like, *I don't know. Find a God's Brain.* The fact is, Dad's put *everything* in the mix. The truth that'll set you free, and all that sorta thing, it's in there, but, well, He says that people'a gotta pull things apart to look for it. Apparently they need something to work toward. And I mean He's probably right 'cause Citizens are made in His image, and that's the way Dad is. He's a workaholic.'

Jesus took another sip of booze then said, 'And I know how you feel about coming to terms with the fact that everything ends. But so does everyone else who's ever lived, and they're all still goin' back for more, so, what does that tell us?'

Walter said, 'I have no idea.'

'Well, until you find out,' said Jesus, 'you shouldn't put your money on anything except for this: When people wanna offload all their grievances, and they sit down across from Dad, it's not Him who comes out different. So slummin' it on Earth, just for the novelty, can't be all that bad; yeah?' He raised his bottle. 'Can I hear an amen?'

Walter shook his head as though his conscience wouldn't let him agree.

'Well, the upshot is,' said Geoff, not unkindly, 'if you *really* hate being alive, you can always kill yourself and spend *all* your time in Heaven.'

Walter laughed without humour and said, 'I already did that. The first part, anyway.'

'No Shiite,' said Geoff. 'Was it over a woman?'

'No,' said Walter, as if the idea was ludicrous.

'Then why'd you do it? And *how'd* you do it?'

Even though it was something he didn't want to talk about, Walter said, 'I was diagnosed with something you don't really survive. My dad had it and that's how he died. I didn't want my family to have to watch it take hold of me. I know it's pretty clichéd, but, I jumped out of a window. Technically it was off a balcony, while I was pretending to wash a window.'

'And you regret it?' asked Geoff.

'I tried to make it look like an accident,' said Walter.

'But now you're thinkin,' said Jesus, 'the people you left behind aren't stupid. And you're wondering if they hold what you did against you.'

Walter nodded, then said, 'That's not a nice thing to have pressing against your mind. I don't know what I was thinking. I'm not usually so...un-clear-headed.'

'Expectations, m'man,' said Jesus. 'Everybody's got 'em. People get around you and tell you who you are, how you act. Pretty soon you start thinkin' it's the truth. The trick is, though, to not give a damn about what people say.'

'Are we talking about the whole Messiah thing?' asked Walter.

'Maybe we're just talkin' about the whole *face-o-me in the grain o' cereal* thing,' said Jesus. 'People see what they wannoo. And before you ask, *Do I think people's beliefs are justified because of their experiences?* let me say that in my case it's something I'm yet to decide on. But in *your* case, obviously you think people *were* justified in believing you'd act a certain way – i.e. that you wouldn't kill yourself. Yet here you are. I'm not meanin' to be nasty about it, but, Mrs. Roosevelt's saying kinda goes the other way, too: People can't make you feel *su*perior without your consent.'

Jesus folded his legs, settled into a more comfortable position, then said, 'Anyway, Walty. On to a less draining subject. Y'might be dead and regretful, but there is *some* good news. *Because* you're a Suicider, it's one o' the Heavenly rules that you and all of your existential concerns are going on a relaxing, fun-filled, all-expenses-paid vacation to Sheol, where all of your questions will be answered.'

'Sheol?' said Walter, his face turning even more serious. 'You mean...*Hell?*'

'Now before you start to panic,' said Jesus, 'let us just tell you, many of the things you've heard about Hell, are—'

'Misinterpreted,' said Geoff.

'That's right,' said Jesus. 'All o' that stuff about heat and fire and brimstone, it's all true, but, well, what *else* do y'expect to find in an engine room?'

'An engine room?'

'That's what Hell is,' said Jesus. 'It's the place where the power from all o' the Physical Universes gets converted then sent into the Heavenly Realm. Without it, everything'd shut down.'

'And by everything,' said Geoff, 'he means all of Creation, which is what people go to Hell to learn about.'

'That's right,' said Jesus. ''Cause that's where y'get gobsmacked by all the systems and everything. And it's actually where Lucifer's been working, now that I'm thinking about it. But anyway, they'll set you straight down there. Give you a bit of enlightening.' He laughed at Walter's expression and said, 'I know. You're going to Hell. It's heavy. But at least you don't have a phobia about bald people.'

Walter chuckled and Geoff said, 'What're you talking about?'

'Never mind,' said Jesus. 'I shouldn'a brought it up. My mouth's got a mind of its own half the time.'

'Nah nah nah,' said Geoff. 'I wanna hear about this. What? Are you scared of going bald?'

'No,' said Jesus, as if the idea was ridiculous. 'I'm the Son of God; I can bring on a miracle.'

'Then what?'

'Bald people remind him of Buddha,' said Walter.

'Not *bald* people,' said Jesus. 'People with shaved heads. Which...'

He tried to brush the subject away, but Geoff said, '*And?*'

'Well, it's not too hard to see the logic if y'peel back the layers, Geoffrey,' said Jesus, digging inside his jeans and coming out with his packet of cigarettes. 'Buddha—the fat degenerate—is bald, and Naysayers are always nay-sayin', "Look at him—he's practically got as many people following him as *you* do, Mr. Christ. And he's barely even *real*. They had to *scramble* to prove he ever actually lived." And that throws a bit o' self-doubt in my head, I am not too shy to say.'

'Oh my Half-Brother's Father,' said Geoff. 'And people think *I'm* a psychological minefield.'

'Hey,' said Jesus. 'At least I don't continually request to die during the act of love-making.'

'It's the ultimate high, bro,' said Geoff. 'Y'can't let wounding a woman's psyche keep you from trying it.' He cackled and said, 'But man, I think you need to get over that little prejudice.'

'It's not a prejudice,' said Jesus, grinning as he held the flame of a match to his cigarette. 'It's an insecurity. And yes, it needs to be dealt with, but now is not the time to start layin' down the plans to do that. We have got bigger fish to beat the crap out of.'

Jesus took a deep drag of smoke and blew it toward the stars, then settled back comfortably on the inflatable woman. Seemingly thinking better of it, he pulled the cushion out from under himself, threw it over to Walter and said, 'Courtesy o' the Morning Star.'

'I'm all right,' said Walter. 'You have it.'

'Nah, I don't want it,' said Jesus. 'Lord knows where it's come from.'

'You're sure?' said Walter. 'I don't want the Vice President of Creation to have to rough it.'

'Nah don't worry 'bout that,' said Jesus, tucking his forearm beneath the back of his head. 'The VP of C is used to roughin' it. And don't be offering that thing to Geoff; he's a Spirit. To him these rocks are like marshmallows.'

'I only made the fire for you half-mortals,' said Geoff, with mock self-righteousness.

The three of them laughed and were quiet for a time.

Walter then said, 'Sorry to keep asking questions, but, why would an Angel clip its own wings?'

'Because somehow,' said Geoff, 'it's convinced itself that self-denial is the path to fulfillment.'

'Which,' said Jesus, 'to a tiny degree is true. But more often than not that kinda thinking just kicks the whole Angry Loner factor into gear. 'Cause most o' the idiots who go around denyin' 'emselves things are usually preoccupied with how noble they are. So they're actually doin' Bad by bein' Good. Clip the self-circumcised Angel is a *Bythebookist*, and has been for quite a while now. I reckon the best word to describe a *Bythebookist* is maniac. Or retard. 'Cause they can't think for themselves.'

'And how come,' said Walter, 'we can't just call a bunch o' *non*-maniac Angels to come and help us out? In place of the Holy Spirit, I mean.'

The two half-brothers began chuckling. Walter couldn't help joining them. Jesus stubbed his cigarette on one of his wrist scars and said, 'Walter. Y'ever hear about the Great Battle between Michael and Beelzebub? How Michael cast Lucifer down from Heaven? Well, as a matter of actual fact, that whole ordeal was nothing more than a very heated, very anticipated, very boring to *me*—'

'And *me*,' said Geoff.

'—fashion-modelling tournament,' said Jesus, who burst out laughing at an obviously-hilarious memory.

'You shoulda seen it,' said Geoff. 'Michael only won because he was wearing the outfit that Lucifer *wasn't* wearing. You remember how in the Book of Revelation it talks about a beast with ten heads?'

'Seven heads,' said Jesus. 'This I *do* remember. 'Cause seven's Dad's favourite number, n' everyone thought Lucy was tryin' to brown-nose his way to victory.'

'I'm surprised he didn't make it,' said Geoff. 'Those shrunken cat craniums hanging off that horned collar were just so elegant, with their dreadlocks and buck teeth.'

'And those bear-feet boots,' said Jesus, 'and the lion-tongue vest. It all went so well with that woolly-leopard-skin jacket. I can still see it.' Jesus began laughing so hard that he looked as if he was grieving. Rolling onto his side, he tried to re-claim his breath, but sounded as if he was failing.

Geoff appeared to abruptly realise something. Picking up a small rock, he threw it over at Jesus to get his attention, and said, 'Hey, J., remember what Lucy said to the judges after he lost the final round? Said the laughter'd be "echoing out the back of their denigrating heads," because his next— soirée or whatever— was gonna slap 'em silly.'

Jesus gradually stopped laughing as he thought about that. 'Maybe that's the reason he's doin' all this,' he said. ''Cause we laughed at him.'

COURTNEY TAYLOR

Chapter 19

Flocking through perfect blue skies, above rolling green fields that bumped away for kilometres, were tens of thousands of instrument-clutching Angels, practicing their newest aerobatical musical number.

'Swan's Lake,' said Lucifer, caressing the air as he listened. 'For some reason it always reminds me of— springtime.'

He was moderately impressed when his former bandmates, doing nosedives and barrel rolls, executed a succession of fly-throughs that saw them shooting between one another, avoiding collisions by only inches. After a few bombastic cymbal crashes and drum slams, the squadrons all gathered into a gigantic many-stranded helix that twisted upward and then dispersed, ending with a collective groan because someone in the trumpet department had hit a wrong note.

'Okay guys, let's take a break,' said the band leader, a dark-haired Angel who was speaking through a golden megaphone. 'But be back in the air in ten minutes, no later. Otherwise we're gonna lose the groove.'

The disbanding Angels swooped down to the ground, laid their instruments on the grass, and immediately began fanning themselves with their wings. Lucifer watched the leader and saw where he landed, then extended his wings and slowly jumped through the air like he was walking on the moon.

'Well well well,' said Michael the Archangel, when he saw his former colleague approaching. 'If it isn't my old study buddy Lucifer. Who let *you* back into the Music Realm? Didn't come up here for a re-match did you?'

'Ha,' said Lucifer, with insincere affection as they air-kissed each other's cheeks. 'You wish.'

'Well, if you want your old job back,' said Michael, 'then take it. *Please.*' Waggling his conductor's baton, he said, 'I thought you were just being *dramatic* when you said these things were a terror to hold onto. All of those G-forces; my knuckles are feeling like they have a bending disorder. I'm actually thinking about taking some time off, so they can recover.'

Lucifer provided a short-lived frown of sympathy, then said, 'Thank you, Michael, but no thank you, Michael. These days I'm quite happy down in the Re-education department.'

'I heard you were teaching classes down there,' said Michael, putting a hand on his hip in a tell-me-more posture.

'Mostly admin work,' said Lucifer. 'Not really my calling but lots of promotions, which, hey, that's actually the reason I'm here. I have a proposition for you. Recently, my department has...Hang on. Let me start again. God wants us to put on a concert.'

SAINT WALLY

Chapter 20

Jesus woke in the grey and cold morning, took a deep and grumbling sniff of the air, and only raised his head when he heard someone say, 'Heht-hem.'

'Petey. How'd you find us?'

'Pride is always predictable,' said Saint Peter, who was sitting on a nearby rock, throwing small stones into a campfire that was now just a puddle of ash.

Jesus laboured to a sitting position and looked at him blankly.

'You don't remember?' asked Saint Peter, gesturing at the surrounding desert. 'This is where Lucifer tempted you with women and wine.'

'That explains the gifts,' said Jesus, kicking the empty bottle, and yawning as he looked over at Walter, who was asleep on the plastic woman.

'Your Father was monumentally proud of you that day,' said Saint Peter. 'He had us all down here watching, and then straight afterward signed us all up to be Pilgrims, so we could watch it again in the Database.'

Jesus, who looked as if he'd spent the night in a very thin shrub, rubbed his face and gave a weak smile. It vanished when he asked, 'Is there any news? On anything?'

'There is some,' said Saint Peter, reluctantly. 'The Bureau of Physical Monitoring has garnered some information you're going to find very interesting. And also, the board has found out about everything that's going on.'

'Crap,' said Jesus.

'They've called a meeting,' said Saint Peter, reaching for his pocket watch. 'It's in forty-five minutes. Thank God for Mr. Hitler, otherwise I wouldn't have found you in time; I thought you'd all *left* me back at that restaurant.'

'Sorry 'bout that,' said Jesus. 'I think I mighta got a bit impatient when—' he rolled his eyes as he realised '—*again*, Lucifer tempted me.'

Saint Peter bobbed his head, gently implying, *It happens.*

'But Petey,' said Jesus. 'We've been talkin' about some o' the potential repercussions, and, y'haven't seen anything out o' the ordinary up in Heaven, have you? I mean in the way that people'a been treating each other?'

'Personally,' said Saint Peter, 'no. But Inaugustus informed me that several Philistines broke into one of the art museums. Apparently they

114

trashed everything. Carnal reversion? A Physical flare-up in their sub-DNA, perhaps?'

Jesus got to his feet and was contemplative as he said, 'I dunno. But I'm gonna have to make a few propositions at this board meeting.'

'You're the second in command,' said Saint Peter. 'Right after God. Don't just *propose* what the board is going to do.'

Jesus smiled and said, 'Thanks, Sheriff. But I'm not sure if that's how things work.'

Walter sat up and looked around with bleary eyes. When he and Saint Peter had traded pleasantries, they together wondered where Geoff had gone.

'He's big into meditation and all that sort o' thing,' said Jesus. 'Probably exposing himself to the sun or something like that. We, in the meantime, are tryin' to figure out the next plan of attack.'

'Uh,' said Saint Peter. 'Might I...fire off a suggestion?'

'Just don't aim it at my Testiclees,' said Jesus.

'Well, uh,' said Saint Peter. 'Perhaps we should consult the official document pertaining to these matters, to perhaps get a sort of indication as to which direction we should be taking.'

Jesus' jaw tightened, and he said, 'I'm guessing you're referring to the Book of Revelation.'

'The prophetic, *divinely inspired* Book of Revelation,' said Saint Peter.

'Divinely insp— Petey. You *do* know Johnny was on mushrooms when he wrote that thing. I should know; I was the one who gave 'em to him.'

'Yes, but, the Lord *does* work in mysterious ways, yes?'

'We have not got the time,' said Jesus, 'to be putting our confidence in something that is not built on practicality.'

Geoffrey son of Joseph, looking pretentiously peaceful, wandered into the slightly tense conversation and said, 'Good morning, everybody. What's the plan?'

'We're takin' off back to Heaven,' said Jesus. 'They've heard about what's happened.'

Geoff nodded and asked, 'And then what?'

'Well,' said Jesus, 'I'm thinking we should see if anyone's got any ideas.' Saint Peter went to say something but Jesus added, 'Any *rational* ideas. Because *I* don't, and things are startin' to get pretty serious.'

Chapter 21

Ten of the twelve Patriarchs of Heaven were seated around a circular conference table, inside a boardroom that was more like a ballroom. It was a grandiose, high-ceilinged, marble-floored chamber, close to the top of Heaven's Main Office.

'This is, of course, unprecedented,' said Pleebus, a purple-haired being that looked like a conflation of man and furless koala. 'And completely unanticipated.'

Derdinand Schopals, who in his most recent life had been a Tallaweigian businessman who'd done a lot of good work with inner-city youth, said, 'We have to pray that the Good Lord will be restored, and soon.'

'Praying is for *victims*,' said three bearded men sitting next to each other—Abraham, Isaac and Jacob, who were father, son and grandson, and all looking the same age, about forty. Isaac continued by saying, 'And who in this instance would be praying *to*?'

'Pardon the interruption, my brothers,' said a slow-talking transparent man named Alexandrius, 'but I very much feel my spirit is telling me to—'

A medley of mumblings drowned him out, because the Apotheothorists were famous for—and quickly becoming resented because of—their über-holy approach to literally everything. Solomon, a tired-looking Patriarch who was casually picking through a tray of croissants (seeing if there were any chocolate chip ones) murmured, 'All you need is *love*.'

'There *has* to be some kind of a contingency plan,' said Nelson Mandela, who, looking about twenty-five, had an over-sized afro that he'd always wanted to grow but previously couldn't because he'd had to look "respectable." 'God knows everything, so it is safe to assume He knew what was going to happen.'

'Maybe God *doesn't* know everything,' said Pleebus. 'And maybe that's what He's trying to teach us right now.'

'That,' said Isaac, pointing an angry finger, 'is nothing but heresy. If you were living in *my* time—'

'If I was living in your time I'd be using my own finger as toilet paper.'

The table descended into a rowdy bicker-fest of accusations and insults. At one point somebody threw a sandal.

'Gentlemen,' said Jesus, who was sitting to the right of his Dad's empty throne. 'Please. This meeting hasn't even started.'

'Well, what are we waiting for?' asked Abraham, Isaac and Jacob.

'Gandhi and Paul,' said Solomon.

'I don't think Gandhi's coming,' said Jesus. 'He's not answering his phone. And how the hell is he even a board-member if currently he's a Physical?'

'You don't think something's happened to *him*, do you?' said a completely naked man named Ricky. (He was a Televangelist, so as a rule wasn't allowed to wear clothes up in Heaven). 'This whole situation could be a— an attempt at getting rid of the *board*. What if there're explosives planted beneath our seats!?'

'It's not an assassination attempt,' said Jesus, grimacing as though he couldn't believe he was dealing with such idiots. 'And even if it was, it'd probably land on the decoy twelve. Look. We all know what Gandhi's like. He's probably teachin' naked women how to set up bazookas or something like that.'

'Then where's Paul?' asked Jacob. 'He's the glue that holds us together.'

'Paul shoulda been here ten minutes ago,' said Jesus. 'And when he gets here he gets here. In fact, I think we should start this meeting now—without him and Gandhi; we've waited long enough.'

'*Without* them?' said Abraham, Isaac and Jacob. Abraham continued with, 'How would you like it if we started a meeting without *you*?'

'If y'ever even *think* about doing that,' said Jesus, levelling a finger at the ornery man, 'I will drag you out that door and show you the *true* meaning of circumcision. And I'll count it a perk o' the job.

'Okay. I say we've waited long enough, and we're not gonna wait any longer. Now. I wanna hear what you guys have to say about—'

Suddenly, the massive wooden doors of the boardroom swung open; and into the chamber, striding like owned it, entered a man with slicked-back hair, wearing an obviously-expensive suit.

'Sorry I'm late,' said the Apostle Paul, placing a leather folder on the table. 'I was just going over some of the stats from the guys down at the

Pilgrims' Passage. I've had them analysing the whole situation, trying to see if there's any way of finding out where Lucifer took God.' He sat down at the table, reached over to a silver carafe, poured himself a cup of strong black coffee, and drank it in a single, no-nonsense gulp. 'Aaah. Also, I've just spoken to some of our guys down in the Dimensional Development department. They've told me something that...' He paused dramatically.

'What?' asked Alexandrius.

'This is quite serious,' said Paul. 'And I *am* going to tell you all what happened. But I want every single individual to promise they will respond calmly. Can you each do that for me?'

The Patriarchs all agreed. Jesus rolled his eyes.

Paul composed himself before saying, 'At 0951 this morning, the official time of God's abduction, the Double-D. department recorded a..."tremor." It was felt all throughout Heaven, and for very good reason. At 0951 this morning, Creation stopped expanding.'

A chill ran up the back of Jesus' neck, and he suddenly felt very alone. Each of the Patriarchs was looking to Paul and one another for clarification of what had just been said. Ricky asked, 'How could— how could something like *that* happen?'

'You've all seen the footage of God's capture,' said Paul. 'You all know that right now He's caught inside a, well, we don't yet know what the thing is, but we've got our people trying to figure that out. This thing, this box, when it came down on the Almighty, it separated Him from all of Existence. That rumbling, which we all felt...it was Heaven contracting. Because...the Creator has been cut off from His Creation. Completely.'

There was a shocked and disbelieving silence, until Derdinand Schopals said, 'I don't understand. This means Heaven is now...*shrinking*?'

'It's not shrinking—not yet,' said Paul. 'It just isn't growing. The Giver of Life isn't here to *give* life. Energy isn't being regulated, so the Barriers of Eternity...will be reached.'

Jesus veered away from that scary and mind-boggling thought by asking, 'Does— does this lack of growth have any bearing on how much energy Hell's getting, from the Physical Dimensions?'

Paul seemed slightly rankled by the interruption, but replied, 'So far there's been a *slight* decrease in Hell's productivity. But the numbers are telling us it's going to get worse, and quickly. Though interestingly, at the moment Hell's being supplemented by reserve power. Several independent auxiliary Dimensions kicked into action at 0939—twelve minutes before the tremor.'

'You mean the Good Lord saw this coming?' asked Nelson Mandela.

'Someone must have,' said Paul. 'Whether or not it was God the Great and Powerful perhaps remains to be seen.'

'Well who else could it have been?' asked Ricky. 'And what happens if *our* power runs out?'

'You mean *when* it runs out,' said Solomon. 'If we don't get God back.'

'Obviously that's the worst-case scenario,' said Paul, 'and if it *were* to happen, we'd be talking about...'

'What?' asked Abraham, Isaac, and Jacob.

'Well, we'd be talking about the end of everything,' said Paul. 'Because if nothing's powering the Spirit Realm, then nothing's powering the Spirits inside it.'

A silence fell over the board members. Pleebus said, 'Effectively, you're talking about Heat Death. For the Spirit World.'

Paul nodded and said, 'It's why we have to get proactive, because if we don't *do* something about this, first of all the lights will go out; then the Citizens are going to—'

'They're going to start attacking each other,' said Jesus.

'Why do you say that?' asked Paul, again annoyed by the interruption.

'*My* people,' said Jesus, 'who've been on the ground, they've told me Negative vibrations'll soon be permeating the Spiritual Realm. As we know from history, when that happens...'

'Things turn ugly,' said Alexandrius.

Paul drummed his fingers on the table before flipping open his leather folder. 'If this is true,' he said, his tone of voice transmitting his doubt, 'then we'd have to close off the Physical Realms.'

Jesus shook his head and said, 'If we do *that*, Heaven won't be receiving any energy at all. And the Physical Realms'd be left to their own devices.'

'We'd also be saving ourselves from the Bad Karma,' said Paul. 'And the Physical Realms are designed to be self-sufficient, so they really aren't our concern right now.'

'Everything in Creation is interdependent upon everything else,' said Jesus. 'Right now the Physical planes are dipping toward chaos.'

Paul smiled cutely and said, 'Is this the Son of God demonstrating No Greater Love on a collective scale?'

There were a few chuckles, mostly from Abraham, Isaac and Jacob. Jesus tried to think of a quick riposte, but there were no knives in the drawer: his mind was a flawless blank.

'What're we gonna do?' asked Ricky, his question directed toward Paul.

'That,' said Paul, 'is something we're all going to have to agree upon. But I personally think that if we can track down Lucifer, then we can interrogate him, or negotiate with him, and somehow extract the information we need to crack that box containing God.'

Pleebus said, 'I don't think Lucifer actually knows what he's dealing with. Something bigger is at work right now.'

Paul didn't respond to that. Neither did Jesus. The VP was staring at the shiny tabletop, which was embossed with an image of a compass, so big that it filled the table's entire surface. The Son of God shifted in his chair, and movement from the compass caught his eye. Looking more closely, he noticed that its *north* needle was pointed at...at him. Jesus leaned closer to his Dad's empty throne. The needle on the tabletop followed him.

'In situations like this,' said Paul, 'sacrifice is often a necessity. As we all know—'

'We're not closing off the Physical Realms,' said Jesus, looking up from the tabletop. 'Not now, anyway. If things get *really* bad, *then* we'll think about doing it. But *until* then—'

'Until then the board decides what we'll be doing,' said Paul. 'And if a decision is made, it's going to be made by a vote. Anyway, even your *Dad* closed off a Dimension when it started leaking Bad Karma. Do you seriously want to go against what He in His ultimate wisdom thought was the best thing to do? All those in favour of—'

'There is *not* going to be a vote,' said Jesus. 'Because *I* am the one in charge. Check the manual, or whatever it's called—'

'You mean the Bible?' asked Ricky.

'—and you'll see it printed very clearly,' continued Jesus. 'In situations when the CEO, i.e. the Creator, isn't able to perform His duty of leadership, that duty passes to the current Vice President.'

'And *I* propose,' said Paul, 'that the current Vice President isn't fit to be occupying a role of such consequence.'

'You can make proposals until the day *I* come back, Paul,' said Jesus, staring fiercely. 'But the sad-for-you fact o' the matter is I'm the one holding the reins, and there is no way I'm gonna be cutting off the Spiritual influence to those Realms.'

'If we don't do what we *have* to do,' said Paul, 'then we are going right down *with* those Physicals. Already the Limbo Lines are overfilling with victims of this whole debacle.'

'I would rather be responsible for the total shutdown of Hell,' said Jesus, 'than to see the look on my Dad's face when He learns we didn't trust the design of His Creation.'

'Please,' said Paul. 'Preciousness isn't your forté, Mr. Christ. I should know because back on Earth, when I was following along behind you and sweeping up all of your little misinformations, I got a pretty decent perception of the real Son of Man. If *anything*, right now you're just trying to cast away your responsibilities. Because if the board would permit me to enlighten them, I'd like to draw their attention to a little edict the Son of God gave this morning, at about 11 o'clock.'

Looking around the conference table, Paul asked, 'Have any of you gentlemen been down to the Waiting Room recently?'

None of the Patriarchs had.

'Well, if you *were* to visit that section of Heaven, you'd find that right now it's filled with steel platforms, which practically reach all the way to the ceiling. The Vice President knows what I'm talking about, because according to my sources, he was the one who ordered the scaffolding to be shipped there.'

'To deal with the overflow,' said Jesus, who wanted to throw something at this usurping Apostle.

'Which is fine,' said Paul. 'The initiative is respected. But what *I'm* wondering is: if you knew the Saints were missing, and God was being held prisoner, why didn't you alert the board? I mean, *I* found out from a *psychic*.'

'I was stuck in one of the *Physical* Realms,' said Jesus.

'And that's happened twice now, hasn't it? In the past eighteen hours?' Paul was reading from the opened folder in front of him. 'And in between those forays you were lunching at—'

'What, you had me *investigated*? I'm the Son o' God for God's sake.'

'And don't you think,' said Paul, 'that *as* the Son of God, perhaps you have a responsibility to ensure that the Citizens of Heaven are kept safe? Led to a place of, I don't know, *greener* pastures?'

'Not just the Heavenly Citizens, Paul,' said Jesus. '*All* of Dad's creations.'

'This is not the time,' said Paul, 'to be getting high-minded.'

'But it *is* the time,' said Jesus, sitting up taller in his chair, 'for you to shut your mouth and accept the fact that *I* am the one sitting at the right-hand side of my Old Man's throne. *I* am the Son of God and *I* am the Vice President, and *I* don't care if *you* don't like it.' Looking around the table, he said, 'If any of you gentlemen don't like the fact that I too am the I AM, then all I can say is—deal with it. By lifting your cheeks off those chairs and walking out that door. Because He, "in His ultimate wisdom," Paul, is the one who appointed me to this position.'

None of the Patriarchs said or did anything. Some of them were looking at the tabletop, while others (like Solomon) were smiling amusedly.

'I am very glad to see that no one is choosing to wipe the dust from their feet,' said Jesus, his eyes conveying a new intolerance for detraction. 'Now. One of the main disagreements me and my Dad have is secrecy. God's opinion is treat the Citizens like mushrooms. Mine is we should show 'em the way. As you know, the Almighty isn't here right now. And that is why *I* am telling you the first thing we're gonna do is inform the Citizens of Heaven about what's going on, because there are measures we can take to slow the processes of Bad Karma.'

'Do you know what's going to happen,' said Paul, 'if the people of Heaven learn that God is missing? They're going to panic. They're going to bounce off the walls and sink their teeth into each other's faces. Don't cut the head off the messenger, I'm just saying it how it is.'

'Whether you are or not,' said Jesus. 'It doesn't matter. Because as I've said, in a situation like this, the responsibility falls onto *my* shoulders.'

'And we all suffer Heat Death if you don't deliver us,' said Paul, with mock happiness.

'May be,' said Jesus. 'But once upon a time you were willing to chuck yourself into a gamble that said I *would* deliver.

'*Gentlemen.* We have got a Deity to rescue and an Existence to save. If there's anything else you'd like to say then please keep it to yourselves...unless of course it's productive. All right.' He rapped his knuckles on the conference table. 'First thing we're gonna do is organise a gathering.'

SAINT WALLY

Chapter 22

Billions of Citizens were crowding the inner balconies of Heaven's Main Office (many of them were VIPS—those mentioned in a religious text). Wondering aloud why a mass gathering had been called, they looked out over the railings, at the giant bronze homeless man wetting his pants, and saw that the statue's arms were lowering hydraulically, his wrists rotating so that his placard came to be laid flat. The statue's REPENT sign was now a stage; and within it was greenroom, in which Jesus, sitting in a make-up chair, was being tended to by stressed-out cosmeticians, and advised by anxious Patriarchs.

'Okay,' said Jesus, taking deep nervous breaths. 'Public speaking. Haven't done this in a while.'

'You'll be fine, bro,' said Geoff, massaging his half-brother's shoulders, and nodding for Walter to agree. 'Just remember: big loud voice—like you know what you're talking about.'

'Just like back in the day,' said Jesus, noticing in the mirror his expression of casual terror. 'Um...Do we know who's gonna be introducing me?'

The Patriarchs looked back and forth among themselves, and were all too terrified to put up a hand. Saint Peter, leaning on a watercooler, said, 'I can do it if you want.'

'Petey,' said Jesus. 'Y'sure? Public speaking's difficult. A lot o' people get up there and freeze. It's actually happened to me a couple o' times. 'S why I had to break out the ol' HP card and slip through the cr—' Jesus' eyes suddenly widened, and he hoped to his Dad that Paul hadn't found out about the whole *Son of God losing his Heavenly Privileges in a card game* incident.

'No no no, it'll be fine,' said Saint Peter, spilling water from his plastic cup as he waved away the VP's concern. 'I've read a few books about public speaking. They say the best thing to do is get up there and imagine everyone's naked and in wheelchairs. Besides, remember: I used to do a bit of it back on Earth.'

Jesus gave a tepid smile and said, 'I might hafta try that technique myself. I'm still debating whether or not to ask for public opinions. Somethin's tellin' me it's the right thing to do.'

'Intuition, you think?' asked Walter.

'Could be that,' said Jesus, staring into space. 'Or it could just be that I'm totally out of ideas.' He snapped to attention and said, 'All right. Let's get down to breakin' the news.'

Saint Peter and the Patriarchs stepped onto a platform that rose through the greenroom's ceiling and then stopped with a *clang*. Now level with the bronze stage, they were back-dropped by the gigantic head of the homeless man (who appeared to be howling) and looking up at billions of Citizens loaded upon balconies, stairwells and escalators.

A few metre's from the front edge of the stage was a plexiglass pulpit. Saint Peter treaded over to it, tapped its microphone, then cleared his throat and said, 'Hello, uh, greetings, everyone. Thank you all for coming here today to show your support. All of Creation is much obliged. Could we please have it that all tongues are kept motionless; the Vice President of Creation will soon be making an address.'

Down in the greenroom, Jesus was standing in a corner, trying to memorise a few sound bytes. Feeling a tap on his shoulder, he turned around and saw the Angel of Death. Happily surprised, he said, 'Grimmy. What're you doin' here?'

'I just came around to see if you're nervous,' said Death, smiling as Walter and Geoff made themselves scarce.

Jesus gave a *so-so* gesture and said, 'Just can't wait till all o' this is over. Provided we get Dad back, of course.'

'You will,' said Death. 'Good always wins.'

'And the bad guys always wear black hats,' said Jesus, wishing it was that simple.

Death, with unconcealed disdain for the VP's torn jeans and grubby wife-beater, asked, 'And is that what *you're* wearing?'

'Why?' said Jesus, defensively.

'Well, you are royalty. Don't you think you should be, keeping up appearances—just a little bit?'

'Whatta ya think I'm doin' by gettin' on that stage?' said Jesus, smiling.

'So, without delaying things any further,' said Saint Peter, who'd begun to quite enjoy his role as herald, 'I'd like to introduce God's Only Begotten Son, the Vice President of Heaven, Jesus H. (H. is for Hosanna—don't laugh) Christ.'

Jesus, who now wished even more that he didn't have to take the stage, said, 'That means I gotta get up there.' He hurried over to a platform that had begun ascending without him; and stepping onto it, said, 'Wish me a bit o' fortitudinity, eh?'

Death said, 'I don't think that's even a word.'

'Who said it needs to be?' said Jesus, a moment before he was lifted out of sight.

A small pattering of applause greeted the Son of God as he appeared on the stage. Waving at his loyal subjects and padding over to the pulpit, he leaned in close to its microphone and said, 'Thank you, Peter.' The booming of his own voice gave Jesus a jolt. He acclimatised to the loudness of the microphone and added, 'And thank you very much everybody for being here today. It's good to see you all. The fact that you took the time to show up demonstrates just how much you have invested in...Creation.

'Uh, I'm moving toward saying something that you might find...hard to process. My intention was to come out here and maybe prime you a bit, so you don't receive the news too badly.

'Uh...and that...attempt at a joke would imply the news is...bad.'

A communal, full-bodied murmur of concern prompted Jesus to hold up a conciliatory hand and say, 'Now, it's nothing we can't handle. It's just...it's something that we as Spirituals have to take care of.'

The collective murmur grew louder.

Jesus looked over at the Patriarchs and saw both anxiety and irritation. He also noticed that standing alongside them were Geoff and Walter, who must have found a way to sneak up here. Geoff gave a thumbs-up. Jesus went to return it but then instantly forgot to.

It had been over two thousand years since the Vice President had had to make one of these speeches. Yes he'd done informal get-togethers—friends' weddings and birthday parties. But when was the last time he'd had to *sell* something? A long time ago. A *damn* long time ago.

'Uh,' said Jesus. 'There are some things that...we gotta outline.'

He could imagine the Citizens going back to their mansions and saying things like, *How about that speech, eh? One o' the worst I've ever heard. And to think that man used to be one of the world's greatest orators.*

'Uh...'

SAINT WALLY

He only got the job because of who his Old Man is; 'cause Somebody up there likes him.

'Um. Thank you for— for coming.'

He couldn't believe he'd just said that.

He's just as ridiculous as the people claiming *to be him.*

Jesus felt as if he'd been slapped. Had someone said that, or had he just imagined it?

Reaching out and grabbing the microphone for a bit of grounding, he said, 'Okay. There are some precautions we're gonna need to be taking in a little while. And I think everyone's gonna be interested to hear why.'

This is worse than that time we had to stand around singing Holy Holy Holy.

Again, Jesus wasn't sure if he'd heard that or just imagined it. Under the pressure of expectation, and feeling like a performer who'd suddenly developed dementia, he unthinkingly activated his usual recourse: He began whistling *Swing Low Sweet Chariot.*

'Remember,' he distantly heard Saint Peter call out. 'Naked and in wheelchairs!'

The Son of God broke free of an awkward, momentary fugue, and looked up at the overloaded balconies. He tried to visualise the Citizens as Saint Peter had recommended; but all he saw was...sheep: dense-headed fluff bags that he was the God-ordained leader of.

Jesus composed himself; and without a single mite of artfulness, said, 'Two things have happened, ladies, gentlemen, and whatevers. One: the Saints have been stolen. Two: God's been kidnapped—by an Angel who won't be named because I think he'd get off on *being* named.'

A terrified hush fell over the billions of Heavenly Citizens.

And then panic set in.

People started shrieking and fighting with each other, or flagellating themselves with rosary beads, or looking around frantically for materials that might make graven images.

'Hey,' said Jesus. 'This is not the way you were designed to react. Calm yourselves down, please. This is embarrassing.'

Someone with long flowing hair jumped off a golden escalator, plummeted, and collided messily with the stage. The man staggered to his feet, rubbing at his shins, then pulled out a plastic bag, unzipped it, and poured ashes onto his own face.

'Aw that's very classy, Elijah,' said Jesus. 'Exhibitionism is always *so* admirable. And a really good example to set for everyone else—sneakin' contraband into the Echelons.'

Geoffrey son of Joseph broke away from the Patriarchs, ran over to Jesus and tapped him on the shoulder.

'Bro,' he said. 'Mind if I practice a bit of the old crowd-control?'

Jesus took a step backward, saying, 'I defer to my ex chief bodyguard.'

Geoff adjusted the microphone, then poked out his tongue and blew a raspberry. It was loud, and long, and attention-grabbing enough that the Citizens of Heaven stopped misbehaving and began looking around for the source of the noise.

Geoff retracted his tongue, took a deep breath, and wheezily practiced what he preached by saying, 'Everybody. Breathe in, breathe out. Breathe in, breathe out...Because we haven't even gotten to the important part.'

The crowd was silent as Jesus resumed his place behind the pulpit. 'Thank you, Geoffrey,' he said, re-adjusting the microphone. 'And thank you Citizens of Heaven, for reacting with such dignity. Anyway. All of what I've just told you is true. My Dad isn't here, and now *I'm* the one in charge.

'It's been a while since I've had to come up with any new material, but I don't think that really matters. Sometimes the old stuff is so good you don't need to look for new stuff. *A house divided against itself will not stand. How can Satan drive out Satan? Before you break into a strong man's house to steal all his things, tie him up so he can't beat the hell out of you.*

'All o' the above is pretty much what's happening to us right now: Someone—in the form of Bad Karma—is trying to break into our house. It's gonna try and split us up and tie us up, but that's not gonna happen. 'Cause we're the strong people in this parable. We're the ones who'll be holdin' loaded shotguns and stayin' awake to watch the door. 'Cause no frangipani Evil Spirit intruder's gonna weasel its way into our domain. We're death-defyers.

'All right. Now I know there are gonna be lots o' questions, but we need to get some answers, and I got a feeling that all o' you guys is where they're gonna come from. If y'look around you'll see a bunch of Cherubs. Some of 'em have microphones. If anybody has any information about the location of God and/or the Saints, then grab a microphone and speak it out loud. Also, if you have any ideas about how we can get God and/or the Saints *back*, then grab a microphone. But please make sure it's one at a time; I might be related to God but I can't listen to two things at once. Ohr yeah, and some o' you guys are gonna have to go into quarantine as a precaution, 'cause of the nature of your, uh, past-life religions. Some carnal reversions are simply too much of a risk. Sorry.'

A man on a balcony, whose white beard went all the way down to his knees, lifted a hand and received a microphone from a flying Cherub. He tapped the device to make sure it was working, then happily asked, 'What if we send out some doves?'

'Yes!' said Jesus, squinting to identify the man on the faraway balcony. 'I'm guessing that's Noah. Good idea. Can somebody write that down, please? Okay. Anyone else? Any other ideas?'

A nervous man who gave his name as Timothy said, 'Search parties,' and then thrust the microphone back to its Cherub as quickly as he could.

'Good idea,' said Jesus. 'Search parties. That's pretty much what the doves'll be; we'll send 'em out into all the worlds and see if we can catch sight o' something relevant.'

Somebody yelled something that Jesus couldn't make out. 'Sorry, what was that? You'll have to get a microphone. And raise your hands please, people, if you wanna say something.'

The Citizen who had called out was a turquoise humanoid with a skin-flap Mohawk. Receiving a microphone from a cute little Cherub, the being in a white collar office shirt said, 'Hi, my name's Henry—'

Another voice, intoning through a megaphone, interrupted with, 'And I'm an alcoholic.'

'And I was thinking,' continued Henry, when the laughter had settled. 'What if we asked an Info-Brain where to find God?'

Jesus couldn't believe he hadn't thought of it earlier.

COURTNEY TAYLOR

Chapter 23

Thousands of flapping Seraphim used their collective might to push the floating God's Brain into the midst of the lobby. To do this, passageways had had to be opened up, and escalators and staircases had had to be contorted into accommodating positions. The enormous machine, which looked like a glass sultana, blocked out the skylight far above, and cast an eerie shadow over the statue and the thousands of balconies encircling it. The adolescent Angels who'd been pushing the Brain disbanded raucously, their efforts applauded by the innumerable onlookers.

Jesus adjusted the pulpit's microphone and said, 'Hey Dad.'

A blinding beam of light gushed down onto him. Squinting against it, he said, 'We have a question for you: *Where are You; i.e. Where is God?*

With a voice so powerful that the bronze stage vibrated, the gigantic glass brain replied, 'Hmmm. It appears that I'm incommunicado, which means I cannot answer your question.'

There was an audible groan from the crowd. Jesus looked around at the Patriarchs, then out at the gathered Citizens, and said, 'Any other ideas? Anyone?'

Someone on a balcony got hold of a microphone and said, 'Henry again.'

'And I'm still an alco— *Ohw.*' No doubt the anonymous interrupter with the megaphone had been slapped across the back of the head.

'And I'm thinking,' said Henry, when the laughter had again settled. 'What if we *all* asked? You know, strength in numbers; *Where two or more people gather in My name there I'll be.*'

Jesus rubbed at the back of his neck and said, 'Probably can't hurt to try. All right, everyone; you all get that? At the exact same time we'll all ask the exact same question: *Where is God?* On three; ya ready? That's *on* three.

'One...two...'

'*Where is God?*' said all the Citizens of Heaven, in a bass but whispering voice, so thick and present that when it finished it seemed to have only been imagined.

The glass brain replied, 'I am sorry to say the Almighty remains: Incommunicado.'

Disappointment emanated from the balconies. Jesus said, 'Okay. We'll move on to the next thing. But that was good. A good idea. And keep 'em comin', you guys. Even if it's the most bull-spit, outlandish thing y'ever thought of in your lifetime; if there's a chance it might help, bring it up here.'

There were a few more suggestions, some of which were so ridiculous that all Jesus said was, 'Okay. Okay nice. Well, we'll think about that,' and then the microphone travelled over to—

'Henry again.' People groaned, and Jesus couldn't blame them. 'And I know we've tried it before,' continued Henry, 'but, all of the Info-Brains are connected, and the closer they are to one another, the stronger the field connecting them becomes. If we put a whole bunch of the Brains together, we might be able to generate enough of a field that they're able to penetrate whatever's blocking them from connecting to God. Or there's the possibility of accessing the Bank of Inaccessible Knowledge—that's based on the All Knowing but Forgive and Forget principle. It could be the answers are *in* the Brain; it just hasn't been provoked into finding them.'

'I'm just wondering if any of that made sense,' said Jesus. 'And tell me, Henry—how'd you come by all this information?'

'I'm a surveyor down in one of the Double D. departments. Don't really do much because God doesn't make any mistakes. But sometimes He comes in and We talk about things. The Bank of Inaccessible Knowledge seems to be one of his favourite subjects.'

In honour of Henry's boldness, Jesus ordered at least twenty Info-Brains to be brought before him—though he didn't say it as grandly as that. As everybody waited for the Brains to be air-lifted via Seraphim, an expert on Bad Karma, named Mojaribus, gave a talk about how to withstand the temptations of Bad Karma.

'Okay, everybody,' said Majoribus, who was a bipedal pachyderm with hyper-extended eyeballs. 'Now some things you have to remember: When Bad Karma sinks its nails into you, it makes you see things that aren't there. A joke becomes an insult, or a look in someone's eyes becomes a criticism...Before you know it you're strapping bombs to your body because you're offended by somebody's T-shirt. Now, some of you might have already *noticed* such symptoms, maybe in yourself, or in other people, and if you *have*, don't worry, because by taking a few simple steps you can actually *reverse* the effects of Bad Karma, and prepare yourself mentally for any sieges in future. Okay. So the first thing you have to remember is this: Every single person can *choose* whether or not they fall to Bad Karma. We *all* have the power to decide, and there are absolutely no exceptions. Secondly, if we stick together, we have a much better chance of staying sane, because Bad Karma likes to isolate people. It likes to drill its way into their minds in private, where it can corrupt their sub-DNA from the inside out. I know. It is not a desirable situation to find yourself in. Heht-hem. Things to be aware of:

'One of the first noticeable characteristics of a BK manifestation is a person's face. The BK gets hold of the facial muscles and twists them around so the person is very *angry* looking. This is something we should all watch out for. If you happen to see such a manifestation, in one of your friends or coworkers, don't "string the person up" or "burn them at the stake"—simply draw attention to the way they are behaving, very, very gently. Because chances are they think they're behaving *normally*, and that *you* are the one who has something wrong with them. And who knows? Maybe they are right.'

'Thank you, Majoribus,' said Jesus, when the last of the gigantic Info-Brains was pushed to a floating halt. 'That was very informative. And if anyone here would like to learn more about BK resistance, Majoribus and his team are currently teaching classes on that very subject. I strongly encourage you all to attend, because the more bullets we've got, the better the chance of hitting something.

'Okay, then. The Info-Brains. A long shot, but, you all know the way my Dad operates: He's mysterious. All right everyone; same question, same time. Let's hope it works.' He cleared his throat and said, 'Hey Dad, another question. This one's comin' from all of us.'

The twenty new info-Brains shot innumerable blasts of light that fixed themselves upon every individual present. Their brightness was such that Jesus closed his eyes, and in that moment, prayed to his Old Man that they'd get some kind of answer out of all this.

To the billions, maybe even trillions, of Citizens relying on him, Jesus said, 'Okay; on three; that's *on* three.

'One...Two...'

In a voice even louder than before, the Citizens collectively asked a question that made the building shake.

'*Where is God?*'

The Info-Brains began to whirr, then vibrate, and then produce distinctive beeping, clicking and chirping sounds, evidently in communication with each other. Their shared equation required so much contemplation that the beams of light they emitted began to weaken, and soon were entirely gone. All of the Brains' energy was being spent internally. They began to look like bottled, super-charged universes.

The bronze stage was quivering so much that the pulpit shuffled toward the edge of it as if attempting suicide. Jesus grabbed it, steadied it, and looked out at the crowded balconies. People were holding their heads between the elbows. Beards were erupting into flames. The Son of God noticed that his skin had begun tingling.

Suddenly, there was an explosion, and thick crystal shards rained down onto the stage, smashing all around the surprised Patriarchs. One of the Info-Brains above them flickered, went dark, and began to fall. A gaping crack in its side revealed a blinking network of bulky neural connections. The polished, runnelled surface of the Brain whipped past the stage, so closely that disrupted air buffeted the homeless man. His arms shook, threatening to snap backwards and perhaps even tear off at the armpits.

Jesus felt like a man on a demented roller-coaster. The mezzanine tower below him, lashed by the wind, tipped frighteningly backward, and then lurched so far forward that several people on the opposing balconies held up their hands for high-fives. He noticed that fractures had appeared in those balconies, and hoped the same wasn't true for the remaining Info-Brains. Their shared computation was now making them shine so brightly they were all but blinding, and they looked as if they were about to over-exert themselves and plunge in pursuit of their fallen comrade, which was crashing its way through golden escalators far below.

But, instead of malfunctioning and falling, or exploding, the Brains stopped whirring, stopped glowing, and hovered silently.

In a unified voice so deep and loud that people screamed and balustrades split apart, the Info-Brains, with the voice of God, said, 'As the Good Lord is currently unavailable, it is exceedingly recommended that any urgent queries be directed to the Second in Command.'

The disappointment was thick enough to baptise a heathen.

COURTNEY TAYLOR

Chapter 24

Jesus was sitting on his Dad's watery desk, looking down at a slide-show of photographs that was playing across its surface. A photo of him appeared. He was standing in front of his own statue in Rio, imitating its pose, only with both of his middle fingers prominently displayed.

'Classy,' said Walter, who had gotten up from a cloudy lounge chair, obviously uncomfortable with just sitting around.

Jesus gave a weak laugh and said, 'Yeah I'm surprised He's got it in the collection. Usually with Dad it's all about graduations and awards. I'm just hoping He foresaw all o' this crap. That kid from the Dimensional department; he knew what he was after; so...'

'You got your hopes up?' asked Walter.

Jesus was about to reply, but three sharp knocks on the door announced Saint Peter, who stepped into the office and said, 'Noah has organised the search doves; he says they're almost ready to be sent out. Do you think it would be a good idea to...show our faces at the launching?'

'Of course,' said Jesus, pushing himself off the desk and making for the doorway. 'How're things down at the Waiting Room?'

'It's filling quickly,' replied Saint Peter, as they strode toward God's elevator. 'At the moment the Deceased are jammed in so tight it's hard to pick out the OTRs and the foetuses. We've still got power, so we can use the Book of Life to sort them out, but, well, if we have to save energy for what's ahead, we might have to give up on collecting the Surplus Morality. And, uh, *about* the Surplus Morality we've been storing...I've had an idea. Actually, someone I know had the idea. What if we use the Saints for the *Citizens*? Rig up a kind of contraption—like a mask—so that before they inhale any Negativity, a dose of Morality drives it away?'

'Petey,' said Jesus. 'That's brilliant. We'd be using the Saints as like a filter, against the Bad Karma. But have we got enough Morality to go round?'

'I don't think we can manage it for every *single* Citizen,' said Saint Peter. 'But for those fighting the Ultimate Battle, it may just be the needed edge.'

They stepped inside the elevator, Jesus holding back a cynical quip as he pressed a button and the doors closed.

'I was thinking,' continued Saint Peter, as the elevator descended. 'If we raided one of the more advanced Physical Realms for some oxygen masks, that would mean not wasting energy on manufacturing them ourselves. I know technically that constitutes theft, which contributes to the Karmic imbalance, but perhaps we could write it off as one of those grey issues your Father makes room for: *Thou shalt not steal, but if you're stealing to feed your starving family, it's understandable.* I think we can get away with that.'

'I agree,' said Jesus. 'And you've got my full permission, Petey. Go for it.'

Ding! The elevator opened upon a wide corridor bustling with Citizens, many pushing iron cages that were filled to bending point with white doves. The Citizens improved their posture as Jesus strode down the corridor. He wanted to roll his eyes when they started saluting him, but instead did his best to return the gesture.

Moses fell into the same stride as Jesus, Walter and Saint Peter, saying, 'Yeah, the pigeons are all ready to go and the search parties have been sent out; but I'm wondering if there might be a bit o' wisdom in having more than one colour dove. You know, so we don't get 'em mixed up with seagulls.'

'Shut up, Moses,' said Saint Peter.

One of the doorways had a porthole; and beyond its glass there was an eternity of white blankness. Walter noticed the absence of a bird cage, and asked, 'What's this room?'

'That?' said Jesus, turning around but not stopping. 'That's the future. No-go zone.'

A pink, pot-bellied lemur-looking creature was sitting on the shoulder of a man who had a long burnt beard. Jesus addressed the man as Noah, and asked, 'How is everything? Ready to go?'

Noah reached up to the pink creature, took a clipboard from it, and replied, 'Well, we've got a cage next to— not every Dimension, but a lot o' the main ones. The doves are all trained; they know what to look out for and where the checkpoints are. So now we're just waiting for you to give the signal. And, uh, I've prepared something you can do that with.' He sheepishly handed over a small rolled-up flag, which, when Jesus unfurled it, they all saw was emblazoned with a rainbow. 'Your Old Man,' said Noah, 'His implication was: I'll never leave all of you up Shiite Creek...Just some of you.'

Jesus, who couldn't help smiling, said, 'Thanks, Noah,' then looked around for, 'Hey, where's Moses? I saw him just a second ago.'

Moses, who had been rapping his staff against someone else's coop, "inspecting it," strutted forth when called upon. He was suspicious when Jesus said, 'Mo, have you still got that megaphone? Mind if I borrow it?' but reluctantly handed it over–along with a pointed finger that told the VP it was just a loan.

'Thanks,' said Jesus, turning on the megaphone and raising it. 'All right! Thanks everyone for being here! Can I ask if we're all ready!?'

There were shouts of 'Yes!' and 'Partially!'

'Okay, then,' said Jesus. 'As you all probably know, what's happening now is we're gonna open up our Dimension doors and move the cages in front of 'em! Then on my signal, we're gonna open the cages and let loose the doves! Are we ready?'

Again there were shouts of 'Yes!' and 'Partially!'

'All right!' said Jesus. 'Then let's open the doors, n' move the cages into position!'

Thousands of excited Citizens opened the doors they were stationed at, and wheeled the cages so they faced the varying habitats beyond them. Jesus had to admit that he too was enjoying the whole camaraderie thing. It reminded him of his three best years on Earth, when he and his Disciples had hit the roads, heading off into the wild rocky yonder to defy the establishment. 'All right,' he said, when everybody appeared to be ready. 'On my signal, release the doves!'

Jesus lifted his flag, held it high, and then dropped it triumphantly.

Nothing happened. None of the Citizens moved.

'That was the signal,' said Jesus. 'Which...I forgot to tell you about.'

Everybody hurried to dispel the awkwardness by quickly opening their respective cages.

In a Dimension in which a class of Albino orphans was sitting under a tree and learning how to read and write, a Spiritual doorway appeared in the air and produced a swarm of doves that sent the children screaming in every possible direction. In a Dimension in which a homosexual couple was making wedding vows, a suddenly-appearing storm of doves rained fecal matter onto an over-abundance of black tuxedoes. The father of one of the grooms jumped to his feet and yelled, 'Ha!'

'Now,' said Jesus, 'all we can do is wait, and hope they bring something back.'

SAINT WALLY

Chapter 25

In the Music Realm, hundreds of thousands of Angels were cheerfully lending their hands to the building of a monstrous choir platform. Lucifer, poring over the stage's blueprints, gritted his teeth when he heard Osama bin Laden's distant-foghorn voice say, 'Uh, excuse me, leader.'

The Angel turned around and saw that the Arab was backed by nine other Arabs, each hauling camera equipment and staring with awe at the choir platform.

'I have just come back from trading the orphans,' said Osama. 'These are the men you were wanting, for to film your maganum oopus.'

'Excellent work, Oosama. Though you're sure they're the best in the business?'

'The very best. Can work with bombs and bullets and children. Not old people, though. This is Waleed, camera man number one. He is very professional. In fact, is prodigy. Has always been one to watch.'

Lucifer held out his hand so that Waleed could kiss it. Waleed didn't understand what was expected of him, so Osama bolted forward and gratified the Angel on Waleed's behalf.

'A prodigy, hmm?' said Lucifer, looking the portly Arabian up and down. 'Then despite your appearance, Waleed, you and I have something in common. *And*, if you do exactly what I tell you to, we're going to get on like an embassy on fire. Gentlemen, I am titillated to be making your acquaintance. *Now*. Defecating upon all further pleasantries, listen to me as best you can, because I do not like to repeat myself. This is what you are going to do for me.'

SAINT WALLY

Chapter 26

In a warehouse cloaked by nighttime darkness, Hitler trolleyed a pallet-load of boxes into the back of a semi-trailer, then wiped his hands and said, 'Zat is ze last of zem. Vee are now güht to go.'

Saint Peter, who was leading the ten-man operation, closed the back of the trailer—locking his crew members inside it—then made his way around to the prime mover, where he clambered up into its passenger seat and closed the door. To the driver of the hefty truck he said, 'Please tell me again that you did in one lifetime have a licence for this type of vehicle.'

Goliath, who was squashed behind the steering wheel with his head pressed against the ceiling, smiled and didn't reply.

A moment later the truck was skidding through darkened streets, heading for the Spiritual gateway that would take them back to Heaven. Suddenly, Saint Peter shot forward and collided with the dashboard. At the same time, the team members in the trailer fell to the floor and were pelted by a deluge of boxes.

'Sorry,' said Goliath. 'I had to hit the brakes because, well, *look*.'

He was pointing at a main road they needed to cross, which was lined on both sides by huge cheering crowds. Coming up the street, preceded by hundreds of people walking leashed animals, was a tiered float that looked like a slanted leopard-skin wedding cake. All confusion evaporated when Goliath and Saint Peter saw a banner that read, *Welcome to the First Ever Soon To Be Annual Completely and Totally Legal Bestiality* Pride *Parade!*

They didn't know what to say or do, but Saint Peter eventually managed, 'Run them over, Goliath. I don't think the Good Lord would have *any* objections.'

The giant hit the accelerator and ploughed his truck through the middle of the parade, tearing apart the float, and sending fur of many kinds and colours raggedly through the air. Beneath the tyres of his steel behemoth went dogs, cats, monkeys, goats, horses, ducks, hamsters, dolphins in mobile aqua tanks, and all of the men, women and children who had professed their undying love for these animals. Goliath then spun his steering wheel and went for the crowd.

Chapter 27

In the department of Existential Relations, an elevated conference room was surrounded by a busy maze of bureaucracy. Inside the glass room, the Patriarchs were seated around a large circular table. At its centre were holographic charts that the Apostle Paul was explaining.

'The Physical reactions we're seeing do give rise to noble deeds—courage in the face of disaster, etc. But they're also conducive to actions that greatly contribute to Bad Karma's alchemy: things like looting and violence.'

'Is it true,' said Derdinand, 'that soon the Negative vibrations will be strong enough to permeate the Spiritual Realm?'

'Like the Vice President informed us this morning,' said Paul, 'they're already doing that. And that molecular process is something we can't really control. I think you all should know that: Soon the Negative vibrations will be so thick we'll actually be able to see them.'

Jesus used his own name in vain, then said, 'We're really gonna have to keep an eye on ourselves; make sure we don't start doin' stupid things. Speaking of which, any news on the doves?'

Nelson Mandela said, 'Forty percent have reported sightings of Osama bin Laden. Although a hundred percent of that forty percent *were* sent into Arabian nations.'

Solomon said, 'We're gonna need something more substantial than just doves. Even the Sonarian monks aren't picking up any trace o' the Almighty's whereabouts. He has to be *somewhere*.'

'I doubt it's a Physical place,' said Paul. 'My people have been down at the Database, combing through the past six hours in pretty much every Dimension that exists.'

'I'm goin' down to the Passage after this,' said Jesus. 'I wanna be debriefed on all the technicalities o' what's happened. There might be some kind o' heads-up that Dad left for me.'

'I think you mean *briefed*,' said Paul, with a note of condescension.

To avoid any bickering, Pleebus said, 'Something else that I think is relevant: There's been a drastic increase in the number of spontaneous calibrated afflictions, also known as demonic possessions. These are produced at random by the Karmic Regulator, to try and centralise some of the Negativity needing to be dealt with.'

'And let me guess,' said Ricky. 'These afflictions *aren't* being dealt with because people are trying to *medicate* the problem, when in fact they should be calling an exorcist.'

Pleebus agreed, then said, 'And there's been a minimal amount of Divine intervention, which doesn't help.'

Jesus said, 'What, you mean the Angels aren't down in the Present?'

'Well, if they are,' said Pleebus, 'then they're not doing their jobs properly. Perhaps we should we should investigate this issue.'

'Damn right we should,' said Jesus, standing to his feet and catching sight of Moses. The man was outside the conference room, using his wooden staff to threaten the two volunteers guarding the door. 'Send Moses. That man is beginning to irritate me.'

―――――

Moses shambled down one of the Dimensional corridors and eventually arrived at door number 219. He was about to knock, but thought, *I'm a VIP; I don't need permission. So whatta ya think about* that, *Mr. "We can't let you in here because they're having a private meeting?"*

Opening the door and stepping through it, Moses found himself standing on lush green grass, and staring at a trapezoid mountain of scaffolding, in front of which were hundreds of thousands of Angels doing calisthenics and vocal warm ups. Raising his staff in the hope of it (and thus him) being immediately recognised and respected, he clomped down the hill toward a group of men whose ethnicity was similar to his own.

Moses didn't see L. Ron snap his fingers, giving an order; but he definitely observed the circle of Arabs (some wearing headsets) that quickly formed around him. It began to tighten, and he discerned a rapacious gleam in the eyes of its members.

Spinning his staff, whirling it and swinging it, Moses told his attackers with aplomb that he was highly-skilled in the arts of self-defence and matter manipulation.

Regardless, Moses was quickly captured.

SAINT WALLY

Chapter 28

The gigantic crystalline room was empty, save for twenty-five Citizens grouped around a makeshift computer console in front of the only active doorway.

'Bro,' said Geoff, standing up when he saw Jesus and Walter approaching. 'I'm glad you made it. These guys here work for the Apostle Paul. They've been going over the footage, finding out exactly what happened.'

'And what exactly *did* happen?' asked Jesus, after shaking the hands and promptly forgetting the names of every life-form present.

'Well, Lucifer covered his tracks pretty well,' said Geoff. 'He burned all the houses, intimidated the villagers, and like we learned before, even went to the extreme of not leaving behind any trace o' that horse.'

Jesus, intrigued by that last fact, made note of it, then said, 'And what about the whole situation? How did it happen?'

'You remember how your Dad tested out the age-old rock question?' said Geoff. 'Well, it seems He got caught contradicting himself, which is why right now He's trapped inside something that we're all calling a Parabox.'

'Which is Physical?' asked Jesus.

Geoff nodded.

'And it's trapping Him because...?'

'This is just an idea,' said Geoff. 'A totally random theory that people are just throwing out there. So don't go getting offended...'

'Geoffrey, just say it.'

'Well, what if this "Parabox" is something that's designed to isolate a bad element, so it doesn't taint the rest of the mechanism.'

'So, what,' asked Jesus, 'you think Dad's in a kind of...quarantine?'

Geoff nodded, saying, 'If God can't tell the truth about *one* thing, then can He be trusted to tell the truth about anything? If the Physical Realms started thinking about that, they might have gone a bit crazy, so put out an APB on the thing *making* 'em think like that. After all, one contradiction makes room for another, then another, then—'

'Then pretty soon the entire Physical Universe is crumbling into insanity,' said Jesus.

'Exactly,' said Geoff. 'So isolating the problem would be the natural thing to do. The Universe'd be preserving itself.'

'But I don't get it,' said Jesus. 'Dad's heard that question before. We've *joked* about it. And there's another one: If God can do anything, can He make a burrito so hot even He can't eat it? Or, if He's all-knowing, can He remember a time when He *wasn't* all-knowing?'

'We're also thinking,' said Geoff, 'that maybe one of the reasons why things are going so badly in the Physical Realms, isn't just because there's a blockage of Saints. Maybe the Universes are...*experimenting;* questioning the way they've always done things. Because if they got a whiff of the fact that a corrupt being was at the middle of them...Sorry, bro. I didn't mean to say it like that.'

'Y'had to, Geoff,' said Jesus. 'It might or might not be true, but, better that it's out there.

'Have you guys come up with any ideas about how we can break this Parabox open?'

'Someone's got a theory,' said Geoff, 'that if we move it to a Spiritual place, then maybe we can crack it open without all of Physicality crashing down on it. We're pretty sure that's what's holding the box together—the laws that God Himself wrote, which He can't contravene because if He did...'

'The Universe'd fall apart,' said Jesus.

'More like Creation,' said Geoff. 'Which is why we think He might be choosing to stay inside it.'

Saint Peter's distant voice called out, 'Ah. We were told you were down here.' Accompanied by Hitler and Goliath, who both looked excited, he hurried toward the group and said, 'We've just been organising the siphoning of the Morality into the oxygen masks. The first hundred-thousand should be ready in about half an hour. We were thinking: perhaps those on the production line should be the first to receive masks.'

'I agree,' said Jesus. 'That'll free 'em up to keep on pumpin' 'em out. After them, I don't know...Don't hand 'em out in clumps. Try n' spread 'em around to different social groups.'

'So our field of missionaries reaches farther,' said Saint Peter. 'Into as many spheres as possible.'

'Y'read my mind,' said Jesus. 'And good work on all o' that. You've probably bought us a decent amount o' time.' He stroked his chin and said, 'The next thing we gotta figure out is what's so special about that horse?'

'Y'mean the one that pulled the Parabox?' asked Geoff. 'Probably nothing.'

Jesus shook his head and said, 'There's something *to* this. Why would Lucifer specifically order for any trace of it to be destroyed?'

'Perhaps he thinks we'll be able to track it down by using the Book of Life,' said Saint Peter.

'I thought animals couldn't be registered,' said Jesus. 'Somethin' to do with not having Souls.'

'A common misconception,' said Saint Peter. 'On both counts. Animals are actually the only beings pre-recorded into the Book of Life—based on your Father's rather precise anticipations of where the future will flow. They are, however, in a different category to most other Citizens, simply because they're more bound to their natures and don't have as much free will.'

'So what does this mean?' asked Jesus. 'If we could get a sample of that horse's...essence, or whatever, then we'd...'

'You'd know exactly when, how and where it was going to die,' said Saint Peter.

'Holy Shiite,' said Jesus, his eyebrows clenching. 'I think we mighta just found ourselves a lifeline.'

'How?' asked Geoff.

'The horse's information,' said Jesus. 'It's recorded in the Pilgrims' Passage.'

'Though to access your Father's predictions,' said Saint Peter, 'you'd need a *Physical* sample of the animal's DNA.'

Geoff said, 'The details in the Database are just a recording, bro. You can't extract something Physical from something that's just...concept.'

'Says who?' asked Jesus.

'Says reality,' said Geoff.

'I happen to be the Son of the Man Who dictates reality, Geoffrey. We're in need of a miracle, and, I used to be in the business. Call all the Pilgrims out of the Passage. I'm sendin' in the Unknown Disciple to retrieve a strand o' horse hair.'

152

'*Me?*' said Geoff. 'Wh-why would you...?'

'Because *you*,' said Jesus, 'might not have been the first man to step outta that boat, but you *were* the first to try n' do a double-front flip off the top of a breaking wave.'

Geoffrey son of Joseph was obviously touched by the confidence that his half-brother had in him, but still said, 'Bro. This is crazy.'

'Of course it's crazy,' said Jesus. 'But so is everything else that's happening right now. Get those guys outta there, Geoff. Then go inside and get that horse hair. It's gonna tell us where they took Dad.'

COURTNEY TAYLOR

Chapter 29

'You fellas take it easy for a while,' said Jesus, to a crowd of Pilgrims who'd just stepped out of the only active doorway. 'You've done a damn good job and the information you've found is invaluable. Now if you're lucky, somebody round here might start takin' coffee orders.'

Hitler stepped forward and cheerfully set about getting preferences.

Jesus clapped a hand on his half-brother's shoulder and said, 'Geoffrey, you are going into that Database to wrap your Spiritual fingers around a completely conceptual horse hair. You are then going to pass it to me. *Comprehendé*?'

Geoff nodded, then turned and stepped through the steel doorway, into a paused virtual-reality playback of the time and place of God's abduction. The soon-to-be-razed village was covered by liquid droplets frozen in the nighttime air. God, a portrait of nonchalance inside the Parabox, was irritating Lucifer, whose mid-sentence expression would have certainly displeased the Angel, were he to see it.

Proceeding beyond the five unmoving forms in the middle of the street, Geoff headed toward a nearby barn and stepped through its wall as would a ghost.

'Okay,' he said, speaking into his golden trinket. 'You can play it now. And can you turn up the light a bit?'

As the room became brighter, Geoff saw a white horse tethered to a rickety wooden cart. Steaming out of the animal's head were thought bubbles, the biggest of which showed that same horse performing on a stage in front of thousands of other horses.

The people on the other side of the steel doorway, who were grouped around the computer console, heard Geoff say, 'I am approaching the completely conceptual horse. Would you mind turning the sound off? And the Mat5-28 mode? I'm gonna have to concentrate.'

The sound disappeared, as did the horse's thought bubbles. The animal shook its head, which meant that playback had resumed.

'All right, I'm reaching for it...Couldn't touch it...I'm gonna try again.'

Geoff was trying to pinch the horse's mane, but his fingers passed through it as if he or the horse didn't really exist.

'This decision o' mine,' said Jesus, speaking into a small microphone, 'it isn't based on wild guesswork. 78 percent of paranormal activity occurs when the still-living spouse of a Present Pilgrim is...how should I say it?...moving on with their life, in a romantic sense.'

'That doesn't even make sense.'

'It does if y'think about it, Geoffrey,' said Jesus. 'Pilgrims visiting their loved ones see what's happening, get angry and wanna throw something, which is exactly what they do. They somehow, inexplicably, channel enough energy to influence the—'

'Bro, I'm trying to concentrate.'

'Sorry,' said Jesus, who was quiet for a good nine seconds before asking, 'Any success?'

The frustration was evident when Geoff said, 'No.'

The stable door opened and Clip hurried over to the cart. Untethering the horse, he climbed up onto the driver's seat and flicked the reins.

Geoff, his fingers sinking into the horse's head, trudged alongside the animal, out onto the muddy street, where Lucifer was going from house to house, setting fire to the thatched roofs.

'He's about to open up the doorway,' said Geoff.

'Just keep concentrating,' said Jesus.

The cronies loaded the Parabox onto the cart while Lucifer produced a glowing white doorway, high and wide enough for the wagon to pass through.

'It's happening, bro,' said Geoff, as the horse began trotting toward the doorway. 'It's gonna...It's...It's gone, man.'

Geoff stood back and watched as the wagon passed through the gateway, followed closely by Osama, who was carefully treading on each of the muddy hoofprints.

The doorway closed and disappeared. Geoff sighed and said, 'Why don't *you* try it, J.?'

''Cause I'm the one you gotta pass it to.'

'*What?*'

'Trust me. It's just a feeling I've got. Can we run it again? Try it again?'

'This is a dead horse, man,' said Geoff, shaking his head and scoffing at his own lame wit.

Eventually Jesus said, 'All right. Come back outside, then.'

Geoff stepped out of the doorway, weary, rumpled, and disappointed.

Jesus walked about with his arms folded, and tiredly rested his forehead on the active steel doorway. He looked up, surprised by the question, when Walter unexpectedly asked, 'I'm a Hybrid. What if *I* tried?'

COURTNEY TAYLOR

Chapter 30

'All right,' said Jesus, as he draped a Pilgrim's necklace around Walter's neck. 'Go in there and— save me some face.'

Walter stepped into a darkened village that was much more real than he'd expected it to be. Playback was already rolling: rain fell through him as if he didn't exist.

Once inside the barn, Walter made his way over to the horse and tried to touch its mane. His fingers passed right through it.

Before long, Clip was guiding the horse and its cart out through barn doors, with Walter trudging ahead of them, trying and still failing to touch the horse's mane.

Out on the muddy street, Clip stopped the cart so that he and Osama could use ropes and planks of wood to haul the Parabox up onto the cart's tray. That done, they peeled L. Ron out of the mud and laid him without ceremony next to the Parabox.

Walter concentrated on a single hair that was gleaming in the light of the fires lit by Lucifer. He was determined to pinch hold of it...but his fingers plunged through it with every attempt.

A wide glowing doorway appeared in the middle of the street, courtesy of Lucifer. The cart began moving toward it. So too did Walter, who, edging backward through it, entered an unrecorded location. There he watched the front end of the horse become a blurry stub as it passed through the doorway. The back end of the animal remained in pristine focus until it trotted out of existence. Clip, Lucifer and the wagon followed it into oblivion; and then so did Osama, who leapt off the final hoof-print and vanished in mid-air.

'Walter?' asked Jesus via the globe. 'You wanna come back out here?'

There was silence...Then Walter asked, 'Can you rewind? Just a few seconds?'

The doorway reappeared. Osama hopped out of it backwards. The cart reversed onto the muddy road and then froze when Walter said, 'That should be enough, I think.'

Clip flicked the reins and the horse began trotting toward the doorway. Walter repositioned his feet and prepared to grab hold of its mane.

As the horse and its wagon approached him, Walter began to feel strangely. His skin was tingling, and an indefinable noise was intensifying. It sounded like a mist of microscopic bees. He tried to ignore it, and concentrated upon his task.

The horse's head entered the doorway and turned into a blurry mass that melted away into nothingness. Walter, distracted by the noise and the tingling sensation, missed his chance to reach for its mane. But without even thinking, he snatched at what was soon the only remaining part of the animal: its tail, which was bristling with static electricity and levitating laterally as it slid out of existence. He was nearly kicked by a protesting hoof that materialised from out of the doorway. He staggered backward away from it, not quite realising that clamped between his fingertips was a thick brown horse hair, almost half-a-metre long.

'I've...I've got it,' said Walter, in shock.

'Say that again?' said Jesus.

'I've...got it. The horse's hair.'

The world around Walter became insubstantial and ghost-like. A Stonehenge-type passageway had appeared in the middle of the muddy street. Jesus leaned out of it and said, 'Okay, bring it over here, Wally. I'm gonna grab it. And well done by the way.'

The VP's first attempt to get hold of the horse hair was a failure: his fingers passed right through it.

'Try again,' said Walter.

Jesus tried again, and again and again, but the horse hair was untouchable: it disappeared whenever Walter tried to push it beyond the doorway.

'It's not crossing over,' said Jesus.

'Just grab it without even thinking about it,' said Walter.

'Pff,' said Jesus. 'I'm just gonna grab it.'

Jesus reached for the horse hair...and was totally surprised when his fingers grabbed hold of it. He was even more surprised when the hair began to flicker, and then glow like a tiny halogen tube. Some kind of current seemed to be passing between his and Walter's fingertips. The ground began trembling on account of it. Jesus and Walter looked at each other, both wondering if they'd just done something...consequential.

All around Heaven's Main Office, lights exploded, windows shattered, marble pillars fractured, and computer monitors went blank. Citizens who were doing things like whipping themselves in order to restore the Karmic balance began to punish themselves even more fervently, because obviously their deeds were either working or not working. Hitler, who was carrying a triple-decker cardboard tray with about twenty cups of coffee embedded in it, had to widen his stance like a surfer, to avoid falling over due to the shaking floor.

The metal doors of the Pilgrims' Passage were jostling around as if set upon hard jelly. Jesus and Walter were trying to gently drive the radiant horse hair through a hazy barrier.

'Keep pushing,' said Jesus.

'Keep pulling,' said Walter.

'Careful it doesn't break,' said Saint Peter, his eyes bulging aggressively.

The luminous strand began to slide through the air, its middle resisting, as if pinched by invisible fingertips. It was mostly on Jesus' side, so he got a better grip, said a quiet prayer with a few swear-words in it, then yanked the strand out of the Database and into the Spirit Realm.

The horse hair stopped glowing and the building stopped shaking. Citizens gradually ventured out from their many hiding places.

Saint Peter gawped at the VP and said, 'Sir, I think you've just written a new law.'

Jesus gulped and replied, 'I think I might owe Joe Smith Jr a new pair of underpants.'

Chapter 31

'This is still just a poke in the dark you know,' said Saint Peter. 'That horse might live to the age of 1,550, and die in a circumstance completely unrelated to Lucifer's little misadventure. He's probably abandoned the animal by now.'

'He hasn't abandoned it,' said Jesus, as he held open the door of his Dad's office for Saint Peter, Geoff, Walter and then Hitler. 'He still needs it to pull the Parabox. And I *know* this'll be where the horse is gonna die, 'cause I'm the one who's gonna kill it there.'

Geoff and Walter looked at each other, both overtly wondering if that even made sense.

Standing on some of God's paperwork was a slimy escapee from a terrarium—a newly-formed quadruped that bolted when it saw them. Saint Peter pressed a button on the side of the desk, then reached into a square tray—a controlled black hole—that slid outward from it.

'I left it up here so that no aspiring infidel could get their filthy hands on it,' said the old man, bringing out the Book of Life, laying it flat on the desktop and opening it to its middle page. Receiving the horse hair from Jesus, he wrapped it around his thumb and then pressed it to the right-side page. A rap-sheet appeared; he read out the animal's information: 'Favourite colour, most deep-seated desire...Ah, location of demise: Dimension 219, also known as—'

'The Music Realm,' said Jesus. 'Of *course*.'

'Isn't that where you sent Moses?' asked Walter.

Jesus nodded, and said, 'I shoulda put the numbers together: The Angels haven't been intervening down in the Realms; Lucifer's probably holding them captive. I could punch myself for bein' this stupid.'

Hitler, gawking reverently at the artifacts adorning God's bookshelves, overheard Jesus say, 'Geoff, would you mind finding out about that? Quickly? See if Mo's been spotted down in the corridors.'

'Where should I meet you?'

'Uh, where we had that meeting earlier on. I gotta tell the Patriarchs about all this.'

Geoff nodded and jogged for the door. Jesus said, 'The Music Realm. I feel like an idiot.'

'Pride is always predictable,' said Saint Peter. 'However in this case we forgot to make the forecast.'

'At least the Apostle Paul didn't think of it,' said Walter.

'You're right, Wally,' said Jesus. 'You're damn right, actually.'

Bolstered by that realisation, and thinking of something additional, Jesus leaned over and tapped the liquid-looking desktop. It receded from his fingertips and rose into the air like water pushed upward by a leaf-blower. Scanning the information he'd been looking at earlier, he read to the bottom of the page and said, 'Yikes.'

'What's the matter?' asked Walter, stepping closer.

'According to this,' said Jesus, 'we got about fifteen hours till the Bad Karma makes an appearance.'

Nobody knew what to say—least of all Hitler, who wanted to crack a joke to lighten the mood but could only think of inappropriate ones.

SAINT WALLY

Chapter 32

Lucifer spun on his toes to face Waleed and Osama, who were standing behind a large digital video camera mounted on a tripod. Skeptically, the Angel asked, 'And you say you don't need to cut it using an editing program.'

'Everything *in*-camera,' said Waleed, gesticulating largely, trying his best to be reassuring. 'Am confident will not need post production.'

'For your sake I hope so, gentlemen,' said Lucifer, his eyes brimming with intensity. 'Because I've told you I want this to be *the* best hostage video that has ever been made.'

'*Will* be best,' said Osama, enthusiastically. 'Will look like has been filmed— 65 millimetre. Format for *big* screen.'

'Will it win awards?'

'Will win *every* award,' said Waleed. 'Except for the ones about bad production values. I forget what those awards are called, I am sorry.'

Lucifer waved away the man's sense of failure, saying, 'As long as it's gritty and disturbing and people watch it and get shivers because of its boldness and authenticity.'

L. Ron, smiling with confidence, stepped forward and said, 'I think it'll do more than that. Because the lead actor is— magnificent.'

'Thank you, L. Ron,' said Lucifer, placing softened eyes upon his loyal follower. 'That means a lot to me because I trust your judgment. I trust it because you have put your faith in *me*. Now. Is the tape ready to go?'

Osama opened the video camera, took out a small tape and gave it to Lucifer, who held it out to L. Ron, saying, 'This is your time to shine, Mr. Hubbard. Take this to the Patriarchs and make sure they watch it. And re-watch it. And re-re-watch it. Make sure they have a complete understanding of the fact that there is going to be pande*monium*.'

L. Ron reached for the tape as if it was a precious historical document, received it with humility and slipped it into one of his blazer pockets.

Lucifer spoke as if his words were being transcribed. 'Soon you will be venturing into the breach, dear L. Ron. But fear not, my loyal follower, because you will be returning safely. And on that day, we will...' He was stuck for words, but finally came out with, 'Party.'

SAINT WALLY

Chapter 33

Jesus, Walter, Saint Peter and Hitler were rushing past rows of cubicles. Sitting inside them, manning telephones, were Heavenly volunteers who were communicating with clairvoyants in the Physical Realms, telling them to advise their clients to just simply love, forgive and embrace absolutely everybody—even if they *didn't* know what the word *hygiene* meant.

'Petey,' said Jesus. 'Would y'mind finding out what's goin' on with those Morality masks? Have a look at these people.'

Many of the volunteers were gossiping, or arguing, or gavelling themselves in the face with their respective phones, as if they couldn't believe the person they were talking to could be so stupid.

Saint Peter nodded and said, 'I'll find you at the conference room if I need you?'

Jesus winked and clucked his tongue in the affirmative.

'All right gentlemen and gentlemen,' said Jesus, when he pushed open the glass door of the boardroom, 'I've got some news for...' He fell silent, because seated at the conference table, along with all of the board members bar him and Gandhi, was L. Ron Hubbard, who was obviously surprised to see the Vice President.

In answer to the unspoken question, Paul said, 'Mr. Hubbard has surrendered himself. He's telling us he's the bearer of a— what did you call it again?'

Very pertly, L. Ron said, 'I think I might have to rephrase what I just termed it. *Now* it can be described as: Something which the *Vice President* really needs to see.'

Paul flicked a switch on the table, and the lights in the room went dim. A moment later, one of the glass walls became a colourful screen. It showed Lucifer, standing on a bulging green hill, smiling directly at his audience. Behind him was the Parabox, containing God, Who was sitting at a table and writing on a stone tablet. Several kilometres in the distance, legions of Angels were doing star jumps in front of the huge choir platform.

'Are we ready?' asked the on-screen Lucifer.

'Okay, we are ready,' came Osama's off-screen voice. 'When Waleed says go, you go. Not Action, but go. Okay? Okay.'

'Okay now *go*,' said Waleed.

'Hi there,' said Lucifer, grinning cheesily at the viewer. 'I don't think I need to tell you who I am, but just to be safe—my name is Lucifer, and I happen to be the Angel responsible for God, aka the Good Lord, Yahweh, Elohim, the Maker, the Dee'ine, whatever, being—how should I say it?—noticeably absent at this moment in time.

'As you can see, the Deity behind me is fine. However, that may not *continue* to be the case, because at this consequential hour, you, the board members of Heaven, are faced with a very serious decision.

'In *one* potential universe, at 1900 hours today, there's going to be a televised extravaganza—an Existence-wide broadcast that answers the question *What has happened to the Good Lord?*

'In *another* potential universe, at 1900 hours today, the King of Creation—in all of His infinite trapped-in-a-boxness—is going to find Himself being pushed through a doorway. A doorway that leads to...Outer Darkness.'

This pronunciation produced a gasp from the Patriarchs.

'Esteemed Leaders of Heaven,' continued Lucifer, with heightening vigour, 'let it be known that you are hereby charged with the responsibility of bending to my whims. Because if you don't, then I am going to make sure the *latter* Universe is the one that blossoms into being at exactly 1900 hours this evening.

'As of right now, your new mandate and ultimate priority, is to make sure that my new musical number embeds itself deeply into the collective consciousness of the Citizens of Heaven. I presume you're all familiar with my minion, Mr. L. Ron Hubbard? Say hello, L. Ron.'

'Hello, L. Ron,' said the dowdy man sitting in the boardroom.

'This fine fellow,' said the on-screen Lucifer, 'is now the bridge spanning the chasm between us. Anything you have to say to *me*, will come through *him*. L. Ron, could you please tell the board members what it is we need them to do.'

'We want to establish an audio-visual link-up,' said L. Ron. 'A means by which the Citizens of Heaven are allowed a more— *transparent* view of their Creator. We've got the cameras and the crew. What we haven't got is a Creation-wide feed and access to airtime. Needless to say, that's where the board of Heavenly directors steps in.'

'L. Ron's got a whoooole list of requirements,' said Lucifer, a few beats too late because L. Ron was nervous and had spoken his lines too quickly. 'And that'll tell you in detail about eeeeverything we need.

'Gentlemen, I apologise, because time is running slim and I really have to leave you now. But what I'll leave you with is this: If you choose to make the *wrong* decision, and L. Ron is not back by my side within one hour, with all of the equipment and all of the manpower I've asked for, then I will take that as a cue, from you, to start the performance early. As a result, The Lord of All Existence will be drifting on His own, in a never-ending vacuum of blackness, completely and severely detached from His precious Creation. And the performance that you gentlemen will have chosen *not* to broadcast, will make its way around Heaven in the good old-fashioned bootlegged kind of way. Which means I still get my exposure. And that's what's important, I think. So on that note, *Sayonara*.'

Lucifer's lingering smile at the camera collapsed, and he asked, 'How was that? Was that good?'

'Was very good,' said Osama's off-screen voice.

'It wasn't too forced? And I didn't trip on any of the words? Because some of them were quite long, and they were next to— ugly words.'

'No, no, no,' said Waleed. 'Was inta-ra-resting.'

The tape ended and the lights came back on. There were several tense moments...and then Alexandrius the Apotheothorist said, 'The scriptures say, "If your brother sins against you, go and tell him his fault between you and him alone."'

Solomon said, 'Do you know who we're talking about right now? Negotiation is not gonna be possible.'

Ricky the naked Televangelist shouted, 'We need some kind of strategy!', and the table collapsed into a heated ten-way argument. As was the custom, a sandal was thrown.

'Fellas!' said Jesus. '*Fellas!*'

The Patriarchs became quiet. Jesus said, 'The first thing we're gonna do is have a conversation without that son of a spastic listening to us.' He was pointing at L. Ron, who was sitting back in his chair, smiling as though he'd just remembered a joke.

Hitler, standing by the doorway with Walter, marched over to L. Ron and tapped him on the shoulder. L. Ron sneered like a misanthrope, rose to his feet, and was escorted out of the conference room.

'All right,' said Jesus, when the door closed. 'First of all I want everyone to know there is no way we are gonna be "bending to the whims" of that pervert. Lucifer is not gonna be getting his broadcast. What he *is* gonna get is our foot in his face. He *isn't* holding all the cards, 'cause we know where he is.'

'Where is he?' asked Nelson Mandela.

'The Music Realm,' said Jesus.

'What's he doing *there*?' asked Abraham, Isaac and Jacob.

'I don't know and I don't care,' said Jesus. 'But he did say something about a musical number.'

'Which if he doesn't get to broadcast—' said Solomon.

'Then God'll be cast out into nothingness,' said Ricky.

'Uh, excuse me everyone,' said Pleebus. 'Such a concept is frighteningly relevant to something Derdinand and I discovered today. The numbers from the Waiting Room indicate that soon the Room will be full. And then...'

'What?' asked Jesus.

'Well, we know you don't want to close off the Physical Realms,' said Pleebus. 'None of us do. But when the Waiting Room is full, the individual Spirits who are traveling around Creation to get to the Pearly Gates won't have any place to go. They'll...'

'What?' asked Jesus.

'When the doors of the Pearly Gates close,' said Derdinand, 'the Souls of the Deceased won't be able to enter Heaven. They'll drift into the Outer Darkness. So it's no longer a matter of closing off the Physical Realms for the safety of the Spiritual. We have to do it for the Physical. Otherwise those Souls will be lost forever.'

Walter turned and saw Geoff, rapping softly on the glass door and looking confusedly at L. Ron a few steps down from him.

'What's *he* doing here?' Geoff mouthed.

Walter wondered where Hitler had gone to, and mouthed back, 'I'll tell you soon.'

Jesus finally said, 'So how *long* until the Waiting Room is full?'

'Our estimates have it within the hour,' said Derdinand.

'Within the *hour*?' said Jesus. 'Why is it filling up so quickly?'

'Metaphysical pustules,' said Paul. 'Those are the Physical reactions to the Negativity, which are claiming lives at an extremely fast rate. We're seeing drastic increases in End of the World symptoms like natural disasters, terrorists, STDs, obesity-related illnesses...'

'Okay,' said Jesus. 'Then we *are* gonna have to close off the Physical Realms. At least that'll cut down the amount o' Negativity we're receiving.'

'Something else I need to draw attention to,' said Pleebus, 'is the science of what we're talking about. If we close the Death Duct, the Souls of the Deceased won't be able to escape from their Universes. We'd be talking about a Spiritual Abundance, which would effectively tilt the balance of each and every Universe Soul.'

'And what'll happen if *that* happens?' asked Jesus.

'Well, a Universe Soul,' said Pleebus, 'is restricted to the space of its Physical Dimension. The best way to understand a Spiritual imbalance is to think of a very large cat stuck inside a quite small beach ball. When an imbalance occurs, the cat's head, due to gravity, wants to bump against the inside of the beach ball, then slide downward, where it will stop and rest on the bottom. Now, a Universe Soul can't simply do that, because the problem we have is a thing called the Law of Cohesion, which keeps each Universe from drifting away into billions of disparate elements. *Because* of the LOC, when a body of matter—be it Physical or Spiritual—approaches the edge of its Universe, it doesn't ever get to collide with the barrier then break through to the other side, because it falls into a gravitational field that slings it back in the direction it's come from. Do you understand what that means?'

'That the cat's head,' said Jesus, 'isn't gonna bump into the side o' the beach ball. It's gonna go flyin' back over to the other side o' the Universe?'

'Precisely,' said Pleebus. 'And when it *gets* there, it's then going to come flying *back*. And it will do that over and over and over.'

'So the cat,' said Jesus, 'is never gonna stop spinning.'

'It will eventually,' said Pleebus. 'But only because its motion will generate a centripetal force, which in the Physical will draw the cat into a compressed ball of organic material, and in the Spiritual, substantially speed up the alchemy of Bad Karma.'

'How will it do that?' asked Jesus.

Derdinand said, 'When the Good and Evil elements of the Universe Souls are caught by that centripetal force, they'll be put under enormous amounts of pressure, and be so compressed that the Positive and Negative emanations won't be able to run from each other. They'll be forced into fighting.'

'So,' said Paul, 'the normal process of manifestation would be— fast-forwarded?'

Pleebus and Derdinand nodded. Jesus asked, 'And if we close off the Realms, how long till we'd have a manifestation?'

'Because there's so much Evil at work right now,' said Pleebus, 'perhaps immediately.'

Jesus gaped at the strange creature, then said, 'So you're telling me if I *don't* close off the Physical Realms, the Souls of billions are gonna go floating off into darkness. And if I *do* close off the Realms, a Bad Karma storm is gonna explode into reality practically straight away.'

Pleebus and Derdinand nodded. The rest of the Patriarchs were all silent.

'Okay,' said Jesus, trying to think this through. 'Can we stop Spirits from being born—from entering the Physical? That way we could curb the amount o' Souls being introduced, to try n' keep things balanced.'

Pleebus shook his head, saying, 'Contraception would be violating your Father's plans for the Universes.'

Solomon said, 'But if it's gonna buy us a bit of time...'

'Not much,' said Derdinand. 'And the damage to the synchronised birth cycles would be monumental. And that's something we don't want to be dealing with post-Apocalypse.'

Jesus laughed weakly, and said, 'I'm glad to hear you're thinkin' beyond all this.' He walked around, looking at the floor, and began speaking blindly, hoping that in the process a pearl of practicality might accidentally fall out. 'Okay. All right. Uh, same thing as always. The main priority is to find God.

We need to start thinkin' outside the— Parabox. Breakin' that damn thing open's gonna be tricky, but...'

Jesus suddenly had an idea. It must have been obvious because Ricky said, 'You've had an idea?'

'I think I mighta just thought of a way to crack open that Parabox,' said Jesus, with an enthusiasm that surprised the other Patriarchs. 'But first. Closing off the Physical Realms is gonna be the last resort, which we'll only do if Dad isn't out of His cage. Y'reckon we've got an hour till the Waiting Room's full; well, tell that to the people down at the Death Duct. *Actually.* I want this done perfectly. Nelson, find out how many more Souls they can fit in the Waiting Room. Ricky, find out how many Souls are in transit right now. Compare the two numbers, and when you've got the difference, give it to the people at the Death Duct and tell 'em to close off the Physical Realms as soon as that amount's through.'

'That way we'll have locked off both ends,' said Nelson Mandela.

'And the Souls won't be floating around in the Outer Darkness,' said Jesus. 'Exactly.'

Paul, obviously skeptical, was about to speak, but Jesus said, 'And before anyone mentions the reserves in Hell, let me tell you it doesn't *matter* if they haven't got enough power to keep Creation running, 'cause if we can't break Dad outta that Parabox, in that damn skinny window we've been given, then He's stuck in there for good, so Creation's up Shiite Creek anyway. But that's actually not bad thinking. Solomon, find out who y'need to talk to about lowering Creation's consumption levels. That might dim the lights, but it'll put the power circuits into a lower gear, and maybe stretch out the time we're given by Hell's reserves.'

'Can I just ask,' said Paul, 'why, all of a sudden, do you think it's possible to just break your Dad out of His containment, when even He Himself couldn't put a dint in that Parabox?'

'Let's just put it down to God-given intuition,' Jesus replied. 'All right. Everyone who doesn't have a job is comin' with me, to the Museum of Heavenly history. After that we're gonna round up some Citizens, enthusiastic ones, 'cause post hence we are dealing with the problem of Lucifer.'

'Speaking of whom,' said Solomon. 'He's gonna be wanting his manservant and technology pretty soon.'

'Well, he's not getting either of those things,' said Jesus, as he and everyone else rose to their feet. 'But what he *is* getting is a whole bunch o' gate-crashers. Wally, could you please invite Mr. Hubbard back into the room? 'Cause Ricky, I think y'might've just earned yourself a pair o' pants.'

The naked Televangelist nodded with pleasure, because Jesus' meaning was fully received, and L.Ron's cream-coloured suit and matching fedora had been covetously admired.

Chapter 34

Saint Peter and his team of volunteers were manning wooden tables covered with cardboard boxes. Inside these boxes were oxygen masks whose insides were each fitted with a small mesh pod containing a dose of Morality. Before giving a mask to a Cherub, Saint Peter said, 'Just remember—if you see big people fighting, run and get *another* big person, one wearing a mask, because we don't want you to get injured. Do you understand?'

The little Angel nodded earnestly, slipped his new mask over his face, then waddled away from the queue, which was almost as long as a Limbo Line.

'And remember!' Saint Peter called out. 'You're a Keeper of the Peace now! Official role!'

Hitler ran over to Saint Peter, breathing like a marathon runner, and said, 'Excuse me. Saint Peter. Back in Voar-room, I saw videotape made by Lucifer. He vonts, vot is vord? He vonts *exposure*, so zat people vill see vot he's doing. But Son of God I don't sink vonts to give to him.'

Sensing that Hitler had more to say, Saint Peter said, 'Yes?'

'Is ze reason I'm here,' said Hitler. 'In *mein* times, sings like zis vould lead to voar. And don't you sink, if vee are going to have one, zen vee vill need soldiers?'

'You mean to say you're down here to rally up some troops?' asked Saint Peter.

'Zhess,' said Hitler, elatedly.

'Did the Vice President condone your coming down here?'

Hitler looked as if he didn't want to admit that, 'I am only *assuming* he vill vont for people to fight. I am doing like ze prophets, ünt paving ze vay for him. Zhoo know?'

'Unofficially,' said Saint Peter, bureaucratically.

The hopefulness drained from Hitler's face and he looked at the floor.

Saint Peter felt badly for having dashed Adolf's good intentions, so said, 'I suppose we *could* round up a small contingent. Just in case the Vice President does make a few plans. Though I know the man, and I don't think that's likely to happen. He *used* to be a bit more rambunctious, willing to get out there and blow things up. That was a long time ago, though. All right Hittie. Join the lines and start handing out the masks. Tell every single person you come across there's going to be a showdown and we need them on board.'

Hitler was joyous, then worried, and said, 'Zhoo vont *me* to— to try ünt convince people?'

'Why not?' asked Saint Peter, handing a mask to a Catholic priest who was covered with bruises. 'You've got panache and natural leadership abilities. You can manage it.'

'But, I am not exactly popular, zhoo know. My credibility is— *kaput.*'

Saint Peter scoffed as if the notion was noxious, then said, 'Throw the first stone and all that sort of thing. Here, you take over my place, and when you tell people about the Ultimate Battle, tell them it's going to be glorious.' He held up a fist of solidarity, then headed toward a group of Zen Buddhists who were shadow-boxing near a refreshment table.

After happily repeating his new nickname to himself, 'Hittie,' Hitler turned to the next person in the line—a man whose face was covered by a hessian sack with eye-holes cut into it. Hitler smiled at him widely and asked, 'Have zhoo heard ze gühd nyooz?'

SAINT WALLY

Chapter 35

Jesus, Walter, Geoff and Paul—along with most of the Patriarchs—hurried up a deactivated golden escalator, beneath which was a huge lava fountain, its jets clogged with offerings meant to appease angry gods. At the top of the escalator, on a vast marble balcony, there was a crowd of chattering Citizens, many wearing war-paint. Jesus spotted Saint Peter, who was standing next to Hitler and Goliath, and called out, 'Petey! What're you all *doin'*?'

'Ah,' said Saint Peter, holding down the midsection of his robe as he hurried forward. 'We were just on our way to find you, Mr. Vice President. Mr. Hitler and I took the liberty of organising a militia.'

'What for?'

'Well, you're going to need people to help you take care of Lucifer, aren't you?'

'Yeah but, Sheriff, I was gonna send in like a strike force. Y'can't just go in there and swing away at somethin' like this. It needs to be handled with a bit o'...delicacy.'

'What's the problem?' someone called out.

'Nothing!' said Jesus. 'It's just, I don't think we're gonna need this many people!'

'What, you mean we won't be able to fit?'

'You'll be able to *fit*,' said Jesus. 'But...'

'But what?'

A storm of annoyed whispers made Jesus hold up his hands like a Pacifist. Paul stepped closer and quietly said, 'Just them being there, might be enough to do a bit of intimidating.'

'Yeah, come on, man,' said Goliath, almost whining. 'We're all psyched up and lookin' for someone to *beat* up.'

'I know you are,' said Jesus. 'That's the Negativity in the atmosphere at work. And let me just say: it's good to see so many Morality masks.'

The crowd groaned. A dark-skinned Aborigine named Jonnaban Clibe said, 'You bin padronize uz.'

'I'm *not* patronising you,' said Jesus. 'I'm just tryin' to keep the Citizens of Heaven from degenerating into a society of mobs.'

'Fight fire with *fire!*' someone called out.

'What does *that* even mean?' said Jesus.

'It means stop bein' agnostic about the whole situation!'

'Look, I am not being agnostic; I'm being...' Jesus was about to say *reasonable*, but abruptly realised that staring him full in the face was a ready-made army—exactly what he needed—and he was about to send it back to the many places from whence it had come. He groaned, then said, 'All right. You guys've got a point. I *do* know where Lucifer and my Dad are. But if we're gonna do this together, then you're all gonna have to listen to me, 'cause I can't have people runnin' around actin' like vigilantes. This sorta thing has to be coordinated, which means that *you all* toe the line. Does everyone understand that?'

'Yes!' said the Citizens, some with enthusiasm, others with pouts.

'Okay then,' said Jesus, before drawing a deep breath. 'Well, we're back to the basics of Come Follow Me. But keep your mouths shut while you're doing it, 'cause I'm startin' to get a headache. Now, we're all gonna proceed to Door 219—that's the Music Realm—where Lucifer is. We're gonna bust in there and drop the pants o' that sack o' crap. But first we're gonna go n' pick up some explosives.'

The excitement was so palpable it could be bottled, sold, and sprinkled onto the penitent.

COURTNEY TAYLOR

Chapter 36

In the Museum of Heavenly History, an Angel security guard was sitting behind an information desk, reading a newspaper headlined with *GOD STILL MISSING—PRESUMED DEAD*. He startled with fright when the bronze doors across from him burst open, and into the museum's lobby flooded thousands of wild-eyed Citizens, many with glowing oxygen masks strapped to their faces.

Raging past the information desk and then all throughout every level of the museum, knocking over tall velvet partitions and sending up clouds of ancient dust, the competing, unruly Citizens rebounded off each other as they ransacked the museum for anything that could be used in a fight.

Superstition ensured that jawbones were a valued commodity. Along with tent pegs, daggers and slingshots, they were exchanged for various types of currency until no more buyers presented.

The display case housing the Armour of God was smashed to pieces and then oraided. The Boots of Peace were claimed by a lady named Susan. The Breastplate of Righteousness was put on the wrong-way-round by a long-eared Angorathon named Crainius. The Sword of the Spirit changed hands several times, until it was swung at the head of an escaped Muslim woman. She suffered a major concussion because her equally-escaped husband wanted to send a very strong message to every *other* person trying to snatch the sword away from him.

Fifty metres above the pandemonium, hanging by wires from the ceiling, were the almost-petrified remains of Noah's Ark. Perhaps because the fossilised Ark looked remarkably like a giant ribcage that had been deep-fried, several people of a certain complexion, all at different places, pointed it out simultaneously and shouted, 'Hey y'all!'

'Ohhhr yeah,' said Goliath, as he climbed onto a platform covered by armour-wearing mannequins. Stomping over to a dummy as big as himself, he said, 'Time to resurrect the Glory Days, baybeh!'

'Bro,' said Geoff, looking around at the looting Citizens. 'Maybe we should check out one o' those You are Here type signs.'

Such a sign shortly led them to a golden treasure chest that looked like the coffin of a wealthy midget.

'Careful, fellas,' said Jesus, as he stepped up onto its display platform. 'Remember the Ark o' the Covenant's keyed to my sub-DNA, meaning until I say otherwise, only *I* can touch it.'

As if to emphasise his point, an animatronic dummy reached out, touched the Ark, and fell to the floor in a shower of sparks. The two golden statuettes adorning the Ark's lid–a pair of boxing Angels–bumped their fists to announce a job well done.

'Exactly,' said Jesus. 'Okay, let's do this.'

Back in the lobby, a loud whiplashing sound announced the plummeting of Noah's Ark, which had just been severed from the ceiling by a cackling group of interDimensional transvestites. The monstrous wooden boat frame tumbled down onto the marble floor and smashed into thousands of brittle pieces, all of them summarily rummaged through because somebody had floated the idea that the Book of Revelation mentioned something about flaming swords.

Jesus, Walter and the Patriarchs, now bearing the Ark on a stretcher laid out across their shoulders, came upon the chaotic entrance hall and could barely believe their eyes. Jesus, after directing the others to gently place the Ark upon the floor, made his way over to an empty plinth labelled *The Missing Link*. He climbed up onto it, and shouted to get everyone's attention. He was completely ignored–until Geoff rushed over the information desk, grabbed hold of its microphone, leaned in close to it, and blew a long, loud raspberry.

People stopped what they were doing and looked around for the source of the noise. It reverberated through the entire museum, so out of place that the security guard emerged from beneath the info desk and looked at Geoff incomprehensibly.

When it was quiet enough for Jesus to be heard, he shouted, 'Thank you again, Geoffrey. And once again everybody else, thank you for reacting with such dignity. You've probably destroyed a whole bunch of artefacts that are priceless, but how 'bout we blame it on the atmosphere.'

'Das is a güht idea!' shouted Hitler, who had the technicoloured dreamcoat tied around his neck. It was now called the Cape of Courage, and considered by Adolf to be a necessary component of the Armour of God.

'All right,' continued Jesus. 'How 'bout all those who don't have a Heavenly Privileges card, look around and find someone who does, and buddy up with that person so y'can go through a doorway together.'

Hands went up and Citizens drifted toward them. It was obviously a bit of a popularity contest, as some groups were bigger than others.

'Okay, that's good,' said Jesus. 'That's...Goliath! What're you doing? Odour of God, put that thing away!'

Goliath had clomped into the room wearing his old armour, and was carrying on his shoulder the two intersecting planks of wood that Jesus had made famous.

'We need something to represent us,' said the giant. 'This thing's perfect.'

'It's not perfect,' said Jesus. 'Y'ever thought about what it actually symbolises? It was a very painful time for me. Not only that, they used the same damn symbol in the Middle Ages, and d'you think I endorsed *that* whole situation?'

Contributors to that portion of history did one of two things: they either became shorter, or raised their hands to provide some qualifying information.

But someone called out, '*This* is a crusade! What we're doing right *now!*' Someone else said, 'Yeah.' And then more people said, '*Yeah!*' And then pretty soon everyone was shouting, '*YEEEEAH!*'

'Well, if that's what it is,' shouted Jesus, 'then guaranteed it's the first and last crusade that *I'm* ever gonna sign my name to!'

'That's not what *I* heard.'

Jesus was momentarily stunned, and said, 'Who said that?'

'Who said what?' asked several people, looking around as if they thought the VP was losing his mind.

'Look,' said Jesus, labouring to stay focused, 'we haven't got time to be quibbling over this Shiite. Bring what y'want. But listen, on the way there, if people annoy you, or if you have the urge to smash something, fight the temptation. Does everyone understand that? Promise me you won't pick fights with each other.'

The crowd grumbled a promise, so Jesus said, 'All right. Now ladies and gentlemen, and Whatevers, we have picked up our secret weapon and we are takin' it to the Music Realm. Is everybody ready?'

Sticks, swords, slingshots and jawbones went high into the air. So did a unified shout of, '*YEAH!*'

'Then let's go!' yelled Jesus.

SAINT WALLY

Chapter 37

Millions of Angels were standing on the colossal choir platform, waiting patiently for their conductor to take the stage.

'I don't know why he wanted *that specific* stage,' said an Angel named Brucé, referring to a cube podium directly in front of the choir. 'I mean it's tiny. And in my opinion, ugly. Nothing but a box with a blanket covering it. *Yowch.*'

Lucifer smeared some rouge onto his lips and then puckered them. Mascara was thick around his eyes, glitter sparkled across his cheeks, and he was deeply engrossed in a mirror that was nailed to a wooden staircase at the back of his stage. When Clip entered his field of vision, a look of horror on his face, Lucifer raised his hands as if threatening to cover his own ears, and said, 'I really don't want to hear what Moses said to you, Clip. As long as that fat boy is locked inside that costume box that is all I care about. L. Ron hasn't returned, and you *know* what that means.'

'Should we wait?' asked Clip. 'Maybe he's—'

Lucifer spun around and nearly shouted, 'We are nine minutes away from the deadline I gave those Patriarchs and we are *not* pushing it back for *anybody*. L. Ron has failed, and the only thing we can do is let that be a lesson to the rest of us: If you can't keep the pace, history will leave you behind.' He took a deep breath to relax himself, then said, 'But don't worry, Clip. If something's happened to L. Ron, we can always swap him for Michael. Has the Angel been behaving?'

'He's standing very still in the middle of the empty aisle,' said Clip. 'I told him—too much movement and the bus'll fall off the mountain.'

'And an Angel trapped in a small falling space,' said Lucifer, 'might as well have no wings at all.' He laughed like a fey aristocrat, then paused somberly before adding, 'I'm sure that's how L. Ron would have wanted it. Now, would you do me a favour, my loyal follower?'

'Anything, my leader,' said Clip, bending slightly at the knee, and relaxing now that he wasn't being admonished.

'Would you mind going over to Oosama? Just ask if he and his crew are nearly ready. I'd ask him myself, but, I don't want the choir to see me till I get up on the stage.'

Clip bowed his head and shuffled backward.

'And Clip?' said Lucifer, as he returned to his mirror. 'Tell them not to worry so much about reaction shots. Close-ups of *me* are more important. It adds...*gravitas*.'

Osama, doing a white balance on camera two (the one that was locked-off and getting coverage of the entire stage) paused for a moment to shake his head with admiration. The sleek camera in front of him, its Capitalistic logo covered by a piece of electrical tape, was a good weight, and had features that the former Taliban leader wouldn't have even dreamed about twenty years ago.

'The Morning Star would like to know if you're nearly ready,' said Clip, smugly approaching.

'Is nearly good to go,' said Osama. 'Am just checking colour balance. Little bit technical but nothing to concern.'

'And everyone else?' asked Clip.

'They are ready,' said Osama, gesturing at the nine Arabian cameramen positioned all across the field. 'Excited, too.'

'Excellent,' said Clip. 'Because Lucifer will be ascending the podium in exactly six minutes. And if the cameras aren't rolling...Need I say more?'

Osama shook his head and gave a thumbs-up.

Lucifer gently cricked his neck and told himself, 'You were *made* to do this.' He giggled, then added, 'Of course your *Maker* didn't realise that, but, oh well. The blind will eventually see.' Running his fingers across the glimmering sequined patterns on his black kimono-cloak, he checked his pocket watch and said, 'All right. Show time.'

The Angel delicately carried himself up thirteen wooden steps that led him into the scrutinising gaze of millions of his duped peers. Some of them were close enough to see what he was wearing.

'Oh my *god*. He looks like a wing'd glam-rocker.'

'Why is he all dressed up? It's only a rehearsal.'

'I think the sequins are a bit much.'

'All right everyone,' said Lucifer, speaking through a microphone on a stand. 'Thank you very much for being here today, at this, our first rehearsal. I thought we might begin things by singing a song we all know, and then we'll step into the new stuff. Don't mind all of the brown gentlemen with the video cameras. They're just recording us so that in future we can iron out our mistakes. If we find any. Haha. Okay then. Everybody, please turn your hymn books to page one.'

The Angels on the bleachers opened their books and cleared their throats. Lucifer held up his baton, then brought it down, and of course the Angels began to sing *Spirit in the Sky*.

SAINT WALLY

Chapter 38

By pure coincidence—or maybe something more—Jesus' ragtag army was singing the very same song. It was a hodgepodge madrigal that made the Son of God smile, but at the same time cringe because hopes were getting high.

Saint Peter bustled to the front of the mob, where Jesus was bearing a corner of the Ark, and said, 'Now, I know you don't want to hear it, but I've been thinking. You know how the Book of Revelation says—'

'Aw, Petey.'

'No, no,' said Saint Peter, 'just listen. This isn't— Well, all right, it *is* a little bit of a crackpot idea, but in the Book, at the final Battle, it says you've got a white beard and a white robe. And...' He reached into a pocket and came out with a fake white beard, which prompted Jesus to groan, 'Petey.'

'Your Father likes to give people the full Saint Peter experience when they come through the Gates. I keep a spare, just in case I need to deputise someone. Looking the way the prophecy *said* you would, might improve our chances of Destiny coming to pass, don't you think?'

Walter said, 'Might hedge the bets.'

The Apostle Paul added, 'And disguise and surprise *is* half the battle.'

Jesus shook his head as if Saint Peter had no morals. The old man incredulously asked, 'What've you got to *lose*?'

'I'd be losin' my self-respect,' said Jesus. 'I'd be lookin' like a damn bearded Albino.'

'Ay!' said a nearby Citizen, who happened to be such a person.

'Sorry,' said Jesus, who then pointed at the Albino and said, 'Hey what if we use that guy as my decoy. That way I'd be able to stay in the background and organise things from a distance, like a general. Maybe *that's* what the prophecy was—'

'Don't be ridiculous,' said Saint Peter. 'Now you're just making fun of the entire prognostication.'

'Jeezus, Petey. Don't be so upti—'

'Well I think somebody *should* be uptight,' said Saint Peter. 'You've got all of these people following you, and *obviously* Armageddon's going to happen

192

the way it's been predicted, and *I* think that if you *really* cared about what your Father—'

'*All right,*' said Jesus, frowning angrily. 'Give me the Daddamn beard.' He took the beard from Saint Peter and slapped it on his own chin. '*There,*' he said. 'Are you— fulfilled now?'

'I'm starting to feel that way,' said Saint Peter. 'But the Book also mentions something about a—'

'*Whatever,*' said Jesus, every syllable making the fake beard flap around. 'Just put it in front o' me and I'll sign it. *Gawd.*'

Several minutes later, a trio of Morality-masked Buddhists was kneeling in front of the VP, presenting him with a white garment that they had appropriated with more force than was necessary. Despite their religion, Jesus thanked the men, and asked that they give the robe to Saint Peter, who had commissioned it, because his own hands were full.

'Now,' said Saint Peter. 'You're going to need somewhere to change into this, so, might I suggest we make a detour? If we go to where I'm thinking, we can also procure something that'll help you take care of that horse.'

'Aw yeah,' said Jesus, who had forgotten about that detail.

Several thoroughfares and a security door later, the Vice President found himself looking up at a dense wall of naked, unconscious Citizens, so high that it literally touched the Waiting Room's ceiling.

'Holy damn,' said Jesus. 'And this goes all the way back to the Pearly Gates?'

Saint Peter nodded, saying, 'And if the ones at the front try to step past the yellow line, my Deputies will make sure they regret it. ' He gestured toward the Art Deco wall, at a long row of Saint Peters who were armed with shotguns.

'Yikes,' said Jesus.

'All right,' said Saint Peter. 'You slip into your robe while I get the weapon. And then from there—'

'We're gonna meet Lucifer,' said Jesus, his white beard coming half unstuck.

Saint Peter hurried over to his desk, scratching at an eyebrow to avoid making eye contact with anyone in the bottom front row. Reaching into a drawer and emerging with a handgun (a .44 Magnum that he always made sure was loaded), he noticed, before turning to leave, that his pot plant was looking a bit dry. He solved this dilemma by donating the plant and its attendant spray bottle to the closest applicant.

'Bless you,' said Saint Peter, before departing the confused Neanderthal.

'Here we go,' said Saint Peter, presenting the handgun to Jesus, who was now wearing an ill-fitting white toga that made him feel billowy and uncomfortable. 'Tuck it in your underwear or something.'

Outside the Waiting Room, where the armed rabble was babbling excitedly, Saint Peter stepped out of an opening security door, amid a cloud of disinfecting mist, and was met by disappointment. The army had expected Jesus.

'Uh, you might want to step back and give the man some room, don't you think?' said the old man. 'And *please!* Don't look so bug-eyed. You're going to scare him.'

When Jesus stepped through the doorway, waving disgustedly at the weird-tasting fog, he bobbed his head and lifted his hands, silently asking the crowd what they thought of his costume. The other Ark-bearers looked him up and down, nodding as if they thought his new apparel was pretty decent. The thoughtful consensus provided by the Morality-masked mob was, 'Yeah. *Yeah.* YEAH!' The soldiers howled, shook their weapons, and head-butted each other joyously. A Nuwaubian named Dennisyte got so excited that he had a seizure, fell to the ground, and was picked up and carried hero-style by a group of Samaritans.

'All right then!' shouted Jesus, no longer feeling like Creation's biggest oddball. 'Now that we're all dressed up and lookin' for someone to *beat* up, how 'bout we track down Lucifer n' kick the livin' *Shiite* out of him!'

'YEEEAAAHHHH!!!!' shouted the VP's followers.

SAINT WALLY

Chapter 39

'Gentlemen,' said Lucifer, when the Angels' fourth song ended. 'That was superb. And now if you'll all be so kind, please turn to the second-last page, and we shall begin the first of our *new* songs.'

His millions of former colleagues turned the pages of their hymn books, and each arrived at a sheet that had been glued into place by Clip, Osama, L. Ron or an orphan.

Lucifer lifted his baton. The Angels cleared their throats and sang:

This is an ode to Lucifer,
The Angel who got God
To bend His knees and accept the pleas
Of those who say He's not
Able to do all He says He can do,
But that is just the start,
Because Lucifer He is reigning,
Over all that once was God's...

The confused choir Angels looked down at Lucifer, who was holding up his arms as if the emotional power of the music was simply overwhelming him. Opening his eyes and grinning evilly, he shouted, 'Come on, boys, let's sing it in the face of GOD!'

The Angel jumped into the air, extended his wings, and pulled away the tarpaulin he'd been standing on, revealing that beneath his feet, trapped in a glass box, was the Creator of All Creation, God Himself.

There were girly screams and gagging noises. Several Angels fainted and rolled over the choir members beneath them. Lucifer dropped lightly onto the Parabox, again closed his eyes, and blissfully absorbed the sound of gossip, buzz, and notoriety, all mixing into a substance more precious to him than any other ever created.

However, his supply was rudely cut short by the Almighty, Who, crouched and peering up the Angel's robe, shouted, 'I always knew you were hidin' something, Lucy! I just didn't know it was– female anatomy!'

God started laughing. The Angels began to join Him. The sound of it plunged Lucifer deeply into a traumatic memory: He was standing on a narrow stage, bright lights beating down on him. From all directions came buffets of ridicule, directed without pity at the costume he'd put the essence of his essence into designing.

Lucifer wrenched himself into the present; and trembling with agitation, said to God, 'Let's see how much everybody's laughing when the Lord of All Creation takes a little tumble off the edge of Spirituality, hmm?'

The Angel waved viciously, giving the prompt that directed his followers to detach their cameras and relocate. One of the Arabs hurried over to the choir platform and untethered a white horse that was standing beneath it.

'All right, Yahwie,' said Lucifer. 'Your little enunciation was our cue to exeunt. Hope Y'don't mind. Actually, I don't really care if You *do* mind.'

The Arabs gathered around the Parabox and peered up into Lucifer's nostrils as he gave a speech for the benefit of the one sound recordist. 'Gentlemen,' said the Angel. 'I am so glad you could be here to partake in this moment of history. Because when the future looks back on this moment, it will see that—'

'Excuse me!'

Lucifer, extremely miffed at having been interrupted, turned around and squinted against the sunlight. He saw a figure in a white robe, standing on a grassy hilltop, about a hundred metres from and directly facing the choir platform. One of the camera-men ran toward the stranger and lay down on the grass, then propped himself with his elbows and started filming him.

The white-bearded stranger asked, 'Any of you gentlemen seen a...horse around here?'

One of the Arabs whacked a mare on its rump, causing it to trot out into the open, dragging a different Arab with it. The stranger in white lifted a silver handgun, took aim...and then shot the horse squarely in its head.

The choir Angels gasped and wondered aloud about what kind of extremely rude parasite could *do* such a brutal thing.

Lucifer gave this newcomer his complete attention. Extending his glittering wings, he stepped into the air, floated down to the grass, and said, 'Excuse me, *sir*. Do I *know* you? Or perhaps I'll just *rephrase* that— were you *invited* here?'

A lack of any reply impelled the Angel to say, 'You know it's rather rude to not answer a question when it's asked.'

Again, the stranger failed to reply; and due to the sudden rumour that the current situation was merely a theatrical performance, one of the choir Angels shouted, 'If this is a comedic piece then whoever's in charge really needs to work on their *timing!*'

'Camera five,' said Osama, into his headset. 'MCUs of Lucifer; reaction shots.'

One of the Arabs hurried to a new position and started filming Lucifer. Every other camera, though, was focused upon the stranger in white, behind whom there began to appear a long line of doorways, manifesting in the air, at ground level, in the hundreds. Out of them began emerging tens of thousands of unkempt Heavenly Citizens. Most were sporting glowing oxygen masks, and brandishing rusty weapons or smoking sticks. These last items (meant to be flaming swords) were lengths of petrified wood that had been wrapped in ancient parchments and lit on fire.

The man in white began bouncing on his feet like a child fighting internal energy. His fist suddenly went skyward, and for the benefit of the Citizens behind him (many of whom were wearing war paint) he shouted, 'KUMBAYA YOU SONS O'—'

The ragtag army of the man in white gave a scream just as primal, lifted its many weapons, then raced down the hill in pursuit of its leader, who was sprinting in Lucifer's exact direction.

The Angel looked around and saw that his camera-men were scattering, some climbing up onto to the Parabox for fear of being trampled. Panicking, he reached into his pocket, brought out the HP card, searched its location tab, selected the first option he saw, then looked up and realised that the man in white was all but on top of him.

Lucifer collapsed into a huddled crouch, shrieking and raising his arms in terror. The HP card, upright in his hand, was punched by the man in white, who slang his fist at the Angel's head but missed by several millimetres. The activated card flipped through the air, slashing at it, creating repeated golden doorways that overlapped each other. Together these doorways looked like a crooked length of thickly barbed wire whose blades were rectangular. Those rectangles started bending and wrapping around each other like cloths being wrung. The space they occupied then disintegrated; and from that blank line there emerged a sparkling gash which began tearing in opposite directions. A crack in reality had formed, and was opening up violently.

This supernatural schism caused the grass to ripple like a carpet being flicked. The man in white was lifted into the air. He dropped to the ground, his forward momentum stolen, and turned to see that his army had also undergone inertia. This was evidently fortuitous. Had the rabble not been halted, it would have barrelled off the edge of a cliff. The metaphysical gash was peeling two membranes of Ality fabric away from each other. Being revealed, several kilometres beneath, was a whole other world: a never-ending patchwork of buildings, streets, moving cars and tiny people.

The man in white said, 'Aw crap.'

—————

The first person to photograph the Kingdom That Had Finally Come was a Japanese tourist named Kabuto, who had been standing on top of Metropopopolis' highest building, aiming his camera at an adventurous dove (that might have been a seagull). A flash of golden lightning had torn the sky in half; and Kabuto, in his shock, had captured the supernatural convergence as it actually happened. After that, because the Ality fabric was now so weak that the Physical were able to perceive the Spiritual, it was a free-for-all: News crews, people with trendy phones, and copious numbers of tourists, were quickly out in force, clamouring to film and repeatedly photograph the apparition that had suddenly manifested above their world's biggest city.

Chapter 40

Jesus ripped off his fake white beard and threw it to the city beneath. He was irritated, but also grateful that he hadn't been barged off this Dimension by his own soldiers. He could imagine them cascading in pursuit of him, all the way down to the streets below, and whistled at how closely it had come to that. To his eyes they were all now standing upon a floating grassy island: a torn-off portion of the Music Realm that was hovering solidly.

A vaguely familiar voice yelled out, 'None of you heathens move, otherwise this fat boy goes right off the edge!'

Clip the Bythebookist Angel had hold of Moses, and was inclining the terrified man toward the precipice. Moses was tied up with floral scarves, and gagged with a sparkly glove.

Lucifer, still huddled with his hands up, became instantly emboldened. Rising from his crouch, he strutted into the limelight of his loyal follower, and said, 'Yes, we're sorry to amputate the amusements, everybody, but we need to be doing some– *negotiating*!' He pulled out the canister of Saints and held it over the edge of the Dimension. The VP's army gasped. Jesus said, 'Don't do anything stupid, Lucy.'

'Hmph,' said Lucifer. 'Unlike you, stupidity's not my strongest subject. And before anyone can think of a witty reply to that, I want you all to take a calm step backward, and look around for the Heavenly Privileges card I misplaced.'

'Before we do that,' said Jesus. 'Maybe we *should* negotiate. 'Cause we have something you might just want.'

From out of the armed rabble was pushed L. Ron Hubbard, who was completely naked, save for the sticky tape that he was bound and gagged with.

Lucifer scoffed with incredulity; and after looking back and forth from Moses to L. Ron a few times, said, '*This*, gentlemen, is a non-*event*. Throw *both* of them off this— this *thing*. I'll do it myself if it's such an issue.'

The Citizens who had marched L.Ron to the edge of the Dimension obviously took that statement as their cue. Before Jesus could order them not to, they shoved L. Ron off the edge of the floating island, and saluted him goodbye as he plunged ungratefully the long way down to the city beneath.

'Okay then,' said Lucifer. 'Now that you people *officially* have no leverage, how about we return to the part where I was saying, *Find that Heavenly Privileges card, or you can pick up these Saints one by one all the way down there.*'

As the followers of Jesus scanned the ground for the HP card, Jesus himself, standing tall and refusing to search, locked eyes with Lucifer. The Angel, referring to the VP's ambitious swing at his head, said, 'You missed. For the first time for the last time. 'Cause there's never gonna be a next time.'

Thankfully, Jesus didn't have to think of a comeback, because someone called out, 'I've found it!' That someone had a hessian bag covering his head, and a name tag reading *John Smith*. He was a member of the prophet protection program, incognito because carnal reversions had influenced certain people to try and scrub off his facial features.

John Smith looked toward Jesus, asking for permission to give the card to Lucifer. Jesus gave it by way of a nod. Smith advanced, but Lucifer halted him, saying, 'Uht-uht. *Oosama!*'

Osama bin Laden stood to his full height, camera on shoulder, and wove through the crowd, sad at being called away from getting low angle shots. He received the card from Smith, said, 'Sank you,' and headed toward Lucifer...until a technicoloured blur shot from out of the crowd and crash-tackled him!

'Hittie!' shouted Saint Peter, as Hitler and bin Laden tumbled off the edge of the Dimension. Their locked forms plummeted as one toward the cityscape far below. The Cape of Courage fluttered wildly.

The HP card, knocked out of Osama's hand, was spinning through the air, unnoticed by all but one. Lucifer saw that it was ripe for the plucking. He lunged and snatched hold of it, then activated it, and opened up a golden doorway.

Jesus glanced away from the Dimension's edge and saw that Lucifer and Clip were slipping through a doorway, their hostage, Moses, discarded on the grass. He noticed that, as they stepped through it, they lost their footing and went floating–in darkness. That darkness was what stopped Jesus from chasing them. It didn't, however, stop Walter, who shot past Jesus, raced for the door, and leapt through it.

Walter's bare feet left the grass, and his entire body became enveloped by darkness. Someone–or something–grabbed hold of his ankles; and because of this he didn't go floating away just as Lucifer and Clip were doing. Walter stretched out and grabbed hold of Clip's wing stump. He pulled the Angel toward him; and for a moment, because Lucifer and Clip were holding tightly to each other, the three of them were drawn into a deranged knot of limbs, wings, and angelic panic. It ended when a blinding flash of white light (the canister of Saints floating out from under Lucifer's jacket) caused Walter to shield his eyes. He lost his grip on the Angels and they spun away into darkness. But something had come off in Walter's hand. It was small, light, and moderately pliable. He believed he knew what it was, and made sure to keep hold of it.

An eternal but brief moment later, Walter abruptly found himself sitting heavily on soft, springy grass, barely recalling what had just happened, but understanding that in his hand he possessed...the VP's Heavenly Privileges card.

A crowd was gathering around him. At the front of it was Jesus, his toga flapping in the wind. Walter held up the card and gave it to him. The VP smiled gratefully, but his solemnity couldn't be hidden. That vacuum of pure darkness, still visible thanks to the open doorway, had eaten up their hopes of getting back the Saints.

Jesus walked over to the doorway and used his HP card to close it. The golden, electrical frame disappeared, taking with it the blackness beyond. The Citizens appeared to be relieved, perhaps because they, like Walter, and like Jesus, shivered to imagine the Parabox being pushed through that doorway.

'Okay,' said Jesus. 'I'm gonna need about six volunteers to step back into Heaven with me. The first hands I see are the ones that're comin'.

'We're gonna blow open that Parabox.'

COURTNEY TAYLOR

Chapter 41

Less than six minutes after the first official photograph of Jesus Christ's return, churches, temples and synagogues all around that Physical world were crammed with Long Term and Last Minute Believers. Those most angered by the Heavenly appearance were the citizens of Jerusalem, who gawked at their TV screens with gobsmacked indignation, because *they*—the *Jerusalites*—were the ones supposed to be getting all of the attention. Many an interviewed intellectual went on the record to speculate that, 'Perhaps we should have seen this coming. Perhaps we should have used the collective unconsciousness of our species to *predict* the real location of Christ's return. After all, where does modern cinema most often *locate* its "End of the World" disaster movies? Metropopopilis, of course.'

The Worldwide Society of Atheists gave one public statement—that they suspected this was some rich person's idea of a practical joke, so more proof would be needed before any of its managing members would be changing their opinion regarding the existence of God, Jesus, or any *other* usually invisible person. Scholars and religious experts were quick to claim that, what with the recent worldwide spate of hurricanes, earthquakes, famines and serial-killers, this was all to be expected, and was perhaps occurring a little bit later than it should have.

Teenagers all around that planet were being advised by their parents to keep their hands in the open, because what with the situation in Metropopopolis, their chances of getting caught in the act by Jesus had become a very real possibility.

As millions of people stocked their fallout shelters with tinned food and bottled water, the Pope hobbled to the edge of his famous balcony, tapped its microphone, and said, 'Brothers and sisters. What can I say but...We *told* you soooooo.'

Chapter 42

After a split-second age of floating limply in pure darkness, Lucifer stopped weeping, and said, 'Clip, my beloved myrmidon. Do you love me?'

'Of course I love you, my leader. You are the one who saved me. Who showed me the light.'

'Then give me your hand.'

The two Angels floated cheek to cheek, until Lucifer asked, 'Clip? Do you think Heaven can be found in the darkness all around us?'

The wingless Angel didn't have time to answer, because Lucifer grabbed him by the collar, planted his feet against his chest, and then used him as a launching platform to kick off into oblivion. Lucifer laughed as his screaming disciple tumbled away into the darkness, and thought, *He sounds like a crazy person. One being teased by intelligent children.*

Congratulating himself on such a creative little analogy—*Is that what it was? An analogy?*—Lucifer reached between his legs and took hold of the canister. It was jostling erratically, owing to the Saints within it, which were driving themselves at one side of their container as if to break through it. Lucifer knew what the particles were doing: they could detect Unredeemed Individuals and were trying to get to them. If Lucifer was to follow their lead, it would bring about a rolling-with-the-punches that would simply be *vainglorious*. His accidental selection of a pre-entered doorway *might* have incurred for him an outcome meant for the Almighty...But here was Lucifer coming out on top anyway. And that said a *lot*.

Lucifer, the glad bearer of a super-charged light, held the bottled Morality out in front of himself and glided through the darkness, trusting the intuition of the Saints, and heading happily, he was sure, toward Creation.

COURTNEY TAYLOR

Chapter 43

'Well well well, if it isn't the Reason for the Season,' said God, as the Ark of the Covenant was placed on the ground and then tipped onto its side, its lid facing the Parabox. 'Come to bust Me out of this thing, eh?'

'We're gonna try,' said Jesus, looking closely at the Parabox, then rapping his knuckles on it. 'My guess is it needs atomic reconfiguring, but from the outside.'

God rubbed His hands together and replied, 'I'll push against the glass so I don't get blown away.'

Goliath, Paul, Geoff and Walter were stationed behind the wooden handles of the Ark's stretcher. Jesus crouched down next to Goliath, directly behind the Ark, and said, 'All right, fellas. This thing's probably gonna kick. But let's do our best to hold it. Ooh, Wally; being half-physical, this might get ugly for you. Wanna maybe wait back in Heaven for a few minutes?'

'I'm gonna regenerate, yeah?'

'That you will,' said Jesus.

'Then I might as well take the hit,' said Walter.

Jesus laughed at Walter's lack of concern for his mortal form, then said, to the milling Citizens nearby, 'Hey, all o' youz, remember: give us some space. When this thing goes off it's really gonna go off! There's a chance y'might get incinerated!'

Goliath had borrowed someone's robe, torn it in half, and wrapped it around his hands: to ensure that he didn't get zapped by the Ark's security system.

'Okay,' said Jesus. 'I rigged this thing to make a bit o' noise, so, don't be surprised when it does. I'm gonna open it on three. That's *on* three.' He gulped and said, 'Alright, let's do this.'

Jesus reached over to the other side of the Ark, groped for one of the Angel statuettes, found its boxing glove, and turned it. The lid of the Ark unlocked.

'Alright,' he said nervously. 'I'm droppin' the lid on three.'

What with how the surrounding militia was edging backwards, the eight or so Arabs huddled on top of the Parabox were sensing that explosives were involved in the current operation. They were proved correct a moment later, shortly after the captive beneath them had looked up and said, 'Gesundheit.'

KABOOOM!!!

A huge blast of chunky white mist exploded out of the Ark and slammed against the Parabox. It and the huddling Arabs went spinning away into the distance, while the Ark launched into the air and whizzed about like a heavy, wayward, bipolar firecracker.

People of the nearby Physical Realm, most watching via TV screens, saw scruffy militants ducking and covering as a golden, glinting object zipped around and above them like an insane housefly. It was spewing out curlicues of white smoke that quickly engulfed the floating island. Its tirade ended when it fizzed straight upward like a rocket, coughed out a few last puffs of smoke, and then plummeted, straight down, toward a crowd that somehow saw it coming and broke apart.

The Ark slammed down onto the grass, leaving a steaming dent. Jesus and the other Ark bearers had been thrown thirty metres backward–into a crowd of Hare Krishnas that had been brave enough to try and catch them. Staggering to his feet, waving groggily at the smog, the VP squinted through stinging eyes, and saw that Goliath was convulsing, Paul was smacking his tongue as if he'd been sprayed in the face with pesticide, and Pleebus was groping at his own head to see if it was still intact. Angels were shrieking as if traumatised, apparently because of how closely the Ark had come to colliding with their platform.

'Sorry everybody!' shouted Jesus. 'That didn't happen the way I expected it to! The materials, they must have expired! Has– has anybody seen my Old Man?!'

The Parabox was soon found, teetering on the edge of the foggy island, by a search team that (like everyone else) looked as if it had been in a flour fight. The members of that team had emphasised the seriousness of their cause by re-lighting their flaming swords. Fortunately no one had done the same thing to the wooden cross that Jesus had wanted to leave behind, because, aside from the negative connotations that would be aroused by a flaming cross, a practical purpose was found for it.

A hearty group of volunteers reached the crucifix out beyond the island and hooked its crossbeam around a corner of the Parabox. With several collective pulls, they tipped the cube safely onto grass, and bowed humbly to receive the applause of their peers.

'Did we even crack it?' asked Jesus, as he wiped residuum from the Parabox's surface to inspect it.

God shook His head.

The VP stepped backward and reached for his handgun. The toga was in the way so he angrily ripped it off. Pulling out the .44 and bringing back its hammer, he let off a round that ricocheted off the Parabox and over the heads of the Citizens. The second shot did the same. The third bullet was flat but resounding–like some kind of death knell.

Jesus was calm for a moment, but then relented to his frustration and kicked the Parabox as hard as he could. It felt good, so he did it again, and again and again, even though it had no effect.

A mauve midget with orange cornrows approached the Vice President, holding out his Morality mask as a gift. Jesus was touched by the offer but declined it.

The rimed crowd parted and through it came Geoff, leading a pale horse by its reins. Making his way over to Jesus, he quietly said, 'I don't know if this is the best time to say it, bro, but, I think you killed the wrong horse.'

Jesus looked blankly at the animal, then clenched his fists and shouted a very loud swearword that echoed several times in the adjacent Dimension. It was, of course, detected and analysed, with surprise, by all of the major news networks.

COURTNEY TAYLOR

Chapter 44

Jesus was sitting with his back against the Parabox, looking out at the city. A news 'copter buzzed past. He gave it the finger.

'So whatta we do now?' asked Walter.

'Well,' said Jesus, 'I'd ask the Old Man, but, He appears to have made Himself absent.' He knocked on the Parabox, showing Walter that it was empty, and added, 'Musta shrunk Himself down to a molecular size or something. He's famous for doin' that sorta thing.'

Walter waited a moment, then said, 'The heads-up He gave Gandhi...do you think that means we should head to the Pearly Gates?'

Jesus kicked at the grass and said, 'Considering that nothing else has eventuated the way it "should" have, I say let's just sit here and wait for the Unavoidable.

'But don't worry, m'man; Dad can make Existence again. Might be a little bit smaller 'cause it'll be inside that Parabox, but, as y'can see: He's not really worried by Time and Space and that sort of thing.'

Walter presently said, 'So, what if in this Smaller Universe, the Smaller Lucifer steals the Saints again? Is the Smaller You just gonna accept that?'

'Daddamn,' said Jesus. 'We're gettin' pretty philosophical *now*, aren't we. But you tell me, Wally, 'cause the Now Me won't exist, and the New Me'll be someone totally different. But anyway, let's not look at things too deeply, all right, 'cause when people start fixating on things they lose their brains. It's called *Idealotry,* or whatever. And please don't give me any biblical analogies to try and inspire me. I'm the Son of God; I could beatitude *anyone* senseless.'

'Then how about a more contemporary comparison,' said Walter, 'relevant to what we're talking about with the Paraboxes:

'You get smaller and smaller if you don't do what you should.'

Jesus jumped to his feet, his eyes ablaze, and said, 'You think I'm small? You seriously think I'm *small*? In my time on earth I was a Daddamn terrorist; I chopped that planet in half. So stick that in your sphincter and smoke it at your bank. Let me tell you something, brutha: had it not been for that Last Daddamn Supper you would be eating those words, 'cause we were there, and we were ready, and all o' this Shiite about Who Believes What and

213

Who Believes What Else, it woulda been put to bed with a pillow over its face.'

'Excuse me, gentlemen,' said the Apostle Paul, 'we're all standing back here, listening, waiting for some kind of directive about where to...carry our cross.'

'Thank you, Paul,' said Jesus, tartly. 'As always, your input is appreciated.'

Paul nodded and made his way back to the nearby soldiers. The mist had extinguished their flaming swords. Even the ones that had been re-lit were now nothing but charcoal.

'Look,' said Walter to Jesus, 'with whatever you're talking about, maybe right here is your chance for redemption. You *are* known as the Redeemer. And maybe keep in mind the logic I think *I'm* extracting from this whole weird scenario. Might be a bit glib, but: Could it be that bad things happen to good people because they're the ones who can defeat the badness?'

Walter turned and trudged away, joining Paul, Saint Peter, John Smith, and Geoff, Geoff who still held the reins of a horse that might have been the "right" one.

The VP's mind was assailed by unintelligible prompts as to what he should do. He thought of the Israelites who had wandered in the desert because they hadn't kept their eyes on the prize; and of how Elijah had stood around looking like an idiot until the fire of Heaven came tumbling down onto his project. He thought of the walls of Jericho crumbling into dust, all because whatzisname and his merry men had taken a deep breath and gone-for-it on their trumpets.

Trumpets.

Didn't the Book of Revelation say something about trumpets?

Jesus looked over at the gigantic choir platform loaded with Angels. There was a whole trumpet-playing section, he noticed; along with sections devoted to every other kind of instrument.

'Should I take that as a sign?' asked Jesus, looking sideways at the empty Parabox.

As he'd expected, there was no answer. But if the Book of Revelation was right about the trumpets...maybe the note his Dad had left for him could be trusted, too.

Before Jesus knew it he was grabbing the reins of the "right" horse and hoisting himself onto its back. There he stood up like a novice surfer and looked out across a lumpy field of chalky faces. They leaned toward him eagerly. He took a deep breath then called out, 'Hey everybody! I think my Dad's given us a heads-up as to what's happening next. If we're all gonna have the– faith to follow His prompt, then, we've gotta make sure the people of this Dimension get the spectacle they've been waiting for. I say we give it to 'em. Can I hear an Amen?'

The force of the replying *Amen* almost knocked Jesus off his horse. He was surprised by it, and said, 'Well, then. In the immortal words of myself: How 'bout we get this rock rolling.'

A shout of *Yeah* accompanied him as he dropped down off the horse and grabbed its reins. Leading the animal to the edge of the floating island, he stopped, turned to his army, and shouted, 'If Dad says the Pearly Gates is where the showdown's gonna be...Well, this is what *I* think.'

Jesus took a bolstering breath, lifted his leg, and kicked the horse square in the ribs. The mare whinnied, tipped off the Dimension, and plunged the long way down to the city beneath.

The Heavenly Citizens were abruptly horrified; and Jesus, who knew from experience that crowds could easily turn on a person, explained his action by saying, 'We had to kill that horse for the Book of Life to make sense. Remember?'

Only a few people knew what the VP was talking about. The rest were looking at him as though he was some kind of lowbrow sex-offender.

'Well, take my word for it,' shouted Jesus. 'It was part o' the plan. And listen closely 'cause another part is this. Where's that Albino I bumped into earlier?'

Chapter 45

There was no such thing as Time or Space in the Outer Darkness, so for what felt like a thousand years but only a few moments, Lucifer floated through nothingness, until the Saints projected a milky patch of light onto something distant ahead of him.

The patch grew in size as the Angel approached Creation, his feet extended before him as he braced for impact. He cried out lamentably when colliding with a brushed steel surface, and began rolling weightlessly across it, the canister clipped to his belt floating about like an unruly bell clapper.

Scrabbling for a handhold but unable to find one, Lucifer made desperate unrealistic promises to a silent higher power. Perhaps these promises ensured what followed: Lucifer brushed against an object which he instinctively grabbed hold of. The light of the Saints showed it to be the rung of a ladder. He laughed in delight, picked one of the two directions the ladder led, and pushed off from the rung–his course, he believed, heading upward.

A split-second age later Lucifer grabbed hold of a rung to stop his momentum. Doing so flipped him over and bashed him against Creation. He collected himself and used the rungs to backtrack, till he came to the feature he'd overshot. It was a hatch with a glass porthole. Beyond it was a corridor, flickering due to smashed ceiling lights.

Lucifer grinned when he spotted a doorbell. He pressed its button, and heard an electronic rendition of *Ha-lle-lu-jah*.

'Handel's *Messiah*,' said Lucifer, with poise he couldn't help but appreciate. 'How quaint.'

The doorbell chirped eerily through many corridors, staircases and seminar rooms, most of which were empty and trashed. In the department of Reincarnational Statistics, it was heard by a group of Cherubs who were sharing a Morality mask beneath a conference table. The little Angels looked at each other, wondering if and or how they should respond.

COURTNEY TAYLOR

Chapter 46

Jesus, Walter, Geoff and Paul were navigating through murky corridors, bracing against Negativity so putrid and thick that the men appeared to be on the verge of vomiting. The lights inside Heaven's Main Office had been decreased to a low level of output. The same was in fact the case for all of the celestial components of Creation: When they came to a vast and grimy window they saw that the closest sun was weak and low hanging. The sky surrounding it was green, sickly, and shimmering on account of the poisons leaking through the Ality fabric.

Beneath it all was a tableau of chaos: ruptured crystal towers, demolished golden highways, and mushroom clouds of feathers that erupted when chariot bombs went off. A jumbo jet commandeered from a Physical Realm sailed heavily into a building, but failed to damage it because the Realms weren't yet interactive. It wouldn't be long until they were, though, Jesus knew. A manifestation of Bad Karma might be only seconds away.

'All right,' he said, looking away from the bedlam. 'Me and Wally are going to the Gates. Geoff, Paul, if Nelson's closed 'em, re-open em–but only the outer panels. And be ready to close 'em quickly. If we lose the Saints in the Outer Darkness, we're finished.'

They were about to split up and leave, but were prevented by a circumstance they hadn't been attuned to. The walls, pillars and windows of this part of Heaven were marred by graffiti, much of it the symbols of a particular gang. A member of that gang appeared on a nearby banister, and whistled loudly. Within moments, countless Apotheothorists appeared, their once crystal forms now polluted and grotty, their eyes filled with hatred.

'Don't worry, fellas,' said Paul, as a crowd of shadowy figures tightened around them. 'I've got an idea.'

'Look!' he shouted, and pointed. 'A child we can sacrifice!'

In one collective snap, the heads of all the Apotheothorists turned to look in that direction. Paul utilised the distraction by bending down and picking up a chunk of concrete (which may well have been a sacred rock). He lobbed it into the midst of the gang, and triggered an internecine ripple of fisticuffs, so vicious and consuming that Paul led the way through it unnoticed.

'Alright,' said Jesus, when they'd made it beyond the gang. 'Well done, Paul. Okay, me and Wally to the Gates; you guys to the Gates' control room. Good luck and Dad-speed, fellas.'

SAINT WALLY

Chapter 47

'For a long time it seemed nothing was happening, Denise. And then of course one of the visitors kicked a *horse* off the apparition. Sadly to say, a Metropopopolis paramedic has just declared that horse officially dead.'

'That *is* very sad news, Tom. Is there any news on— Oh. I'm sorry. We're now crossing live to the President.'

The United States of Babylonica's First Black Lesbian President took the stage and addressed a roomful of journalists. 'Ladies and gentlemen,' she said, in her baritone voice. 'Let it be known, because re-election time is fast approaching: I *do* believe in Jesus, that he *is* coming back. But for reasons I cannot divulge, I also believe this apparition is a threat to our nation.'

———

'Excuse Me, Peter,' said God, Who had reappeared in His Parabox. 'Y'might wanna start spreading the word: Those helicopters are vacating.'

Saint Peter clapped his hands and shouted, 'All right everybody, show-time is approaching. Let's all take our places and do what we have to do.'

The choir Angels found the right pages in their hymnbooks and cleared their throats. Everybody else, now marching in malformed lines, began waving their weapons like background actors in a third-rate play. There wasn't a lot of order among the ranks, but there was definitely a lot of passion, mostly because people were having contests over who could take off their Morality mask and go the longest without being affected by the Negativity.

One of the choir Angels pointed his flute at a small black triangle in the sky, and asked, 'What's that?'

Saint Peter gave the distant aeroplane a cursory glance, then re-faced his choir and said, 'Don't worry about that. I'm sure whatever it is, the Vice President's got it under control. Now remember: *Amazing Grace*. Key of D minor. If that even makes sense.'

'Hey look, it just dropped something,' said another of the Angels. 'It might be a welcoming gift. A *We Come in Peace* sort of thing. Although technically, aren't *we* the ones coming in peace?'

As the atomic bomb descended, one of the Angelic trumpeters cheekily began to bugle the Cavalry Charge tune. Several other Angels joined in; and soon, with a refrain that sounded a lot like the William Tell Overture, Saint Peter's entire band was heralding the descent of a nuclear missile that was headed right for them.

That missile fell from the sky like a giant concrete tear and landed directly on God's Parabox.

KABOOOOOM!!!!!

A monstrous erupting fireball turned the air to quivering liquid amber, and blew apart the choir platform. Multitudes of Angels and their instruments went flying. So too did the scattered Arabian cameramen (who were precisely the reason the island had been bombed). With them went a white, grazing horse. This pale neighing creature shot across the sky like a flaming comet; and by happenstance, collided with the Reincarnation of Gandhi, who was entertaining a group of heavily-botoxed women on a nearby penthouse balcony.

The next thing Gandhi knew he was naked, and careening headlong through the Death Duct, the valve of which began closing because Ricky the no-longer-naked Televangelist had reached his quota of Souls. Before Gandhi could count to one, he'd spent what felt like several billion years circumventing half of Creation, and was banking toward the Pearly Gates. Their huge ivory columns whooshed past him as he sailed into the Waiting Room, wherein billions of naked bodies were stacked upon tens of thousands of scaffolding levels. Consigned to a lowly position among those bodies, Gandhi shrugged apathetically, and allowed himself to be taken over by a Soul Sleep.

However, Nelson Mandela and his over-sized Afro nodded to an engineer in the Pearly Gates' control room, and a glass wall at least ten metres thick began rising from the floor of the entrance bay, directly behind Gandhi. His bum cheeks skidded against the glass as he was pressed into the posterior of the person ahead of him. Because that person looked like a glazed sumo, and because Gandhi knew it would be very difficult to get back to sleep, he swore in his most recent native language, and refused to contemplate if his actions might have led him to this situation.

COURTNEY TAYLOR

Chapter 48

A chubby red-headed Cherub had left his peers beneath a conference table, the deal being that he would take the Morality mask on his mission, and return with it once he'd helped the person who was locked outside Creation. So far he'd slipped through the barbed wire fences of a newly demarcated holy land, and escaped the lascivious clutches of a group of men wearing white collars. Now, leaning out from behind a corner, he peered down a corridor, at a porthole at the end of it, his mask held to his face because its elastic band had broken.

A fan of feathers pressed against the glass, pursued by a face that the Cherub didn't quite trust. As he treaded closer, he saw that the Angel outside appeared to be wearing...make up.

An intercom next to the doorway suddenly crackled, saying, 'Oh thank goodness you're here; I've been locked outside for*ever*! Can you open the door; *please*? And *hurry*!'

Opening the hatch would require two hands, so the Cherub took a deep breath and placed his Morality mask on the floor. He tried to open the door but found that its handle wouldn't shift. Returning to his mask and taking a deep gulp when it was back in place, he said, "I think I might need some help. Don't worry, I won't be long. I'm just gonna get some of my friends.'

'*Hurry*,' said the voice from the intercom, with pronounced impatience. 'It's *freezing* out here.'

Had the Cherub glanced back while rounding the corridor's corner, he would have seen the eyes beyond the porthole rolling with contempt at how *annoying* some people can be.

COURTNEY TAYLOR

Chapter 49

The public outrage was widespread, because what type of moron drops a bomb on God? Around that Physical world there were protests, riots, burnt flags, car bombs, mass suicides, prayer meetings, end of the world dalliances, countless numbers of rapes, disapproving self-righteous celebrities, naked people giving out free hugs (many of whom of course got raped), people in home-made bunkers shooting their children so as to save them from the Time of Tribulation ahead, and people in bars and taverns ordering reckless quantities of the strongest drinks possible. As well as all that, those who happened to die found themselves rejected by the white light at the end of the tunnel. It had shrunk and disappeared, meaning the spirits of those in transit had to return to their carnal capacitors. *Zombie apocalypse* quickly became the most searched-for term in history.

On the floating island above Metropopopolis, where the US of B's bomber had struck, the gigantic burning mushroom cloud rolled up into itself and rumbled out of existence. Left behind was a deep black pit, at the bottom of which was a puddle of melted glass: the atomically reconfigured remains of the Parabox.

God was sparkling clean and hiking happily through the fallout zone, waving at His charcoaled soldiers as they rose to salute Him.

'Good to see You out of captivity, my Lord,' said a blackened Saint Peter, as he fell in line with God's stride. 'Might I ask what the next move is?'

God arrived at the edge of the Dimension and replied, 'We wait.'

In the bureau of Physical Monitoring, holographic readouts showed updates of Universes and the bloated Souls within them. Each top-heavy U-Soul was writhing as though in anguish. Their respective movements obviously affected each other. When their holograms were overlaid, it was clear that they were locked into a pastiche that had begun spinning.

'Ohhhh this is not good,' said a Citizen called a Gangababorian. 'The Law of Cohesion is well and truly having an effect.'

One of his co-workers—a Spanish-looking woman with a pair of eyebrows that wrapped around the back of her head and then plaited into a long ponytail—asked, 'What's the timeframe on a manifestation?'

'About half-a-second from now.'

On the planets of so many Dimensions that only God could count the number, Physical beings unexpectedly disappeared into thin air. This occurred because latent specks of Negativity buried deep within their Spirits had been boosted into overdrive by the gravitational compression created by the movement of the Universe Souls. Citizens handing out pamphlets which predicted this mass disappearance had no idea that they were now inhaling the remains of the Carnal Capacitors that had vanished. Nor did they realise that the piles of clothes left upon the ground were a prelude to something very bad.

KABOOOOOM!

The flagpole at the middle of all the Dimensions went flipping like a meat cleaver when a vile black substance exploded into existence. The Bad Karma, which looked like an angry churning planet of oil in zero-gravity, was a monstrous unholy mass that chewed and clawed at the many membranes of the Ality fabric, feeding on the Positive and Negative vibrations being drawn toward the centre of the Universes.

On trillions of planets in billions of Dimensions, small white beads of light suddenly jettisoned from untold numbers of life-forms. These particles of Morality, part of a Creational contingency plan, launched out of their respective Carnal Capacitors and zipped through tiny wormholes that momentarily opened up in front of them. At the centre of the Universes these Saints joined forces, becoming a huge cosmic aggregate of holy electricity. Their pale crackling cage surrounded the Bad Karma, and then collapsed on it, igniting a white-hot war of Good and Evil.

Geoff and Paul were racing up a huge wide staircase that abruptly began trembling. The giant fresco high above them (which showed God, scantily covered with greenery and doing a bodybuilder pose) was cracking and raining chunks of plaster.

From out of an adjacent corridor came a sprinting Cherub, who tripped on the stairs, bounced repeatedly, collided with Geoff, and then sprang up with a fist pulled back, his face like that of a demon.

Geoff and Paul didn't have the time or courage to deal with the little maniac. They continued up the stairs, but only until the Cherub leap-frogged over their heads and landed heavily in front of them. Pressing a broken

Morality mask to his own face, the Cherub said, 'I know you, you came to my squadron's graduation, and you cut the ribbon for the opening of the new obstacle course.' He was pointing his chubby finger at Paul, who obviously had no recollection of the events. 'You've got to help me. There's someone outside and their trying to get in. They need help.'

Geoff and Paul looked at each other; then Paul said to the Cherub, 'What do you mean *outside*?'

Chapter 50

On the outer balconies of Heaven's Main Office there was a far-reaching and many-tiered garden, in which Citizens who had recently undergone rehabilitation would sit in groups and talk about the ways that Sheol had changed them. Normally this place of green pastures and still waters was a lush and tranquil safe haven. Now it was a stack of denuded wastelands seething with those-yet-to-be-reformed, who were addicted to the heady fumes of Negativity, and more than happy to submit to the Carnal urges of their sub-DNA.

Citizens who in previous lives had been Rapists, Peadophiles, Mass-murderers, Governmental Lobbyists, Brutal Dictators, Slave Traders, Negligent Parents, Gang-members, High-school massacrers, Mercenaries, Lawyers, Pharisaical Journalists, Warlords, Cannibals, Atheists, Speciesists, Feminists and Masculinists and Unscrupulous Capitalists, were all forming coalitions and raging against anyone who was different. The only ones not joining forces and fighting were the Pacifists, whose concentrated evil was on full display in the form of their apathy.

Thousands of Puritans from various Dimensions had banded together, knocked over a tremendous statue of Smith Wigglesworth, and used it as a battering ram. Their mission finally succeeded when an unexpected earthquake cracked open the hinges of their target. With one last scream and a self-righteous rush, the Puritans charged the massive Gates of Hell, smashed them open, and unleashed upon the Echelons a stampede of unrepentant sinners.

COURTNEY TAYLOR

Chapter 51

Lucifer was beginning to think that that stupid little Angel had forgotten about him, and wondered why Creation had started shaking. The door handle was tickling him so much that he had to constantly change hands, and even grip it with only one hooked finger at a time.

The intercom suddenly crackled to life and said, 'Hello?'

'Yes yes, hello,' said Lucifer. 'I'm here. I don't know where here is, but, surely *someone* must.'

The voice, more mature than what Lucifer had expected, asked, 'What's the number on the panel?' When the Angel read out the number etched beneath the intercom, the person said, 'Okay, I see where you are. This'll be quite easy. All you have to do is go upward. Don't even have to turn.'

'W-what's upward?' asked Lucifer.

'It's the opposite of downward.'

'Ewr,' said Lucifer, disgustedly. 'Charming.'

As the Angel gained upward momentum by reaching out and pushing off the rungs, he waxed philosophical as though in an in-depth interview. 'I wouldn't trade those days of difficulty for anything,' he said out loud. 'They formed me. And allowed me to become who I was supposed to become. You see, *without* that adversity, I wouldn't be where I am today; *who* I am today.'

A deep rumbling interrupted him. Grabbing hold of a rung, he flipped over sideways and crashed into Creation, but stopped himself ascending and trained his ear toward the sound. Quickly deciding that the people "assisting" him must have opened up some kind of doorway, Lucifer pushed off from the ladder and again floated upward.

In not long he was rising above a dark rectangular lake: a huge black floor, which aggressively met his feet when gravity rudely took hold of him. Landing with unbent knees and an unsteady spasm, the Angel wobbled, gained his balance, then ran a hand across his hair and looked around for any spectators. He quickly saw that he would have had billions, were they not all turned away from him. They were pressed against glass and stacked upon thousands of levels, their naked bodies jiggling due to the shaking floor.

It wasn't until the Saints began ramming the inside of their container with heightened ferocity that Lucifer realised where he was.

Lucifer laughed out loud and slapped his knee, then leapt into the air, extended his wings, and exulted in his own powers of attracting good fortune. Unexpectedly, the scaffolding beyond the glass wall abruptly collapsed, and the billions of naked bodies crumbled into a dense pile that smoonched against the glass–so heavily that Lucifer could hear the weight of it.

Laughing at the misfortune of those in the Waiting Room, Lucifer searched for an exit, and found it in the form of a security door to the right of the glass wall. With a graceful flap he sailed toward it. He was about to land, find the correct button and saunter through an opening doorway...but the door slid upward on its own, revealing Jesus, who was aiming a chunky silver handgun directly at Lucifer.

The Angel screamed and took off like a panicking bird, the strokes of his wings becoming more controlled the higher and safer he got. When feeling that he was out of bullet range, he suddenly recalled that Spiritual beings are immune to Physical things like bullets, and reconsidered the tactic of interposing distance between himself and his would-be attacker. Remembering his advantage, he unclipped the canister of Saints and hugged it to his chest, then reached beneath his cloak and produced his own silver handgun.

Lucifer raised his wings till their tips almost touched; and in that pose he descended delicately. Landing lightly upon the shiny black floor, the nozzle of his gun pointed at the canister of Saints, he called out, 'You do of course know that that thing in your hand is *useless*! I'm *Spiritual*!'

'The fabrics are breakin' down, Lucy,' Jesus replied, moving closer. 'You me and this thing are all on the same wavelength now. Want me to prove it?'

'Ha!' said Lucifer. 'Want *me* to prove it?' He was about to pull back the hammer of his pistol to exhibit his seriousness, when suddenly, he was flicked in the head by what felt like a giant steel finger, and a gunshot boomed throughout the entrance bay.

'OUCH!' shouted Lucifer, rubbing with rage at this forehead. 'I swear to your Old Man, try that again and I will *blow* these goodie-goodies into the next room!'

Another booming noise flooded the entrance bay–this one coming not from any handgun, but from the Pearly Gates, whose two gigantic ivory panels had been travelling to meet each other since the Angel had first touched down in the entrance bay. Lucifer jumped as if slapped on the rump, and soon realised what was happening. He knew he had only one legitimate recourse, and he was proud that he wasn't afraid to use it

'You might think me spiteful for saying it,' said Lucifer, as Jesus stalked closer, his gun trained steadily, 'but it's my personal opinion that every now and then, we all need to go out with a *bang*.'

The Angel pulled his trigger and shot the canister. Its integrity corrupted, the entire jar burst apart, exploding so violently that Lucifer was knocked off his feet and thrown through the air. He landed heavily on the floor, amid a storm of blazing white beads that immediately began attacking him. The Saints pulled at his clothes and dragged him around, attempting to redeem him thanks to confusion brought about by the weakening Ality fabrics. The Morality could sense the Angel's misdeeds but didn't know he was a purely Spiritual being, removed from any Soul Cycle.

The Saints apparently decided they could multi-task. Picking up Lucifer in a sparkling mass, they compounded around him, and then jetted toward the Unredeemed Newly Deceased in the Waiting Room. Their radiant torrent of Goodness slammed against the glass, so powerfully that cracks formed. Lucifer, pinned at the epicentre of those cracks, woozily witnessed the Saints regathering, their intention to blast him from front on.

The Angel screamed and the Saints rushed toward him.

————

The moment the Saints had exploded from their canister, Jesus knew he had a fresh problem. How would he get them to the Bad Karma, if and when it manifested? Indeed, had it *already* manifested? Was that why the floor had begun shaking?

The Saints had become a blurry white storm cloud with extruding channels that looped around to circuitously and repeatedly assail their target. A shining spider web of lengthening fractures was spreading out over the glass wall. If the Saints broke through that wall, and redeemed the Newly Deceased, there'd be nothing left over to administer to the Bad Karma.

'So whatta ya think we should do?' asked Walter, when Jesus re-entered the corridor. The security door slid upward and locked against the ceiling. They peered through its glass slit, which was trembling.

'I-IIIII...have got no idea what to do,' said Jesus, his mind completely empty of ideas.

Walter looked around the corridor, spotted an air vent, and asked, 'Is this compartment used for quarantining?'

'I-IIIII...presume so,' said Jesus.

'If we could trap the Saints in here,' said Walter, 'is there any way we could...vacuum them up?'

'Um...' said Jesus. 'I...suppose so. Surely there'd be some kind of...decompression function.'

A nearby computer panel gave them all the information they needed. Luckily for Jesus, who hated computers, it recognised his HP card and customised his interaction with it.

'All right,' said Jesus. 'Just to clarify this for *me*. We close the doors at both ends of this section. We trap the Saints, then grab 'em through the vents, and store 'em in a decompression tank.'

Walter, looking as nervous as Jesus felt, replied, 'And we use an Unredeemed member of Creation to get them in here.'

They agreed on what they were doing, and set about doing it.

Jesus lowered the security door and they both stepped into the entrance bay, where a huge, pure white fireball, radiating hoops of glowing energy, was pounding repetitively against the glass wall, hoping to penetrate Lucifer's form and smash through to the Unredeemed.

'Lucky you're the faster runner, eh?' said Jesus, as he edged backward for the control panel on this side of the door.

Walter treaded toward the Saint storm, which apparently sensed him coming. It paused and appeared to look at him. A moment later it was jetting toward him, intent upon redeeming him. Walter flung himself into the corridor and sprinted down it, not looking back, racing for the hallway's second security barrier. Jesus, peering into the corridor, felt the Saints rush past him—with such force that they nearly sucked him into the hallway. His feet lifted off the ground and he grabbed hold of the control panel to stop himself from flying away.

Above the roar of the Saint storm came the shrieks of Lucifer, who was a dark, thrashing blur getting dragged into the corridor amid a blinding concentration of white light. The last of the Saints rushed into the passageway and the suction outside of it ended. The feet of Jesus touched the ground and he pressed the button that closed the security door. Hopefully Walter had made it to the other side and closed the door there. Jesus peeked into the glass slit and saw that the brightness was diminishing: the Saints were being vacuumed into the air vents, as per the algorithm he'd created via the control panel.

When there was nothing left in the corridor save for an Angel whose clothes were bleached; whose head was bald; and whose wings and eyebrows were completely plucked, Jesus lowered the security door, stepped inside, and made his way over to a fuse box. Behind its door was a wall of technology: buttons, switches, levers, dials, and oxygen tanks emblazoned with Hebrew text. One of those tanks was rattling as if filled with jumping beans. Jesus detached it and slung it onto his shoulder.

'So now we've gotta track down a Karmic Regulator,' said Walter.

'That's exactly right, Wally,' replied Jesus. 'You and me are off to Hell.'

Chapter 52

Jesus and Walter picked their way through corridors crowded with naked upright Citizens, many awakening because of how drastically Creation was shaking. These individuals were overflow from the Waiting Room, positioned here no doubt by Saint Peter's deputies.

Jesus, with a tank on his shoulder and a silver handgun tucked into the back of his pants, led the way to a murky transport terminal, in which a bank of chariots (most upended or set on fire) gave them hope of quickly making it to Hell. He and Walter loaded Lucifer onto what appeared to be the only functioning chariot, followed him up onto it, and then hung on tightly after Jesus had keyed in their destination. A plume of flame sputtered out the back of the vehicle. It took off into the air and headed for the opening of a glass tunnel.

The crystal pipe led through several empty departments before looping around, exiting the building, and nose-diving. As the chariot plummeted down the outside of Heaven's Main Office, Jesus and Walter looked out across blackened skies, toppled skyscrapers, and grimy golden streets filled with billions of warring Citizens. The many suns of Heaven were like sickly dollops of lava floating in putrescent water. The withering Realm seemed beyond both restoration and redemption.

The chariot reached a hyper speed and slipped beneath the ground level outside the Main Office. Racing past pipes and steel walkways, it levelled out and took them alongside a row of gigantic glass cylinders. Inside of them, floating in softly glowing liquids, were huge fluctuating machines.

'Welcome to Hell, Wally,' said Jesus. 'Those're the engines that power Heaven. Usually y'gotta wear sunglass goggles and radiation suits; 'cause o' the whole fire and brimstone thing.'

The chariot had just enough energy to make it to their destination: a room that was like a hibernating mission control. They dismounted the chariot, which sank to the bottom of the glass pipe the moment they left it, and headed for an elevator on the other side of the room. They were joined in their rapid stride by Paul, Geoff, and a dozen sprinting Cherubs sharing a single Morality mask between them. Without being asked, the Cherubs surrounded Lucifer, lifted him onto their little shoulders, and carried him.

'The Karmic Regulator's on the ninth level,' said Paul, pressing the button for the elevator, and holding open its door as everyone flooded through it. They were only just able to fit; and to the frustration of everyone present, Lucifer, who looked like a traumatised, crowd-surfing chicken, began to distantly sing elevator music as the numbers above the doorway increased in value.

The doors opened upon a large workspace filled with beeping machines and flashing red ceiling lights. A group of Citizens wearing Morality masks was gathered around a console, above it a hologram showing the layouts of various Dimensions. At the centre of the images was a black-and-white blot, representative of the war between Good and Evil.

'Ladies, gentlemen and whatevers,' said Jesus, 'how do I get this,' he brought the tank off his shoulder, 'into that,' and pointed at the stain on the screen.

'Normally a Karmic Regulator would do that job,' said a turquoise humanoid with a skin flap Mohawk, stepping forward. 'There's one here, but, currently I don't think it'll suit your purposes. It's being fed by reserves; from auxiliary Dimensions that are practically out of power. We've got about three minutes till the Regulator shuts down completely. When that happens, Hell's engines...die.'

'But if the Saints are administered to the Bad Karma,' said Jesus, 'that'll stop the U-Souls from spinning, and that'll reduce the pressure that's causing the Bad Karma to...metastasise. Yeah?'

'Yes and no but mostly no,' replied the humanoid. 'Even if the U-Souls *do* stop spinning, and the pressure's relieved, the Bad Karma's at such an advanced stage that the Regulator isn't gonna have time to do what it needs to do. The Saints'll be *on their way* to having an effect, but they won't get to *have* that effect. It's too late for that.'

'So, what,' asked Jesus, suddenly crestfallen, 'these Daddamn things,' he shook the tank, 'are useless?'

'An hour ago,' said the humanoid, 'they wouldn't have been.

'Sorry.'

The humanoid's voice broke as he apologised. It caused Jesus and everybody else to look at the floor.

Jesus then asked, 'Why is your voice familiar to me?'

'I'm Henry. The "alcoholic." I was the one who thought it'd be a good idea to try and access the Bank of Inaccessible Knowledge. There's always a Plan B, with your Old Man. What that plan is now...I simply don't know.'

Jesus turned and concentrated upon the growing darkness at the centre of the hologram. The way it was mauling the light almost made him shiver. He had, in his hands, the remedy for the ailment he was looking at. But there seemed to be no way to administer it. Unless...

'Hey Henry,' said Jesus. 'What if we bypassed the Regulator and applied the Saints directly?'

'How would we do that?' asked Henry.

Jesus delved into his jeans and emerged triumphantly with his HP card. Henry only shook his head, and said, 'Every time a card like that performs a task, the action has to be ratified by Creation's mainframe, to make sure it won't damage the system. Right now, the Realms are too volatile for us to access them. The shifting Alities effectively mean that connecting point A to point B would be like...like trying to dig hole through water. The mainframe wouldn't consent because it knows it'd be damaging its own configurations.'

'Can we ask it for a bit o' lenience?' asked Jesus. 'Or hit some kind of override button?'

'Not without God signing off on it,' said Henry.

'Is there any...any kind o' loophole you can think of?' asked Jesus. 'Some kind of, I dunno, miracle?'

'A miracle?' said Henry, thinking through the question. 'A miracle is a contravention of the natural order, requested, and made possible by the permission to *override* the natural order. If we can't get the permission to override...we're locked outside of where we need to be.'

'Is there anyone...*inside*...you can think of?' asked Jesus.

'You mean *part* of the natural order,' asked Henry, 'as opposed to *experiencing* it?'

Walter stepped forward and said, 'What about Death?'

The eyes of Jesus widened in hope. Turning to Henry, cringing in fear of a negative answer, he asked, 'Would Death be able to...get us where we need to be?'

'Theoretically,' said Henry... 'Maybe. I think. I could be wrong, though.'

'Paul,' said Jesus, 'are you able to get hold o' Death? (There'll be less questions if she talks to you instead o' me). Tell her we need her down here in Hell, and that all other priorities should be abandoned without question.'

As Paul contacted and conferred with Death, a hologram of the Spiritual Realm superimposed itself onto those of the Physical Universes. This three-dimensional x-ray of Creation had a blurry nub at the centre of it, indicative of where the Bad Karma was so potent that it was about to burst through into the Spiritual Realm. The nub was blackening; and all watching on knew it was a frightening portent of things to come.

Chapter 53

In the lobby of Heaven's Main Office, where untold zillions of Citizens cowered in fear, there was a horrid explosion, directly at the place where the homeless man was usually wetting his pants. The bronze statue was torn in half by a hateful dark energy that immediately started gouging the fabric of the Spiritual Realm. It heaved toward itself anything it might devour, effecting the destruction of the marble balconies, and tearing the golden escalators from their mounts. The mezzanine tower began to collapse, its highest levels slamming down onto the ones beneath. Citizens jumped off it for fear of being squashed, but were plucked out of the air by the Bad Karma and dragged up into it.

The outside windows of the building shattered, and toward their gaping openings flew anything that hadn't been nailed down by a Lutheran. Piles of confiscated Morality Masks flew en mass toward the Main Office, lifted by the suction of the Bad Karma, or propelled by the fighting spirits of the Saints within them, or animated by both these influences. Horned citizens who'd been elevated to positions of godhood condemned the masks' disobedience, but graciously consented when seeing that even stolen military aircraft were powerless against the suction. In fact, even the suns and stars were moving toward the centre of Creation. The suns began flickering...and then went out. Every educated Citizen knew what this meant: the engines in Hell had just died.

Chapter 54

The lights cut out the moment that Death entered the room.

'Y'know I am pretty busy,' she said, with irritation.

'So are we, Grimness,' said Jesus. 'We need to get *this there*. It's full o' Saints. And I don't have time to reason with you.'

Death looked at the blemish at the middle of the holographic screen and said, 'You're insane. A Spiritual connection to that thing would probably drag all of Heaven into it.'

'That's what's happening anyway,' said Jesus. 'As of two seconds ago.'

Death could obviously see that he was right. She nodded nervously then raised her khopesh.

'Hey everybody, maybe stand back,' said Jesus. 'Y'don't wanna get dragged into this thing.'

'Are *you* intending to get dragged into that thing?' asked Paul, apropos of the way that Jesus was holding the tank close to him.

'I get the feeling that's how it's meant to be,' said Jesus. 'And hey, if it doesn't work, we *all* get dragged into it. Nobody misses out on the fun.' Turning to Death, he anxiously nodded for her to make the incision. Death aimed her golden blade, smiled sympathetically (and maybe even a tad respectfully), then nicked the air in front of Jesus.

The VP was torn off his feet by a roaring blot of suction that threw him instantaneously into a storm of un-synced metaphysical layers. The Ality fabrics were cartwheeling all around him, each a unique configuration of matter that was smashing against the others, forging a confusion of sparks and liquid ripples that rolled about like the undersides of gargantuan waves.

Ahead of him was a monstrous conflagration of Good and Evil– a galaxy-dissolving tempest that looked like a yawning, many-dimensional, evil-looking Yin-Yang symbol.

Jesus retrieved the silver handgun from the back of his pants, put its barrel to the nozzle of the tank, and prayed to his Old Man that he wouldn't accidentally shoot himself. He barely heard the gunshot, but he certainly heard the Saints break free of their captivity. The twinkling gems formed a glittering cloud that grew and grew: Apparently he had the whole subatomic compaction thing on his side. Whether or not there'd be enough Goodness to deal with the manifestation, he didn't know; but he threw away the tank in celebration, unloosed several rounds, and screamed with laughter as he and the Morality plunged headlong into the storm.

The Saints all around him began shaking, and crackling. Jesus knew intuitively that this was the moment wherein all would be decided. He had one bullet left in his gun, he believed, and he wasn't gonna use it without coating it in a bit of style. Aiming his handgun at the evil he was plummeting toward, Jesus quoted his own favourite line when playing video games. He pulled back the pistol's hammer, and said, 'Eat this lead in remembrance of me.'

KABOOM!!!!

An almighty eruption of Goodness slammed into Jesus and continued on past him. It wasn't his bullet that had caused the sudden reaction, but the contingent of Saints. They had collided with the very centre of the conflict, the place where the centripetal forces generated by the spinning U-Souls had crushed the Positive and Negative vibrations into a highly combustible stasis. Essentially, the man of Calvary had arrived with the cavalry: the extra Saints had triggered an instant metaphysical reaction.

Chapter 55

An explosion of holy white light washed through every single inch of every single Dimension, rendering translucent the countless Physical worlds whose Citizens were watching on in terror. Even individuals without working retinas, on hemispheres facing away from the supernatural storm, were able to watch as Good triumphed over Evil. All they had to do was look at the ground, and there they saw the faint ebbing form of what had once been an immense inky tumour.

Innumerable microscopic balls of bitterness ignited and then fizzled out of existence, often leaving behind habitats completely decimated of all life. These specks of Bad Karma had passed, via inhalation, from one raging Citizen to another, until frequently there was nothing left of an eco-system but an atmosphere of deadly black motes. Now those motes were gone, and the air (or its equivalent) was clean and free.

Scrunched Ality fabrics so deeply creased that they'd cracked straightaway began relaxing. Dimensions that had been grating against each other, often tearing and flooding one another with foreign matter, began to slow and settle. The fiery firmamental refractions cast by fabrics' conflict were dwindling. All who had beheld these colourful rippling waves had sought religion. The only exceptions were of course hardened environmentalists, who could only blame their own species for the current catastrophe.

It soon became apparent that the Universe Souls had stopped spinning. So, from out of taverns and temples and bunkers and brothels emerged Citizens who only moments ago had been on the verge of either murder or self-compaction. Reconsidering their words and actions, and in most cases even apologising for them, they agreed that giving was a superior ideal to taking, and that toleration was preferable to annihilation (if the circumstances so permitted). They joined hands, sang impromptu hymns of thanks, and looked upward as debris rained downward. Many were hoping that the apocalypse was just pausing for dramatic effect, because if it wasn't, those last minute acts of charity were really going to sting.

God, Who was observing all this, turned to Saint Peter and said, 'The VP'll be arriving shortly.'

COURTNEY TAYLOR

Chapter 56

Jesus H. Christ was a glowing blue spectre in glowing white underpants. He was hurtling through space like a lukewarm believer, so deep in galactic backwaters that he quickly decided his only recourse was to call upon the being that hadn't been answering his previous calls.

The tune he began to whistle was warbled by the speed at which he was travelling. *Swing Looooow, Sweet Charioooooot, comin' forth to carry me—*'

A portion of space next to Jesus burst open as though by a shotgun blast. Out of it flapped a resplendent white cockatoo that squawked, landed on his head, and beamed a telepathic greeting into his mind.

'Ho-ly Sh-pirit!' Jesus shouted. 'Where've you been?

'Whatta ya mean it's classified? I'm the VP—I'm privy to everything.

'Whatta ya mean not this?

'I think I *will* ask Him. And when I do...But anyway. Dad's been kidnapped. We have to—

'What? Just then? What'd He say?

'Are you serious? Well, what about the whole Armageddon situation?

'Ha. Typical. What— He's waiting now?

'Might as well. Not really doin' anything else.'

Jesus grabbed the bird's feet and hung onto them. It squawked, and ahead of them there appeared a Dimensional tear, which they passed through. Suddenly they were soaring over Metropopolis, toward a levitating slice of blackened land. Apparently not all of this world's satellites had been vacuumed into outer space. Jesus could see a screen, and on it a fuzzy linkage to a news report. Footage of him and the Holy Spirit appeared. He looked around for the camera but couldn't see it. Regardless, he let go with one hand, and waved and blew a kiss. This effort unbalanced him and almost put him into a lopsided spin.

Tens of thousands of Heavenly soldiers cheered as the blue glowing Jesus began his approach. Letting go of the bird, he dropped, hit the ground and rolled. When rising to his feet, he was swamped on all sides by people wanting to pat him on the back, touch the hem of his Mormon undies, or, in one case, give him a wedgie.

The crowd soon parted to reveal God, Who looked Jesus up and down, then snapped His fingers, restoring Jesus' physicality to its normal state.

'I was beginning to think I'd have to do this tiresome press junket on My own,' said the Almighty, holding out His arms for a hug. 'And I'm glad to see you dressed for the occasion.'

God and Jesus shared a bearish, back-slapping embrace. When it ended, God admitted, 'I'm proud o' you, boy. Y'handled all this like a true Son of a Me. Couldn'a done it better Myself.'

Jesus said, 'Thanks. I'm proud o' you, too...Old Man.'

God put His son in a headlock, ruffled his hair and said, 'Let's not forget how y'lost your front teeth, eh boy?

'Now. Some o' your friends are soon to be appearing.'

A moment later, a doorway manifested and opened. From out of it flooded Henry and his colleagues, followed by a tide of Cherubs upholding Lucifer, and then Paul, Geoff, and Walter. Jesus noticed that the Cherubs must have been suffering the residual effects of the Negativity: they were maliciously pinching Lucifer whenever they thought no one was looking. The depilated Angel appeared to barely notice. His only protest was a faraway, 'Heh?'

'Okay then,' said God. 'The *next* item on the agenda. I might have to direct this one toward the Vice President, because the people of this Physical world have been waiting quite a while for him to make an appearance.'

God waved His hand as though unveiling the cityscape in front of Them. Jesus stepped toward it and looked out over Metropopolis.

Billions of people all across that planet leaned closer to their television screens, and untold numbers of homeless people all simultaneously said, 'Sshh, it looks like I'm about to say something.'

The Vice President of Creation glanced around at his countrymen, then quietly said, 'I think this might be the whole "bitter scroll" reference.'

Jesus waved.

So did his singed followers.

And that was the final image the people of that planet were given of the Heavenly visitors, because a flashing and lashing cord of rutilant electricity erupted from God's fingertip, and He welded the rapturous rupture in the sky until it disappeared completely.

SAINT WALLY

———

As disappointed zealots abandoned their placards and made their way homeward, they collected, as mementoes, the burnt sticks, battered instruments, and rusty weapons which had fallen off the now-vanished floating island. They didn't seem to notice that these items were becoming less visible. This was occurring because the Ality fabrics were regenerating.

Also fading from sight were two familiar men sitting on a park bench.

Osama was shaking his head and saying, 'You don't understand. In every life I lead, I end up making the wrong choices. In my last life, when I was a boy, all I wanted to do was make fil-ms, and that was how I got caught up in the whole...'

Hitler patted him on the shoulder and said, 'Nein, nein, nein. Ze time zhoo have *ahead* counts for more. *Behind* zhoo is...Vell, ze Vice President, he vonce said to *me*: *Vot is done, is done, is kapüt*. Ünt ze first step for people like you ünt me, is *accepting* zat. So *zat* is vot zhoo have to fookus on, ja? Ze fyoochure.'

COURTNEY TAYLOR

Chapter 57

The many suns of Heaven reignited in the sky, revealing eroded vistas of smoggy, bombed-out mansions, and the Main Office, which was a tall, weary soldier standing among a boneyard of fallen skyscrapers.

For some time now there had circulated the belief that not only was God dead, He hadn't even existed in the first place. When evidence to the contrary boomed out across the Echelons, Citizens who looked like hateful decrepit night-dwellers emerged from their hiding places, eager to see if the disembodied voice was something more than just an auditory hallucination.

'Ladies, gentlemen, and whatevers,' said God, standing upon the highest outer balcony of the Main Office. 'If it just so happens that you have contributed to the decay of morale and Morality up here in Paradise, then here is your chance to redeem yourselves. As of right now, a Kingdom-wide cleanup is taking place. I strongly urge everyone to take part, because as soon as the restoration is complete, We're going to have *another* Kingdom-wide get-together—a celebration to commemorate the return of Me. And a few other things.'

God snapped His fingers and the Pearly Gates began opening. The fractured glass wall within the entrance bay abruptly shattered. Before the naked Citizens could spill backward like potatoes out of a tilting dumpster, a dense river of equally-naked Citizens flew in from the Outer Darkness and slammed into them. This battering ram of nakedites, which had spent an infinite moment going round and round Creation, was the remedy to a clogged artery.

At the very front of the Limbo Lines, where conscious Citizens were still waiting behind the yellow line, the art deco wall split open from a central point, its many features rolling away from each other to reveal the greeting terminal beyond it. A moment later, a colossal force threw countless numbers of the Newly Deceased unceremoniously off the scaffolding and into Heaven. They were saved from any injuries or indignity by a cleansing flash of light, and an unseen power that caused them all to levitate.

The Neanderthal still had hold of Saint Peter's pot plant and spray bottle. With these objects, and now suddenly wearing an ivory tuxedo, he flew to meet his loved ones, who were still waiting for him. They cheekily teased him about his newfound passion for horticulture, and complimented him upon the new sheen of his formerly greying tips.

Now that the Soul Cycle had been reactivated, and the cogs of Creation were once again turning, God felt it was just the right time to look around and say, 'Yes it is good.'

SAINT WALLY

Chapter 58

When the prophet Ezekiel referred to a thing in the sky made of wheels within wheels, he was speaking of a mobile discotheque named Club Elysium. It is worth noting that God's fondness for taking this club out for joyrides accounts for the prevalence of UFO sightings.

Club Elysium looked like an ultra-complicated gyroscope, or a blazing atom with many spinning valence hoops. Its interior was a twisting, pulsing and flashing realm of smooth chaos, in which notions of up and down were completely dismantled. Revellers were overhead, underneath, and on all sides, cavorting and carousing across spacious platforms that connected and disconnected as they circulated around a huge central dance floor.

Performing pillars of cloud and fire politely settled when a burning blue star shone an icy spotlight onto God. It was time to honour some very significant contributions to Creation.

The award for *Most Original Method of Confusing and Reengaging the Attention of a Distracted Crowd* went to *Geoffrey Son of Joseph (AKA, the Disciple the Writers of Scripture were Too Embarrassed to Mention)*. Geoff shook God's hand and received a shiny golden plaque. The Holy Spirit, sitting on God's shoulder, gave Geoff a nod. He returned it.

Saint Peter received the award for *Most Outstanding Keeper of the Faith*. The trophy was a cringing toddler clamping his hands to his ears. Saint Peter looked a bit teary when God referred to him as one of Their best, and agreed with God's statement that he deserved a holiday. God and Saint Peter shook hands; then the latter walked over to Geoff, that they might compare the largeness and shininess of their respective awards.

Best Crash Tackle of the Almost Apocalypse went to Adolf Hitler, whose recognition effected a slight lull in the applause. Hitler, smiling shyly but enthusiastically, gratefully accepted a golden statuette of a mustached man flying through the air with a cape spread out behind him. God patted him on the shoulder, and Hitler was so touched that he accidentally gave a Sieg Heil. At first nobody clapped. But then it was the familiar situation of one person starting, others joining in, and then everyone whooping and slamming their hands like excited chimpanzees.

'I would also like to add,' said God, 'that Mr. Hitler has just been appointed the director of a counselling program dedicated to the rehabilitation of drastically wayward Souls. In his new capacity as chief mentor he'll be reporting directly to Me, and will be overseeing a wide variety of Newly Deceased individuals.'

The Apostle Paul won the award for *Most Beneficial Reference to Child Sacrifice for the Purpose of Achieving Positive Outcomes for Creation and All its Citizens*. He and God saluted before shaking hands heartily.

'And next,' said God, 'we have a man who didn't know what he was in for when he decided to terminate his own life. He was hoping for blackness, but what he got instead was a whole lot of supernatural trouble. Boys and girls, please give it up for Walter Alastair Matthews, who is still Unprocessed, so technically shouldn't even be up here.'

The *Sidekick of the Millennium* award—also known as a *Barnabas*—was a golden sculpture of two mischievous boys, one holding up the other so that he could aim a slingshot. Walter felt extremely flattered to receive it, and didn't know what to say when shaking the Almighty's hand. Looking out at the huge audience (which must have contained at least several billion people) he wondered if anyone he knew might be watching on.

The crowd became raucous when a man on a white horse cantered through its midst, heading over to accept the award for *Most Insane and Needless Act of Sacrifice in the Face of Monstrous Adversity*. Jesus H. Christ, wearing a clean white singlet printed with the words *Come on down and deathdefy*, dismounted, landed heavily, and then clomped over to his Dad. The award he received was in his own image: it was a long, lean and scraggly man holding an oxygen tank and a pistol, his mouth open wide in fun-fueled fear. Jesus smiled, shook his Dad's hand, hugged Him, then went to join the others but was called back. It was obvious that the Almighty was telling His son to say a few words. It was even more obvious that Jesus hadn't prepared anything.

Eventually Jesus said, 'Um...thanks everyone. Especially Death. Without her we'd all be...dead. Ha hah. And Henry, thank you for being the...Runner Up for the Keeper of Faith award.'

God whipped his fingers, and Henry found himself clutching that very award.

'Everyone else who needs to be thanked,' continued Jesus, 'y'can scratch your name onto *my* award, and consider that a mark o' my gratitude.

'Um...yeah. That's pretty much it. If I've forgotten anyone, sorry, but, y'shoulda made more of an impression.' He laughed in a nose-crinkling way and relinquished the stage to his Dad.

'I don't know about you fine people,' said God, 'but I think that was very well said. So let's give these boys one last hand, and then *get back down* to the business of *partying!*'

SAINT WALLY

Chapter 59

The cohorts to whom Jesus was speaking each straightened their posture when God approached, a drink in either hand. Passing one of those drinks to Jesus, God said, 'Mind if I borrow the leader of the Cloaked Crusaders for a moment, gentlemen?'

God and Jesus wandered away from the group. God said, 'I won't say anything about the character of the people you're hanging around.'

'And I won't say anything about potentially having more children to take some of the pressure off me,' replied Jesus.

'Let Me tell you,' said God, downing His drink and creating another, 'one's enough. But listen. I have something to confess. You know how the Holy Spirit was "noticeably absent" during this whole situation? Well, it wasn't answering your calls because…I've been drawing up plans for a new Dimension, and the HS has been overseeing the last-minute details.'

'What, You told it to ignore me?' asked Jesus.

'*You* know the way the bird is,' said God. 'It's the biggest Me-damn gossip you'll ever come across. And it thinks it's an eagle for crying out loud. I just wanted this whole thing to be a surprise, because this new Dimension I've been dreaming up, I was thinking maybe I'd throw the question at you: I design and build; you manage. Whatta you think? Now you don't have to answer right now. It's a lot of responsibility and potentially a lot more—sacrifice. But I'm just saying, it's there if you want it.'

Jesus, who had adopted his "pensive face," asked, 'Will I have a say regarding the, uh, aesthetics?'

'Of course. You've got good taste. You inherited that from Me.'

'How 'bout the choices r.e. religions? 'Cause I don't wanna be tellin' people they hafta do things like, I dunno, stand one leg so that—'

God held up a hand as if He knew what Jesus was getting at, and said, 'Bearing in mind that belief *is* needed to get the job done, and that there'll have to be negotiations about how much lovey-doveyness We chuck into the mix.'

'I totally expected that,' said Jesus.

God stirred His drink and said, 'So whatta ya say? Y'wanna throw in for round two?'

'I think this'd be more like round 350,000-and-two,' said Jesus.

'Pff,' said God. 'You know Me. Lose track of the numbers when You forgive and forget. Easy to do when You're dealing with eternity.'

Jesus confirmed his drink was non-alcoholic, then raised it and said, 'Then here's to Our new Dimension. May it be as diverse and plentiful as the list of Your illegitimate grandchildren. *Kidding*.'

Smiling happily, they tapped their glasses, downed their drinks in a single gulp, and both said, 'Aaah,' at the very same time.

COURTNEY TAYLOR

Chapter 60

Walter shifted nervously when God sat down next to him and ordered a drink called a Sore Altar Boy. The bartender, a three-eyed Asian with a trendy sidewards comb-over, reverently placed the drink on the countertop, which seemed to have live streaks of lightning passing through its black granite.

Before taking a sip of His drink, God sagely remarked, 'A man with his feet on either side of a fence finds that his testicles are the true victims. You're not a man experiencing pain in that particular region, are you, Walter?'

Walter shook his head.

'If I was to inform you of a loophole,' said God, 'do you think you'd step backward through it?'

Walter nodded.

'Before you did that,' said God, 'would there be anyone up here you'd like to re-connect with?'

'I think I'd save that for when I come here properly,' replied Walter.

'Allow Me to throw a wild animal into the kindergarten,' said God. 'The board of Heavenly directors is two men down. Alexandrius volunteered for reincarnation; to help out with some of the recovery efforts. Gandhi is, well, re-learning some things. I wonder if the board might find the Sidekick of the Millennium to be a helpful addition.'

Walter presently said, 'I appreciate the opportunity, but, responsibility and A-list parties have never much appealed to me.'

'Well, I'm offering it not just because of *this* whole scenario,' said God. 'Previously you've been, how should I say it, A Man After My Own Heart.

'Something to remember, though: even if the Big C is down to zero–let's say it's been knocked outta you by your fall, or by the radiation from the Last Battle–I make no guarantees about the future. If a bus wipes out you and your family, a bus wipes out you and your family.'

'I understand that,' said Walter.

'Some of your more recent connections,' said God, 'they might appreciate a See You Later. How 'bout I wait here?'

Walter made his way through a bouncing sea of partygoers, dodging conga lines of peculiar individuals. The roaming dance floors spun around on all sides of him, their crystal bannisters reflecting blades and beams of light of every conceivable colour, their majestic staircases never leading to the same dance floor twice. Miraculously, he spotted Geoff and Saint Peter, standing next to the white horse that Jesus had rode in on. As Walter approached, he heard that they were deeply engrossed in a discussion about predestination in regard to animals.

Walter chose a moment to interject, and said, 'Apparently I'm not quite dead, so, I'm heading back to the Physical.'

'You've *chosen* to go back?' asked Geoff, evidently perplexed. 'Already?'

Walter nodded, then turned to Saint Peter and said, 'Make sure you get your handgun back.'

'Already have,' said Saint Peter, pulling back his cloak, revealing that his .44 was tucked into his underwear.

'And try not to traumatise too many women,' said Walter, to Geoff, as they shook his hands.

'No promises will be made,' said Geoff, grinning.

Walter regressed into the crowd, but first added, 'I'll see you when I make it back up here. Keep keepin' the VP outta trouble in the meantime, hey?'

'I'm beginning to believe it's the reason we were created,' said Saint Peter, raising his bottle. 'And thanks for all your help!'

Jesus was on a lower level, surrounded by a shoal of business types who looked to be trying to sell him on an idea. Instead of interrupting them, Walter caught the Son of God's eye and gave him a wave goodbye. The returning wave was obviously one of Hello, but Walter didn't rectify the confusion. Instead, he made his way back to the bar where God was waiting for him.

'There's one last thing you wanna ask Me,' said God, as Walter took a seat.

The depth of Walter's transparency became immediately apparent to him. Feeling extremely insolent, he said what had been on his mind:

'When You were in that Parabox, and Lucifer was threatening to push You into the Outer Darkness...If he'd succeeded, You probably would have been released, because the only things containing You were the laws inside Creation. Is that correct?'

'In response to your question, Mr. Matthews,' said God, 'My only comment is: *No* comment. Except...that Angel really is an idiot.

'You're a smart little son of a Calithumpian, Mr. Matthews. And as your Creator I'm complimenting Myself by saying that. Now. Back to the business of your Physical life. Are you sure you wanna be rejoined to it? Because you might not be so chirpy seven years into the sentence, when the kids are being snotty-nosed little degenerates you can't get away from, and the mortgage is several times overdue, and all of those uncivilised nations are still behaving accordingly. Life can seem very long.'

Despite such burdens, Walter nodded: he was ready to go back.

'Okay then,' said the Almighty. 'Then by the power vested in Me, *by* Me, I command you Saint Walter to go back into the world and do what you do–only not so seriously. And yes, My reference to children does imply that I took the liberty of un-chopping the chop, so take it easy, M'man; I'll see you when you get back to the Real World.'

God waved a lazy cross and snapped His fingers. Walter was abruptly seized by a white light–one that travelled away from him. Or maybe he was travelling away from it. He seemed to be falling down the shaft of a well. The light grew smaller and smaller and soon became nothing but a faraway star. Before darkness overcame him completely, he heard God say, 'Now. Who do I have to have crucified to get another drink around here?'

COURTNEY TAYLOR

Chapter 61

The next thing Walter knew he was lying in a darkened room, and feeling as though his body was set in concrete. His mouth was dry and every bone was aching. The gradual remembrance of how he'd come to be in this predicament prompted a leaching guilt, one that reminded him of what the Jesus of his dreams had said about hospitals: they were dark places because of all the incisions made by Death.

Death in fact was making an incision right now. Directly in front of Walter's bed there was a gleaming golden blade, cleaving the air like it was cutting into gelatin. The fissure pulled apart and revealed a scruffy man with no front teeth, who goggled with distaste at Walter and said, 'Blasphe*mee*. Wally. Y'look like a frozen corpse that a bunch o' kids've toilet-papered.'

Death leaned out from behind Jesus, cringed sympathetically, and waved.

Walter chuckled, and tried to ask her what a psychologist might make of his imagining Death as a woman. All that came out of his wired mouth was a garbled mash of noises, ending with a sound that might have been a question mark.

'Uh, Grimmie?' said Jesus. 'Would you mind goin' back and gettin' the Holy Spirit for me? I think I'm gonna need a translator. And uh, this might be a private moment sort o' thing.'

Death feigned suspicion before smiling and stepping back through the rift. She wiggled her fingers at Walter, giving him a small wave, then sewed up the Dimensional tear and disappeared.

Jesus brought out Walter's *Barnabas* award and placed it on his bedside cabinet, saying, 'Dad wanted me to tell you: if y'ever start thinkin' this whole escapade was nothin' but a dream or whatever, this thing here's gonna remind you it wasn't.'

'What's goin' on with you, anyway? Leavin' without properly sayin' goodbye.'

'Sorry,' Walter tried to say.

Jesus found a chair and brought it closer. Sitting down, he asked, 'Who's the chick?'

Walter forgot he was telling himself he was hallucinating, and tried to say, 'Can you...describe?'

'Not bad lookin', said Jesus. 'Late thirties. Brown hair. Wedding ring so, damn it.' He grinned. 'How y'feelin'?'

'Won't complain,' said Walter.

A momentary gash of golden light appeared in the middle of the room. Out of it flew the Holy Spirit. It squawked, landed on Jesus' shoulder, and addressed Walter with a dignified bow.

'All right,' said Jesus. 'You guys've already met each other, so, Wally, the bird is gonna tell me what *you* wanna say, and *I'll* tell you what *I* wanna say. Make sense? Okay. This is my way of saying thank you—or whatever—for everything you've helped me with. I'm gonna discuss a few issues, which, as a rule I generally don't talk about, 'cause, everyone's got questions for Jesus, so...Okay. Well. At one point you expressed interest in the reason I'd been crucified, and *I* said I didn't wanna talk about it. Well, I hate it when people leave *me* dangling, so, here comes the reason I got– laid out to dry. Or whatever.

'You remember how in the Book, I'm down at that garden?'

'Gethsemane?' asked Walter, via the Holy Spirit.

'That's the one,' said Jesus, flinching noticeably at the mention of the word. 'Me n' the boys were down there that night 'cause that was our rendezvous point. We were gonna meet our "co-conspirators," Elijah and Moses, and they were gonna hand over the Ark o' the Covenant, so we could use it to...' Jesus looked as though he didn't want to say it, but finally came out with '...blow up the local temples, n' the outstations, n' the courthouses; any authoritative establishment pretty much. The only reason we didn't manage to "fulfill our plan" is 'cause...I sometimes have a fondness for alcohol that...goes a bit beyond what's healthy. And yes, that is the reason my first miracle was turning water into wine—but I'd just earned my HP card. Of course I was gonna celebrate. Anyway. In anticipation of our "bringing down the systems trying to oppress us," me n' the Disciples got together and had a bit of a— premature celebration.'

'The Last Supper,' said Walter.

'Exactly,' said Jesus. 'And you know how it goes. One drink leads to another drink, then another and another, and soon you're so drunk y'start sweating blood...I'll never forget the look on Judas' face, when he found us all passed out in that garden. He'd left the party early 'cause he'd drawn the shortest drumstick. It'd been his job to find the authorities to bring 'em to back to Gethsemane. I was gonna get arrested, then taken to the courthouse. From there I was gonna, you know, pull the pin on my explosives. That was s'posed be the signal for everyone else to do the same thing, all across the city.

'But,' said Jesus, taking a weary breath, 'when I got hauled into that courthouse *without* any explosives, I wasn't sober. They interrogated me, and the now-famous line I happily brought out was, "I'm gonna tear this thing down so not a single brick is standing." They took that to mean I was a "terrorist," so, 'cause o' the, you know, culture, I got nailed to that damn cross. Dad didn't wannoo intervene, 'cause goin' down to Earth had been *my* idea. Me n' J-the-B, we had this big thing about establishing a kingdom before the time we both hit 35. Didn't happen, but, the fun's in the dreaming, yeah?

'Anyway. That's the story. And sfeizz it to say, things'd be pretty different if we'd succeeded.'

It seemed that Jesus had nothing more to say. He distractedly slapped his thighs like a drummer, then worriedly patted his pockets and said, 'Aw Shiite. HS, I think I mighta left my HP card back in the men's room. Would you mind goin' back to Heaven, n' gettin' Death for me?

'I *know* you can give me a ride. But me n' Death'a gotta do somethin' after this. It's more time efficient this way.

'Look. Would you just *do* it for me, please?

'*Thank* you.'

The bird bowed once again to Walter, then squawked, blasted a short-lived portal through the Ality fabric, and flew through it.

Jesus was quiet for a moment, then said, 'If you're wondering why you can see us, it's 'cause you've just re-entered. That won't always be the case, so, enjoy the splendour of my facial features while you can.

'Dad told me y'didn't wanna be a Patriarch. Well, not that y'didn't wanna be one—that you'd rather be down here with all your people.

'Thanks for the help, eh? With everything? I'm much appreciative.'

'Anytime,' said Walter, providing a three-syllable groan.

Jesus was about to say something else, but a golden blade preceded Death, who leaned out of a new rift and smiled compassionately at Walter.

The VP got to his feet and said, 'Anyway, Wee Wally, aka Saint Wally; as the saying goes: *Goodbyes don't really exist, but, See Ya Laters do.* Just don't reincarnate yourself before y'come n' say hello. All right?'

'I won't,' grunted Walter.

'And don't do anything I wouldn't do,' said Jesus, stepping through the rift and turning around. 'Not me, but, the famous me.'

Walter waved a taped finger from side to side. It was a facetious remonstration, but also a *See Ya Later*.

The VP also gave a wave, however it progressed into a *rock on* hand gesture, perhaps because waving was a bit too difficult for him. When Death lifted her golden blade and mended the gash connecting the Physical and the Spiritual, Jesus disappeared, leaving behind a stillness that remarked upon the nature of his presence.

Walter lay in the quietness, his ribs feeling like crumbling chalk, his respiration slowing as his body relaxed. He wondered what kind of Spiritual energies he might be producing, and hoped that they were Good ones. Closing his eyes, and listening to the breathing of the other person in the room, he found that, in spite of his pain, he was glad to be alive.

SAINT WALLY

Chapter 62

A large golden Buddha statue sat fatly and happily in a peaceful, well-tended garden, his bald head gleaming in the moonlight. This all changed when Jesus crept toward him with a substantial rock in his hand, and bludgeoned the Buddha till he was decapitated.

Moments later the Son of God was sprinting across the surface of a pond, being chased by angry monks who'd forgotten they didn't have the same liquid-treading ability as their quarry. After accidentally tromping on a sleeping duck that bobbed back up confused and invigorated, Jesus happily ditched the golden head into the water, wiped his hands of a job well done, then rendezvoused with his accomplice.

Death gave a small curtsy before stepping into Club Elysium first. They headed for one of the many gigantic card tables that had risen from the floor during their absence. God, at one of them, rolled His three dice and it was all sixes.

'Ha Ha!' He shouted. 'How'd'ya like *those* Forbidden Fruits!' Snatching up a cocktail glass, He high-fived Einstein, then linked arms with a pair of burqa'd models and sauntered deeper into the party.

A circle of dancing Citizens had formed around John Smith, who, still with the hessian bag on his head, was break-dancing in outrageous fashion. God jived up next to him and shouted, 'Stand back, moron! I'm gonna teach you all how to *dance! WHOO!*

The Good Lord jumped into the air, did twelve consecutive side-flips, landed by doing the splits, and then lifted Himself off the floor by spinning the strands of His beard like they were helicopter rotors. He then did Russian split jumps, a record-breaking number of windmills, "wormed" His way almost to the ceiling, and Boston-shuffled all across the dance floor. Some of the Almighty's moves were a little bit too "contemporary" for some of His Citizens. But He was pretty acrobatic, the old coot. Even the Atheists would have admitted that.

SAINT WALLY

Epilogue

Lucifer, Clip and L. Ron were sitting in a foul-smelling dusty wasteland, surrounded by flies bigger than coconuts, and mountainous piles of detachable defecation systems. These fleshy organs each needed recalibration, due to a faulty edict from the VP about the permissibility of certain foods. The task of recalibrating them had fallen upon Lucifer and his two present henchman.

Lucifer was flinching and cringing whenever a new star system erupted overhead. God and Jesus were detonating the galaxies of this their newest Dimension. In spite of the distracting pyrotechnics display, the Angel's thoughts obsessively returned to the Crimes Against Creation tribunal he'd been forced to sit through.

Osama's apparent "remorse" had allowed him to enroll in Hitler's program, and in doing so, avoid the current penalty. Clip had been given a lesser sentence than Lucifer, because apparently he'd been "traumatised" by the Outer Darkness. (That didn't explain why he was so rudely un-talkative, though. All that Clip did now was stare into space–and salivate: a practice simply *horrid* to watch). L. Ron *also* had an anecdote pertaining to saliva. When his sentence was announced, he'd spat on the ground in outrage, shouted that his penalty was an injustice, and demanded to be made an Apotheothorist, given that he was the "inventor of the whole *clear* concept." Solomon, who had so annoyingly chaired the tribunal, had replied emphatically that there was, "Nothing new under the sun, capi-tan."

And that was why L. Ron was now sitting in the dirt, as naked as the day that he'd fallen from the sky. Lucifer couldn't be sure, but, L. Ron, and sometimes even Clip, seemed to fix him with stares that one could almost perceive as...resentful. This almost made him question if his devotees were perhaps considering becoming *former* devotees.

But all was not lost for the Morning Star (as he liked to sometimes call himself) because a pair of naked humans came skipping happily from over a horizon formed by bowel piles.

'Gentlemen,' said Lucifer, perking up at the sight of the nudists. 'I am sensing that here is a chance for us to inject a little bit more anarchy into the Mechanism. Whatta ya say for the sake of excitement, we get a little bit...*Luciferious*.

'Excuse me! You two! Yes, over here! No, don't worry about us. We're harmless! We actually work for the Almighty! I don't want to interrupt your, uh, *frolicking*. But I was just wondering if, well, would you like to hear my "rock" question?'

The man and the woman looked at each other; and because they both had quite a bit of free time on their hands, shrugged and said, 'Sure.'

———

'And that, ladies and gentlemen, is the real and genuine story of how Lucifer earned the nickname "Beelzebub," aka, "the Lord of the Flies."

'Heh heh heh.'

THE OMEGA

COURTNEY TAYLOR

Don't miss out!

Visit the website below and you can sign up to receive emails whenever Courtney Taylor publishes a new book. There's no charge and no obligation.

https://books2read.com/r/B-A-HVQAB-AYPOC

BOOKS 2 READ

Connecting independent readers to independent writers.

Also by Courtney Taylor

Where the White Fricks are
Saint Wally
Ted Kelly: The Best Bloke Ever

www.ingramcontent.com/pod-product-compliance
Lightning Source LLC
Chambersburg PA
CBHW022002010726
47494CB00003B/859